CW01333337

BRING THE HOUSE DOWN

BRING THE HOUSE DOWN

CHARLOTTE RUNCIE

b

THE BOROUGH PRESS

The Borough Press
An imprint of HarperCollins*Publishers* Ltd
1 London Bridge Street
London SE1 9GF

www.harpercollins.co.uk

HarperCollins*Publishers*
Macken House,
39/40 Mayor Street Upper,
Dublin 1
D01 C9W8

First published by HarperCollins*Publishers* 2025

1

Copyright © Charlotte Runcie 2025

Charlotte Runcie asserts the moral right to
be identified as the author of this work

A catalogue record for this book is available from the British Library

HB ISBN: 978-0-00-868801-1
TPB ISBN: 978-0-00-868802-8

This novel is entirely a work of fiction.
The names, characters and incidents portrayed in it are the work
of the author's imagination. Any resemblance to actual persons,
living or dead, events or localities is entirely coincidental.

Set in Meridien by Palimpsest Book Production Limited, Falkirk, Stirlingshire

Printed and bound in the UK using 100% renewable electricity
at CPI Group (UK) Ltd

All rights reserved. No part of this publication may be reproduced,
stored in a retrieval system, or transmitted, in any form or by any means,
electronic, mechanical, photocopying, recording or otherwise,
without the prior permission of the publishers.

Without limiting the author's and publisher's exclusive rights, any unauthorised use
of this publication to train generative artificial intelligence (AI) technologies is
expressly prohibited. HarperCollins also exercise their rights under Article 4(3) of
the Digital Single Market Directive 2019/790 and expressly reserve this publication
from the text and data mining exception.

MIX
Paper | Supporting
responsible forestry
FSC
www.fsc.org   FSC™ C007454

This book contains FSC™ certified paper and other controlled sources
to ensure responsible forest management.

For more information visit: www.harpercollins.co.uk/green

To Sean

WEEK ZERO

Saturday, 29 July

1

Alex Lyons opened his laptop and wrote the review in the space of forty-five minutes after the show ended. It was a one-star review. He didn't agonise over that rating – I'd never seen him agonise over anything. The solo performance artist, Hayley Sinclair, had a lot to say about the climate emergency, the patriarchy, and the looming end of the world, which was fair enough, but unfortunately her show was so terrible that, by half an hour in, Alex had decided that he actually wanted the world to end as soon as possible. Then, at least, he'd never have to risk seeing one of her performances again. That was a good line, so he put it in. He wrote hunched on a low wall outside the venue, thinking about where he could get a drink afterwards.

Alex was chief theatre critic for the national newspaper where I was a junior writer on the culture desk. We'd both worked at the paper for years, but that year, for the first time, Alex and I were both away from London, reporting from the month-long arts festival of the Edinburgh Fringe.

I can't give you the name of the newspaper, but let's just say it's considered by some people to be the last remaining newspaper of decency, and by other people to be a rag of unforgivable bias. I'll just call it 'the paper' – that's what everyone who worked there called it anyway.

Alex proofread his review and found no errors, so he emailed it to the editor on duty with the star rating at the top in capital letters, for clarity – ONE STAR – and packed his laptop back into his chestnut Italian leather satchel, a birthday present from his mother. He lit a cigarette and walked down Rose Street, which was full of stag dos shouting in vowels and vomiting into the gutters between the cobblestones.

Edinburgh was a city that Alex knew only in August. I know it a little better, having lived there for a while after university. I've seen it stripped back to its gorgeous Enlightenment bones of dark wet stone tenements in the quiet, endless winters, the yeasty smells of the brewery on still nights, the sea mist over Holyrood, the glass-fronted hotels for the rich rising above lines of addicts queuing for methadone on Leith Walk.

For Alex, like most annual festival visitors, Edinburgh was not a real place, but a mirage, a pop-up of banners and posters, coffee vans and burger vans and street performers, the spats of frying meat and the dank smell of lager.

It was gone eleven and the streets were still full. A rat matched his pace along North Bridge, hunting in the night's street rubbish that spilled across the pavement. Suits, who were either TV journalists or disgraced politicians, strode home from a late broadcast at the BBC studios with their jackets flapping open. Audiences were coming out of theatres.

All this had a glamour for Alex. As he walked, meandering through the streets to absorb the festival air, the city brought him peace after the bad show, and if he doubted his opinion or suspected himself of cruelty, for even a moment, he could rationalise his work as all part of contributing to the culture, to maintaining high standards, and to being in a city full of people chasing their next pleasure. A city situated towards delight, not mediocrity. A place where people wanted only the best of life and it made them honest and free.

It seemed as though everywhere on the Royal Mile, under the clear summer moon in the never-quite-darkness of the Scottish summer night, were actors and actresses coming out of their shows. This gave Alex a jolt of energy. He was always drawn to actresses. All theatre people, with their superficial vanity and deep insecurity, were easy to flatter. But actresses, in particular, offered him something deeper that he couldn't always define. This unsettled him in a way that he liked. Actors and actresses had something about them that normal humans lacked. They had large, expressive eyes. They could sing, usually. They had a warmth that made Alex want to reach out his own cold hands towards them. They held, always, the energy of potential transformation. By knowing how to become other people, they knew the terrible truth of what it's like to taste the life of someone else.

When I first started working in culture journalism, I used to get asked to do a lot of clickbait listicles for the website that nobody else wanted to write – '13 things you never knew about Picasso', and all that. It became a bit of a speciality of mine. So: there are three things you need to know about Alex. The first is that a lot of women fell for him.

'The thing is, Sophie,' Alex had said to me on the train we'd taken together from London Kings Cross up to Edinburgh Waverley two days previously, opening a Raspberry Lucozade he'd bought from the trolley, leaning towards me over the grey Formica train table as if about to reveal a universal spiritual truth. 'Since I turned thirty, getting laid has become *embarrassingly easy*.'

'Yeah?' I said. 'Lucky you.'

He did a little smile and drank his Lucozade. It's this image of Alex from the beginning of the festival that returns to me now: the unseriousness of his eyes, staring at the moving sea through the window of our train.

Previously lean to the point of lankiness, like an ex-racing greyhound, in the last few years he'd gained some muscle, having taken advantage of the paper's inexplicably well-appointed and free-to-access onsite gym that I never used. Alex now looked like the kind of human being they would put in the human being catalogues. Tall, strong, good teeth and slightly curly dark hair, physically independent, no defects. No visible defects.

Alex read what he said were 'proper books'. He always had a line ready on Adorno and Derrida and Stanislavski, and so what if it was always the same line? It wasn't just those guys. He had deferential feminist stuff he could say about Germaine Greer and Judith Butler, and an at-the-fingertips thesis on Sarah Kane. And he could be funny about the lowbrow. He liked panto. He liked characters who wanted you to boo and hiss.

The women Alex went for were educated and arty and ambitious. They were writers and directors, editors and agents. And actresses. He had, he told me, recently resolved to stop sleeping with women under the age of twenty-four after one of them told him he looked like 'such a softboi, but old', and it was like being insulted in an entirely different language.

In general, he had a preference for women around his own age, who had until recently been stuck in long-term relationships with boring men who didn't appreciate them, and who had mostly wriggled themselves loose from their sexless cocoons at around thirty and, drying their wings, found themselves a) horny and b) looking for an intellectual equal. In Alex, they thought they might find it.

He was always briefly entangled with someone. His attitude towards women was something that made it difficult for me to think of Alex as a friend, though it's something you can tolerate in a colleague.

That's the second thing to know about Alex: he was a good colleague. He made me laugh. He'd give me a conspiratorial eye-roll during a forward-planning meeting while he leaned back in his chair with a biro in his mouth. He had a disarming ability to notice and remember people's preferences: he'd do a coffee run for the culture desk and remember without having to check that Graham liked his flat white with oat milk and Nicky on listings always had an extra shot.

And I had to admire his work. He could turn out copy clean as mine at twice the speed. Where my pieces could be tentative and people-pleasing, Alex's reviews were sharp and zingy and held the page.

One time, a few years ago, I'd written a feature about the Venice Biennale that wasn't working. I knew it wasn't working because Paul Ellis, my least favourite of the paper's senior editors, had told me it was shit and I needed to start again. But I'd already rewritten it four times, and I was fighting back tears at my desk, wishing that Graham, the culture editor, wasn't off sick, when Alex dragged one of the wheeled chairs over to me and plonked himself down in it.

'Don't take journalism so seriously, Soph,' he said. 'Can I?'

He picked up the printout of my draft, which was now covered in Paul's red biro crossings-out, lines drawn through whole paragraphs so violently they almost tore through the paper, and read it in about four seconds. He pointed to a sentence halfway down.

'Ignore Paul. Start with this bit. This observation about the city, where it's like a character. It's kind of beautiful. Move it up top so you start with colour, then get the nut graf out of the way, and shove everything else after that and give it to a different editor to sign off. Relax, it's a nice piece.'

He sauntered off for a cigarette. Praise is rare in journalism. That was still the only time anyone at the paper had ever directly complimented my writing.

Alex told me not to take journalism so seriously, but I was never sure whether he took that advice himself. And this is the third thing to know about Alex. He loved writing about theatre. Theatre really mattered to him.

Theatre, Alex once told me when I made the mistake of saying I wasn't all that into it, because exhibitions were more my kind of thing, is different from any other form of art. It isn't like a film or a TV show where everything's been recorded and cut and edited, and someone has already seen it before you. It's nothing like a painting, which is a single, preserved moment of perspective. Theatre is happening to you right now, made real by the people in front of you, never seen before, not quite like this, and never again. Stage performance is the only storytelling art form created in the present tense, Alex said. These people could do anything. They could make you feel anything. Isn't that wonderful? Isn't that terrifying?

As with everything we love, Alex experienced it first as a child. It was a children's show about penguins, which his mother, the actress and director Judith Lyons, had taken him to when he was six years old. She knew it was on because at the time she was casually seeing the artistic director of the theatre in Hammersmith where it was playing. Here, Alex was baptised into the rituals of theatre, which, like the rituals of any religion, are designed to seduce.

There was, before the night even began, the ritual of the ticket. For Alex, this was a paper key to a door that he had longed to open, and which led to the place that was, he suspected, where his mother really lived. The ticket was a promise that he would be welcome at this theatre, at this time, and there would be a seat prepared for him, and light in the darkness.

(As an adult, Alex could do a good rant on the death of the paper ticket stub in the age of the e-ticket. He really got going on it over Friday drinks in the dark, wood-panelled pub round the corner from our paper's newsroom, eyes shining in the gloom, holding a pint of Oyster stout, on and on about how something has been surrendered, and we've now lost forever the printed remains of a time past, a time when magic left real traces in your pocket.)

Alex, at six years old, had arrived at the box office, which was not an office and had no boxes, and was greeted by a front of house assistant in a golden waistcoat. She ripped off the perforated ticket stub and bent to stamp his outstretched hand with an inky purple blotch in the shape of a penguin.

This was before his mother had received her damehood. But even then, she was conspicuous, with a fur-trimmed jacket and high leather boots and a familiar face. She enunciated more than other people. She bought him a striped packet of red and green sweets. The sweets were sour inside but coated in crystals of sugar, to be eaten quietly and not rustled. She was approached by two politely giddy women in the foyer and indulged an autograph request with the fountain pen she carried in her handbag.

'You'll have to excuse me.' She drew the 'J' in 'Judith' with a long tail and dotted the 'i' with a horizontal line. 'I'm here with my son.'

This made Alex feel special and important. The whole interior of the building was velvet, from the carpet to the seats to the curtains to the new texture of his own body in this strange place, and everything was deep red and gold, arched and designed for his delight.

His mother bought a theatre programme in the foyer. The booklet was bigger than any of his reading books at home and filled with shiny black-and-white pictures of the actors in rehearsals, somersaulting and gesticulating and laughing with scripts in their hands. His thumb found a page with more weight than the others, and here was a sheet of penguin and snowflake stickers, opposite a puzzle section with a themed wordsearch about Antarctica.

The theatre was full of children just like him, except not like him, because they didn't have his mother. Alex and Judith sat in a row towards the front of the stalls on the scarlet fold-out seats. Using the fountain pen, he had just circled the words COLD and SOUTH POLE and PENGUINS in the wordsearch when the house lights went down, like the blowing out of a candle.

His mother smelled like a shimmer of flower petals and slightly of whisky. She squeezed his hand and he squeezed hers. The curtain drew back, and the stage lights came up, and there were people up there, real grown-ups, confident and loud and alive, with snow falling on the stage as they pretended to be anything other than who or what they really were. There was nothing between him and the actors. They could touch him if they wanted, and he would let them. All they wanted in return was his applause. This meant they wanted his love. (It was only much later that he would realise he had the power to keep his love from them.)

He didn't remember much about the show itself, as an adult. He only remembered, as he told me when everything was falling apart, the moment when his mother's world became his world, too. The fear and wonder of it. He remembered the applause, and how it connected the audience and the performers in a sacred pact of pleasure. He remembered it every time he reviewed a show.

When I first made the connection between Alex's surname and his mother's, I wondered why Alex hadn't turned out to be theatrical in the way his mother was. In choosing to be a critic, he'd chosen to be an outsider, half in show-business and half out of it. And I wondered if there was, within him, a spark of resentment at a world that he knew to be less magical than it looked. But which still, despite everything, bewitched him.

Dame Judith is now in her seventies and, as it said in the BBC news article when she received her damehood, she is one of this country's finest living interpreters of Shakespeare. She was a single mother, and Alex, who was an only child, grew up in a house full of stars: his mother's famous and semi-famous lovers and friends drifting in and out of his life. His mother's world was self-consciously artistic and outsiderish, he told me, a place where you were free to speak on anything as long as it was entertaining. His mother and her friends had money, but they weren't businesspeople. They set themselves morally apart from people who made a living in conventional, corporate ways. His mother used to say they were like nineteenth-century opera singers, who'd been born in the gutter and risen to dine with kings.

I liked Alex. As hard as that is to admit now, back then, I couldn't help liking him. And if that sounds defensive, there are good reasons. But something drew me towards him with a quiet, addictive dread.

Alex cut across town. He had to wait to cross the road, and he used that time to check one of the dating apps he'd been on since he'd got to Edinburgh. The apps always exploded during the festival. So many unmoored, excitable and creative people all in one place. He scrolled through some pictures, deciding who he'd message when he got back. The lights changed. Because he was hungry, he changed direction towards the Traverse theatre bar, which might still be serving food, and kept walking.

The subterranean Traverse bar, near the flat in Edinburgh that the paper had paid for Alex and me to stay in, was still open, but half-empty. It held the resonance of a place that had recently been packed full of people who'd just now moved on elsewhere, to some other bar, some other show, a bed that wasn't their own. He ordered a Guinness and a steak pie from a boy in a branded shirt who looked about fifteen, and the boy said sorry, but they'd stopped doing food half an hour ago.

He felt the proximity of her a few feet away. Hayley Sinclair, the performer from the show that he had, barely an hour previously, eviscerated on the page, the recipient of his solitary, condemning star. She was drinking gin and sitting with her body turned halfway into the room, watching who came in.

'A Guinness, on your own?' Her voice was deeper than it had been on stage. As he'd noticed during her show, she sounded American, though she used British phrasing and over-pronounced her consonants, as if she'd lived here for a while. It was already hoarse. A voice that wouldn't last the whole month. 'Must be bad.'

'The show I saw wasn't great.' He had been sitting deeply enough in the shadows of the auditorium that there's no way she would have seen him, still less remembered his face. He would reflect, later, when he was telling me all this, that he could have ended the conversation there. 'You?'

'I'm a performer. I just did my first show. You never know how it's going to go down, but I think it was OK. I got here after they'd stopped doing the pies, too.'

Hayley was sitting up very straight and tapping one foot on the bar stool. She was lit with unspent adrenaline, physically almost buzzing. And she was alone. Doing a solo show was a dangerous kind of loneliness. It meant no company to debrief and decompress with afterwards. Alex could indulge that lack, as a form of kindness. She didn't have to know who he was. She didn't have to know that he had even been in the audience.

What he'd taken for a derivative, affected quirkiness onstage – a knowing reclaiming of the manic pixie dream girl aesthetic – was in fact, close up, something more fragile, and less artfully constructed. Every joint and muscle in her body was tense, in need of release. She smelled of something boozy and a little like strawberries. They talked about shows they'd seen. They agreed that Edinburgh during the Fringe was an intense and mind-bending place, a festival city, a place out of time. Through Hayley's green satin top, he could see the outline of a nipple.

'So,' she said, taking a sip of her drink. 'Where are you going next?'

See? *Embarrassingly easy.* Everything he'd written about her on stage was forgotten now, irrelevant, the capturing of a moment of artifice that had dissipated with the last of the summer evening light. Offstage, she was warm and close and uncomplicated. They stood in the corner of the bar, her jacket folded over the crook of her arm, and he kissed her. And it rose within him, that addictive one-night-only falling in love feeling, taking him over like a warm bloom of drunkenness. That feeling of the house lights going down and the stage lights coming up, and a physical presence before him, and the night about to take him somewhere new.

And all that night, while they were together, Alex's terrible, vicious, personal, career-ending words about

Hayley were being printed in black on creamy newsprint. Alex's name was at the top, next to a large, close-up photograph of Hayley's face, duplicated hundreds of thousands of times. In the newsroom in London, the night editor scheduled Alex's words to go online at six o'clock the next morning. And, because Hayley was a pretty girl, he puffed the review with her picture nice and big on the homepage of the website, to be read by millions of readers on their phones as they woke up, to be read by everyone that Hayley had ever hoped she might impress.

2

I woke early, far from home, after staying up to review a mediocre late-night art installation with a silent disco. I was used to toddler hours. It was strange to wake to a quiet city full of adults, instead of to the insistent shouting of a small person in a cot in the room next door. I would call home after seven thirty, after my coffee, by which time Josh would have given Arlo his Shredded Wheat in our tiny flat in Leytonstone.

It had been breakfast time when I'd kissed them both goodbye on Friday, when I'd left for Kings Cross to meet Alex and catch the Edinburgh train. Arlo had tried to grab my keys so he could jingle them and screeched when I'd put them back into my pocket. He hadn't understood the gravity of the situation, that his mother was leaving home for more than three weeks, the longest time she'd ever been away from him. He'd just wanted to jingle the keys.

I set down my phone on the black vinyl counter in the kitchen in Edinburgh. It glowed with an email.

Thanks for buying FLORENCE COTTON PYJAMAS NAVY STARS M from Arabella Ritzy! We'd love your feedback! Please review your purchase. It only takes a minute, and your feedback helps us keep improving! If you enjoyed your item, tell us (and others!) about it! Click here to rate your experience!

I archived the message with a swipe. My editor was never this enthusiastic about my reviews. I'd worn the pyjamas the night before, as it happened. They were only OK.

The flat, absurdly huge, was an Old Town tenement on Spittal Street with gigantic windows of thin glass and flaking wood that shuddered through with the cold winds of Scotland in August. The paper had rented it every year since the 1990s, and whoever it was in the editorial management office just booked the same place every time because it meant they didn't have to change anything except the date on the intranet logistics portal. It was the same place they used to book back when they had a budget to send a team of six reporters to the festival every year. Nobody had bothered to update the records of what was needed now that, for the first time, it was just Alex and me, and I was one of the cheapest full-time writers on staff.

Graham, the culture editor back in London, called us for a planning meeting most mornings after ten. He had only ghosts of grey hair left on his head, a quiet voice and a Welsh accent. He was always the last person to speak in meetings and the only really kind journalist I'd ever met. Having enjoyed reading to his own four children, now long since grown, he reviewed kids' books by obscure debut authors, never the ones with celebrities' names on the cover. If he didn't make the effort to seek them out and give them space, nobody else at the paper would bother.

The flat, managed by an apathetic lettings company and owned by an elderly laird's widow in Angus who had possibly forgotten it existed, was decorated somewhere between eighteenth-century Scottish merchant's house and NHS doctors' surgery, with fire doors and fire alarms and fire blankets installed everywhere, and heavy brass door furniture painted over in thick magnolia gloss. The paper's comedy critic, Mehdi, was in Edinburgh too, and should have been staying with us, but he had a rich friend who lived in a grand set of rooms on Royal Circus who let him stay there instead, so it was just Alex and me.

On our first afternoon there, after collecting my festival press pass and lanyard from the Fringe media office, I'd opened the large brown wardrobe in my bedroom – everything was as if it had been designed for humans three sizes bigger than normal – and a moth the size of a tennis ball had burst out of it. It looked as shocked as I felt as it plummeted to the floor like a live grenade. I have no idea what grenades do when they're live, but this is how scared I was of that moth. It might have been living and growing in the wardrobe, undisturbed, for decades. I backed away and heaved up the sash on the ancient window, to encourage its departure, and a rain-flecked breeze blasted in with the sound of pedestrians and the thick smell of the overflowing communal rubbish bins three floors below. Still the moth remained on the old carpet, wounded somehow, wings buzzing furiously in a blur around its huge, woolly grey head.

'Alex!' I shouted.

With a presence of mind I appreciated, he got a flyer for a hip-hop adaptation of *Twelfth Night* and a pint glass from the cavernous kitchen cupboards – it was the only one remotely big enough – and dealt with the moth by trapping it between both objects and then flinging it out through the open window.

It had felt unfeminist to rely on a male acquaintance for bug disposal, but I was glad the moth was gone.

I'd decided I'd go out first thing every day to buy the newspapers and clutter the kitchen table with them. Not just our paper, but all of them. When print finally dies, I'll miss it all: the spread of messy, tangible knowledge and provocation, and the sound of rumpling paper. And I like doing the crossword and leaving coffee rings on the comment pages.

There wasn't much food in the flat, and after I got back from the Sainsburys Local I wished I'd found a croissant from somewhere as well. I spread our paper out on the wooden kitchen table, smoothing one hand over the fold.

The Fringe takes place over four weeks in August, but, for some reason, the first week is always called week zero, followed by weeks one, two, and three. It's one of the things that makes the whole festival feel as though it inhabits a different plane from normal life. It was still only week zero, but the papers were already full of reviews. My art review had been cut down by the duty editor from six hundred words to barely half that length. Fair enough – it was an equivocal three stars. It was crammed low down on the page underneath Alex's splashy review of *Climate Emergence-She*. On the left side of the page, before his full excoriation began, there was Alex's rating, rendered in a single, small, spiky typographical blob, confirming that the show had earned only one star out of a possible five. The paper didn't allow Alex to award zero stars. Otherwise, he'd do it all the time.

Alex's pieces were always printed at the full heft of their original length, with a luxurious standfirst and enormous picture. This time the picture was of performance artist and campaigner Hayley Sinclair, close in on her face, wispy blonde hair in a candyfloss cloud at either side of her squared-off cheekbones, a nose ring, and one ear frosted with several piercings, her make-up running in a constructed moment of mourning for a world that was about to boil to death. She was a few years younger than us. The editor had pulled a quote from Alex's review to caption the picture in bold.

Tedious and derivative: Hayley Sinclair

I read Alex's review, which was mean in the way that Alex's reviews were always mean, and in a way that I had become inured to.

Clarity is generosity, Alex always said. At first, years ago, if he didn't love a show, he'd give it three stars or four stars and try to write something balanced, making nuanced suggestions for improvement. But that had only made the theatre people angry. That really wounded them. Because how dare he be lukewarm on something they cared about so much? That they'd poured the very blood of their hearts into? And it made his mother call him, especially if the people he was reviewing were friends of hers, and say, 'Oh, darling. Couldn't you have been nicer?'

No, he had arrived at the conclusion that, sometimes, the kindest thing you can do is to be not nice. And so now Alex Lyons was not nice. He was not nice at all.

And as Alex always said, people *like* reading bad reviews. Readers get bored of too many raves, and nobody ever wants to read a three-star fence-sitter. Three stars isn't even a bad review! Three stars is good! He was sick of explaining this to people. Because nowadays, in the context of a mass culture of online shopping reviews, for most people, five stars has come to mean the baseline, rather than the outstanding. Alex did not like being misunderstood, and so his reviews had gradually become more extreme, and eventually, he'd resolved, as far as possible, only to give shows either five stars or one star. Anything in between was air.

The scarcity of the five-star reviews he did occasionally give out made them, he knew, more precious. When Alex Lyons gave something five stars, the theatre world went crazy. They'd emblazon his name and his rating on posters for the show across all the stations of the London Underground. And he liked that a lot, too. The rarer his raves were, the more valuable they became. So they became rarer and rarer.

I turned the page to read the comedy round-up, which was when I had the surreal experience of the face from the previous page appearing in the open doorway.

'Sorry,' it said, in an American accent. 'Bathroom?'

I swallowed my coffee. 'At the end of the hall.'

The face disappeared. I turned back to the page. Yes, it was the same face. Hayley Sinclair. Before I could process this, my phone lit up with an email from work asking me to write an obituary for an elderly TV actress, a household name, who was still alive but who'd had a stroke following her latest divorce, and could die any minute. Then the phone screen changed to an image of Josh's face. It was Josh and Arlo on a WhatsApp video call.

'It was impossible to get him to sleep,' said Josh as soon as I answered. Arlo was in the foreground, frowning at the screen.

'Oh God. Did you have the blackout blind up?'

'Yes, and the white noise.'

'It's just that sometimes you take it down.'

'You're supposed to take it down every day, because of the condensation. I put it back.'

'I guess it could be his teeth again. Did you read that article I sent you?'

'No? I've been trying to get through the laundry. What was it about?'

'Doesn't matter. Just something funny.'

As I was saying goodbye, and I miss you, and I love you, to Arlo's sticky face, pudgy and indignant, and Arlo was saying 'Bah!', Alex entered the kitchen, dressing gowned, fumbling with the kettle. He acknowledged me with an eyebrow raise, which I returned. I ended the call.

Hayley Sinclair turned on the shower, causing the sound of water to shake the flat. The first time I'd heard this sound was on our first evening here two days ago, and initially I thought something catastrophic had happened to the pipes and water was gushing down the actual walls. Googling it on my phone, I learned this was in fact normal with a power-assisted shower running on crumbling old pipes.

Alex had boiled the kettle and was unscrewing the milk.

'Just reading your hatchet job,' I said. 'She seems familiar.'

Alex came over to look, one hand leaning on the table close to me, the other feeling the stubble along his jaw.

He looked up at me, a little conspiratorial smile, a little caught-with-his-hand-in-the-cookie-jar smile, a little oops-now-what smile. Nina, who worked on the features desk, had said a couple of years ago at the work Christmas party, when she'd danced with Alex after drinking a lot of free white wine, that everyone has a bit of an Alex crush. Even the people who hate him.

'You're in trouble,' I said.

'I'm sure she'll get over it. She's a grown-up.'

His voice was naturally quite low and soft most of the time, when he wasn't drinking, so that you had to lean slightly towards him to hear it, and as I did this, I smelled yesterday's cigarettes and the vestiges of something fruity. I tried not to look as though I was smelling a colleague.

'Are you going to see her again?'

He gave a me a look that said *Christ, no*. And then: 'Coffee?'

As he was making me another coffee in the AeroPress, the cascading water sound stopped. I shut the paper and folded it.

'I didn't know people still read those,' said Hayley, in the doorway. She had a towel around her. If I were in her situation I would shuffle to the privacy of a bedroom as quickly as possible with my head down, but Hayley didn't seem embarrassed at all. Her shoulders were bony and pushed down and back with the posture of someone who did a lot of breathing exercises. Even though she was clean, she had a strong smell of something that was not from our shower. It was like spiced fruit tea and a little like sweat, as if she hadn't showered at all, or as if the reality of her was so strong it even eclipsed soap. Alex didn't say anything and she didn't expect us to, so she went back into his bedroom to get dressed.

'Maybe hide it,' said Alex.

He wasn't panicked at all, which is wild to me now. He passed me a mug of coffee and I put the paper in the recycling bin with the red lid, as we had been told to do by the laminated folder of instructions left on the hall table by the flat's owners. Alex went into the shower and took his coffee with him, which struck me as an odd habit. I opened my laptop to start working on the obit.

Since I'd returned to work a few months previously, the obituaries desk had been asking me to write more and more, even though it wasn't strictly part of my job. Obits paid nothing extra and almost nobody wanted to do them. After maternity leave, though, I'd felt a need to make myself as useful as possible at the paper as a kind of atonement for my time away. Serving the dead seemed appropriate, and I found I was quite good at balancing the elegiac and the macabre. This sort of thing interested me now. I'd read an article once about how the brains of new mothers are resculpted by hormonal changes so significantly that they form whole new architectures. The creation of a new life, of Arlo, had, in my case, resculpted my brain towards death.

Often the people whose obits I wrote were still alive, and I had to write something in advance that could be stored in the stocks folder and then published quickly when the time came. That meant I was usually writing about people in the past tense even as they were going about their days in full health, unaware of my existence. Sometimes, writing an obituary made me feel as though I *was* death, lying in wait for the famous, anticipating their end. It was a powerful feeling, to weigh the most significant moments of a person's life and bear the responsibility of distilling their infinite mess and complexity into one clear story.

I liked, also, that the obits didn't have my name on them, because they're considered to be the voice of the paper, not the voice of any particular journalist. Writing anonymous life stories felt like being undercover. When I first started working in newspapers, I was thrilled whenever I got a byline. It was that whole thing of seeing your own name in print. That thrill had faded over the decade I'd been doing it, and eventually I truly didn't care anymore. You want to see your name in print? Just buy a printer, is my advice. Sophie Rigden is a boring name, anyway. I am actually sick of looking at it, especially when it's next to my pieces about shows nobody else can be bothered to review. I sometimes told people I was an art reviewer, which was technically true, but my actual job title, the thing on my payslips and my HR records, was Junior Culture Writer. In effect, that meant I wrote about everything except anything important, which would always be assigned to one of the senior critics.

I got a few hundred words into writing the obit and made notes for what else to research. It was coming easily. There were a couple of hours before I had to see my next show, an installation by a former Turner Prize nominee. Without Arlo to take care of, I couldn't believe the amount of time that I now had in a day, compared with how swallowed up by the functions of daily life I'd been on maternity leave while Josh was at work.

I marvelled at how much sleep I'd had for two nights straight. My skin was better. My muscles felt nourished. It was as if the world had opened a door to me when I'd stepped on the train to Edinburgh after fourteen months of nothing but motherhood, and through it I'd found the same world I'd known before I'd had a child, and it was saying to me, *See? You're still here. You've been here all along.*

Every day, for the next few weeks, I could do anything or go anywhere in the city and eat and drink whenever I wanted, instead of getting breakfast at the same time every morning because that was the time that Arlo woke and called to me. Each day in Edinburgh had ten extra hours in it, a hundred extra hours, all for me.

And what riches they were! What was it like for people like Alex, who had them all the time? Didn't he know? With what did he fill his endless, precious, shining hours? We were the same age, both of us thirty-four, but I couldn't remember ever being like him.

'Where's that paper you were reading, do you mind?' Hayley reappeared, dressed this time. She was holding her phone.

'Sorry, I threw it away.'

'My agent just messaged asking if I've seen it. Is it still in the recycling?'

Damn recycling. I thought of the time before anyone recycled anything, when you could throw a newspaper right into the kitchen bin with everything else, the coffee grounds and the slimy plastic bits of food packaging and the grey fluff that accumulated in the corners of the living room, and nobody would go searching through it all to find some stained newspaper at the bottom. But now newspapers in the recycling bin weren't thrown away at all, but temporarily filed in a clean, dry place for likeminded objects.

She pulled it out, checking the date to differentiate it from the two previous days' papers that were in there with it. I realise I could have plucked it from her hands, but she had an energy that was hard to interrupt. Instead, I watched as she took it back to the table and spread it out next to her phone. She sat opposite me in a thin khaki green top and no bra, her legs folded underneath her on the chair in the way that a child sits in a primary school assembly, a way that I didn't think my knees were capable of any more. She was, what, twenty-six? She licked a finger and whipped through the pages to the arts section and stopped, her hand still in mid-air, above the page with the large picture of her face. The water from Alex's shower gushed and gushed.

She let the page settle onto the table and lowered her hand as she read in silence. I wanted to get up and leave but any movement from me would betray the sin of foreknowledge. I stared at my laptop as if concentrating on something profound, keeping her in my peripheral vision. The expression on her face hardly changed. She breathed out, long and slow, through her mouth.

I wondered if I should find a way to usher her out of the flat before she could take it up with the man currently washing the smell of her body off his in the shower, before considering what I owed Alex, after all. The silence stretched until I had to fill it.

'Not good news?'

'Pretty shit, to be honest.'

'Look, don't take it personally. This is what Alex does – he exaggerates. He gives everything either five stars or one star. Mostly one star. It's like a persona or something. It doesn't mean—'

I stopped because she was looking at me as if I'd just pulled off all my own skin.

'Alex?'

She didn't know. He hadn't told her any of it. Not his full name, not his real job. They hadn't met because she'd known he was a critic who'd come to her show. She had, in fact, until this moment, no idea who he was.

She looked down at the paper, her face so close to the table that it was almost touching her nose, and she squinted at the tiny circular byline picture of Alex beside his name, taken years ago and pixelated in the paper's ever more cost-saving poor print quality, almost unidentifiable as him. Almost.

'Alex Lyons?'

As if summoned by a stage manager's call, Alex appeared in the doorway. I hadn't heard the thunder of the shower stop, but now the flat rang with its silence. He had a too-small white towel tied around his waist and you had to admit he looked incredible, hair wet and tousled like a glossy magazine advert for a fragrance *pour homme*.

'You wrote this?' said Hayley.

Alex froze.

'*You* wrote this?' She said it louder.

He grimaced and raised his shoulders, one hand grabbing at his towel to keep it in place. 'Yeah,' he said. 'But—'

She stood up, pushing the chair back with a shrieking scrape across the vinyl floor. She was shaking. She went into Alex's bedroom and re-emerged immediately, stuffing things into a tattered canvas satchel. She pulled on one scuffed sandal with a hop, and then the other one.

'Hayley—'

'Just fuck off.' She pushed past him.

I got up to follow her, through some guilty flash of sisterhood, though I don't know what I could have said, and anyway she was already at the front door. She slammed it after her and it bounced back off the latch and swung open again, the sound of her clattering shoes down the spiral staircase of the communal hallway echoing into the flat as they faded away.

Alex looked at me, eyes wide in relief that she was gone and that this was about to become a good war story to tell our colleagues back in the newsroom in London. Like the time the previous year when Nina had written a critical profile of a Swedish ballet dancer and instead of emailing or phoning the office to express her feelings, the dancer had sent a fax (a fax!) saying I HATE YOU PLEASE DIE. We only discovered that we even still had a fax machine when a box at the bottom of the stationery cupboard started making a noise that nobody under the age of twenty-five had ever heard before.

'At least she said please,' Alex had said at the time.

We went back into the kitchen. An angry, rhythmic buzzing noise tore into the room. Alex pointed to a glowing phone on the table next to the abandoned newspaper.

'Is that yours?'

I shook my head.

'Oh,' he said. 'Fuck.'

3

Hayley's phone was a different brand from mine or Alex's, and we couldn't work out how to unlock it to mute it, so it kept buzzing all day, as more and more of Hayley's friends sent her messages. Because we didn't have her passcode or facial recognition or whatever she had set up, we couldn't read what they said, and only saw the notifications multiplying. Alex said he didn't understand why people put such tight security measures on their phones. He said he never locked his phone or his laptop. Crazy behaviour, I thought. Here was someone who had apparently never needed to develop an instinct for self-preservation.

 Alex had been smoking Gitanes at the bottom of the tenement stairwell for half an hour, so I took him out to a café round the corner that I remembered with fondness, and which was named after a line in an e e cummings poem. He needed to make some notes on a Beckett play script before giving a talk at an industry event later at the Playwrights' Studio. I took my laptop with me so I could finish my obit. The café had pot plants dangling in macramé holders and bare Edison lightbulbs hanging from a spiderweb of black wires in the sort of lighting arrangement that Josh had wanted to fit in our kitchen but that I'd vetoed on grounds of impracticality. I remembered this place, from my last time in Edinburgh, as being grungy and dark inside, like most of my favourite places in the city, but now its walls had been repainted in bright turquoise and candy pink. There was an enormous pink espresso machine on the counter.

Alex and I had to share a long wooden table with a student fifteen years younger than us on a laptop with wireless headphones, who looked annoyed that we'd sat in his aura. Alex brought over a flat white and a carrot cake on a little blue dish. It was weirdly dainty next to my fat gold croissant, which felt impossibly luxurious. The events of the morning were already shaping into anecdote. 'Can you take her phone?' Alex asked.

'What, forever?'

'Until tonight?' His foot was tapping. 'I've got three shows today and it keeps going off every two minutes. I'll meet up with you later and take it to the box office at her venue.'

'OK.' I cut my croissant into six small pieces, the way I did for Arlo at home. 'I was just thinking, reviews in this country aren't like on Broadway, where a bad review in *The New York Times* essentially closes the production, and a good one makes it a hit. Here, it's more of an advisory thing.'

'That stuff about closing down a production is bullshit wherever you are. Nobody says that about anything else, do they?' He ate some cake. 'A doctor saying that you have cancer doesn't *give* you cancer. You had the cancer already and the doctor just pointed it out. The cancer's what kills you. A bad review can't turn a show bad. It just points out what's already there. A show only closes early if it's crap.'

'Why did you sleep with her?'

'Well obviously I wish I hadn't, now.' He picked up a sachet of brown sugar from a hammered copper pot and shook it back and forth between his thumb and forefinger.

'Have you done this before, with people in shows?'

'Stop interviewing me.' His mouth was full of cake.

'I'm just curious. I mean, is there a line? Would you sleep with someone at the paper, for instance? *Have* you slept with someone at the paper?'

Hayley's phone buzzed in my pocket. The door clattered open as two more people came in and left when they saw there weren't any empty tables.

'I don't shit where I eat.' Alex ripped the end off the sugar and poured it into his coffee and stirred.

By a natural fluke, I have the kind of face that, at rest, appears non-judgemental but a little sceptical about whatever you're saying, and a voice that sounds slightly sarcastic, whether I want it to or not, even when I'm consciously attempting to be sincere. It's quite useful for a journalist – something about this combination invites confession – and although I have an excellent memory, I'm not a natural secret-keeper. My mother used to tease me and say I was an old-fashioned gossip, even as a child, when I would sit on the stairs and eavesdrop while she was on the phone. There were more questions I could have asked Alex, more places I could have taken the conversation, but he bent back the spine of his play script and started reading it in a way that felt final. I wondered how he defined shitting and how he defined eating. I watched him.

Alex did not call me to organise exchanging Hayley's phone so I carried it with me all day, in the opposite jacket pocket from where I kept my own. After fumbling some more with the side buttons, I eventually managed to stop it making the alert noise every time there was a notification, but it still vibrated occasionally. I took it with me to an exhibition by a major ceramicist at the National Gallery of Scotland, which had colourful banners twisted around the pillars at the entrance for the festival. The exhibition itself was full of immense, heavy, carefully misshapen vases painted with bizarre scenes and worth indefinite, large amounts of money.

The last show in my diary for that day was an art installation which only opened for half an hour in the evening. It was in a converted Masonic hall in the New Town and consisted of several interconnecting rooms in which different things were being destroyed. In the first room, the artist herself was standing at the top of a ladder in a dress of deep, womblike pink, with a boned corset and a train that was so long it fell right to the floor. She was turning around in it, slowly, to a recorded soundscape of rainforest noises, as threads from the dress unspooled from her body, like the legs of a spider, onto six gigantic, pendulous wooden skeins suspended from the ceiling. As the dress unravelled, more of her naked body was revealed.

I made a few notes in one of the spiral-bound pads I'd taken from the newsroom stationery cupboard. I wrote, *womblike pink*. And then, *femininity unravelling*.

'Jesus, it's a load of shite, though, isn't it?' The whisper at my shoulder was a voice from ten years ago, Stuart MacAskill. I'd worked with him at my first magazine job after university.

I hugged Stuart. It's not unusual to run into people you know during the festival. Edinburgh is a small city, and the population mushrooms during August with audiences as well as with thousands of comedians, actors, musicians, artists and theatre people, and a lot of journalists, too, from all over the world. Working at the festival, you'll see people you know all the time. And some people who, at first, you *think* you know from work, and then a second later you realise they're actually just a medium-famous comedian you recognise from TV, and you've been staring at them for ten seconds too long at the vegan bagel place.

Obviously all this is really annoying for people who live in Edinburgh. It used to annoy me, then, too. But now it was just another way I'd become what I used to hate when I was younger.

Stuart had been my first editor when I was writing listings at an Edinburgh events magazine in a tiny, freezing cold office in a Georgian building through an archway in the Old Town, and where Stuart had been in charge of the Around Town section of the magazine, taking specific editorial control of theatre and LGBTQ+ events. Born in Glasgow, he was a compact and effusive man, and a keen middle-distance runner, even though he took a lot of party drugs on Saturdays. The magazine has since closed down. Now he was the theatre critic for a rival paper.

'I'm out here spending all my time recognising English people, it's embarrassing. You look stunning. Haven't you just had a baby? No, with that figure? Have you seen the posters?'

He was lying about my figure, which I appreciated. I said I didn't know what he meant about the posters. He took me outside through a side door. Here, a run of wrought-iron railings had been obscured with temporary wooden panels. There were two poster designs glued onto them, advertising two different shows. The first one had a picture of an inflatable red and yellow skull and said: *Bouncy Castle Hamlet: To Bounce or Not to Bounce? (Featuring real inflatables – no slings or arrows please!)*

That wasn't the poster that Stuart meant. Next to it was a poster for Hayley's show, featuring the same haunted image of her face we'd printed in the paper. Above it, there was the title of her show, *Climate Emergence-She*. But I couldn't read that title, because over the top of it and obscuring it, there had been pasted a newer, bright green banner, which said:

Now called:
THE ALEX LYONS EXPERIENCE

Stuart looked both scandalised and thrilled. 'I read Alex's review from last night. Is he involved in the show now? The posters are everywhere today. It's a much better title now, isn't it? Should we go?'

I heard my name called by someone else approaching down the street. Lyla Talbot had worked on the entertainment beat on the news desk at the paper with me and Alex until the previous year, writing frothy diary stories about various developments in pop stars' love lives, mostly. She was a reporter, not a reviewer. She'd been the kind of journalist who had unnaturally good hair and well-maintained teeth and self-esteem, instead of running on coffee fumes and panic, and therefore had just been biding her time in journalism before she could cash in her experience for a real job that actually paid, which she had now done. She was at the festival as a performance agent, and she probably now made a lot more money than I did. She'd sent me a chummy email about some of her clients, full of emojis and exclamation marks, the week before, which I'd ignored and then forgotten about until this exact moment.

She'd always been flirty with Alex, though I wouldn't have said she was his usual type. He'd humoured her when she came over to our desk in the newsroom to complain about the freaks on the comment pages, lingering until someone offered to include her in the next coffee round. I'd suspected, just after she'd left the paper, that she had started sleeping with Alex, because he'd mentioned her once or twice out of context. This was a suspicion that strengthened now as she said, 'Are you going to Alex's show, too? It's starting in, like, half an hour. Come, sit next to me. Let's get tickets now, before it sells out.'

The venue was in fact only two streets away. A tide of intrigue carried me with Lyla and Stuart to the box office, which was a trestle table inside a pub called *The Seven Hills*. The theatre space was a repurposed function room below the pub, accessed via a staircase that smelled of stale beer, with walls covered in thousands of varnished-over posters from gigs and festivals stretching back decades. There was a poster for a Billy Joel gig in Edinburgh in 1979, a 1980s adaptation of *Rebecca*, a production of Chekhov's *Three Sisters*.

Lyla had been right to worry about getting a ticket. There were around fifty people in the queue and no spare seats once we'd sat down. The audience were mostly women my age, a few scattered men, and some older people, too, who, I imagined, might well be readers of the paper. One guy was telling his friend he'd seen Hayley on the Royal Mile that afternoon, flyering for the show in her underwear, which couldn't be right, surely. With the room almost full, the wet heat made me think of the Mediterranean, as if there might be mosquitoes. A black fan was plugged in next to the stage, wheezing an ineffective hum.

The speakers were playing a song I'd only heard at venues and on the radio and had never deliberately streamed, with a globular bassline and percussion that sounded like gum popping, and a chorus about catching feels. Stuart had got us some drinks in plastic glasses from the bar upstairs on the way in. Mine was a beer, not cold enough. I'd found a seat that was half behind a pillar, with Stuart and Lyla on either side.

Stuart leaned across me. 'I hope she *has* changed it. I was booked in to review it tonight anyway. I was dreading it after Alex made it sound like utter pish.'

'It's *so* difficult for the performers, though.' Lyla stirred her lemonade with a candy-striped straw. 'It's not like with a bad review of a book or a film, where the creative work is already out in the world and done with, and the writer or the performer can just shrug it off and go on to the next thing. I can't imagine what it must be like to get a bad review on the first night of your theatre run, and then have to get up again and keep going, putting yourself out there, knowing that people think you're crap.

Especially when it's a solo show. I really feel for them. I do think you need a heart of ice to be a reviewer.' She laughed and touched my knee. 'No offence to you two, obviously. I know you're both lovely!'

'I'm lovely *and* evil,' said Stuart. 'It's a very impractical combination.'

They were laughing. I felt faintly sick. How would I even begin to tell them what had happened that morning? Black paper and fabric had been taped around the walls to hide the ancient pub wallpaper. We might have been deep below the earth. The stage itself, surrounded by a black curtain backdrop with a projector screen hanging down from the ceiling, was black, too, and scuffed by the shoes of twelve performers a day. There was a microphone on a stand in the middle.

'It's weird,' I said. 'Going to see a show without having to review it afterwards. I feel like a civilian.'

'What's in that beer?' said Stuart.

The gum pop music stopped with an abrupt manual fade and the lights went down as Hayley Sinclair stepped onto the stage, holding a newspaper. I could tell from the font and the design, even from where I was sitting, that it was *the* paper. *My* paper. Instead of the thin, worn-out sandals that Hayley had been wearing as she'd left our flat, she was in black heels. She wore high waisted jeans and a silky silver top with mesh panels down each side and a lot of glittering eye make-up. She walked, slowly, in shadow, straight towards the middle of the stage.

I remembered her phone in my pocket and fumbled at it in a last attempt to switch it off, only to see with relief that the battery had died. I decided to leave it with one of the venue staff at the end of the performance so that they could give it back to her.

A spotlight came up on Hayley's face. She was really gorgeous. Instead of the girl in the towel from my kitchen, now she looked like someone I'd been booked to interview for a magazine feature. She was almost vibrating. Her eyes were so wide you could see the whites of them all the way round. She twisted the microphone cable with her finger. She took a deep breath, and began to speak in a voice low, steady, slightly husky, a little sexy, rippled with menace.

'You know how, every so often, one of your friends tells you a story about someone who's done something so horrible to them that at the end, you say, *I cannot fucking believe he did that?*

'I'm going to tell you a story like that tonight. All of it is true. And I want you to listen to every word of it, and then I want you to go and tell it to everyone, so that they look at you, exactly the way you're going to look at me tonight, and they say, *I cannot fucking believe he did that.* And then they'll go and tell everyone they know, too. And so it becomes a legend. A parable. A warning. Do not let the Alex Lyons Experience happen to you.'

Something invisible seized around my throat. I gripped her phone in my pocket. She opened the newspaper.

'Last night, a critic came to see my show. And he didn't like it. Actually, he hated it. And he decided to tell everybody how he felt, without mincing words or sparing anybody's feelings. He told everybody through this newspaper, today, which you can still go and buy right now. The only person he didn't tell, in fact, was me. He didn't tell me that he'd ever seen me before when he picked me up in a bar right after the show and invited me back to his place. He didn't tell me, when he was fucking me in his bed, that just hours before, he'd written *this* about everything I've ever worked towards.'

She began to read from the newspaper. The fan was pointing away from me. The hair around my face slickened and curled.

> Traditionally, a show is called a show because there is something to see. In *Climate Emergence-She*, the only thing to look at, for the entire hour, is an unfortunate person called Hayley Sinclair, droning, in a voice situated on some unhappy plane between high-pitched whine and dead flat monotone, on and on and on, in circles, about how the world is getting hotter, and we're all going to die, and it's all the fault of corporations and governments mostly run by men.

'Just to remind you,' Hayley said, kicking off her shoes to stand barefoot on the warm stage, 'as he was fucking me, he knew that I would read these words. And that my family would read them, and that my agent and the people at True North Stage and the Arts Council and Community Boost who funded this show, would read them.'

> It's a lot to ask of an audience to sit for an hour and listen to the opinions of one person on one topic. The opinions, at least, had better be hot. There had better be action, intrigue, something to chew.

'He knew that all the power was his, and that a bad review could close my show and make sure it never toured or transferred, and my career, which I'd already risked by sinking my own money into venue and staffing costs to top up the funding, would be over.'

Every person in the audience was unnaturally, achingly still, bound together in silence. I'd never heard a hush like the one I heard in the gaps between her sentences. Was this the same performer that Alex had savaged for being so limpid, so unimpressive, so unoriginal? She blazed with fury. Every member of the audience leaned slightly forwards in their seats, as if she held them all by an invisible thread.

> Is there any of this in *Climate Emergence-She*? No. The best you can say of Hayley Sinclair's one-woman show about the looming climate apocalypse and its links to the patriarchy is that she's probably right. Yes, the world is probably going to end at some point. Unfortunately, Hayley herself is so tedious, and so derivative, that after you've endured the first ten minutes of what the venue is loosely calling a 'show', you'll be begging for the world to end much sooner than scheduled.

Someone laughed and shushed themselves with a hand. As she read, Hayley shook her hair loose from her sparkling headband, which she let fall to the floor. It was like watching Botticelli's Venus come to life as a hipster enchantress. She was essential, elemental, primordial with commanding rage.

> We should expect better from this lecture (I can't in good conscience call it a show – reader, I owe you the truth), because she was funded to bring it to the biggest

arts festival in the world by no less than three different funding organisations, and she's still charging punters fifteen quid a ticket to endure the equivalent experience of listening to a self-important niece hectoring her elders at a family barbecue.

She ripped the mesh of her top entirely along the seam on each side. It tore easily and exposed her bare skin, glowing under the stage lights.

I can only assume these funding organisations have never seen theatre before, and gave her the cash purely because she was saying something they wanted to be seen to endorse without having to change any of their own behaviour. Climate change is bad. Yes, correct. Show funded.

She undid a bracelet from around her wrist and let it fall, *thunk*. A woman in the front row flinched. How far was this going to go? Was Hayley going to strip down to nothing?

Sinclair herself just looks like any other identical modern hippy who's watched too many films with manic pixie dream girls in and decided to base her life on that archetype, which was, by the way, devised by Hollywood executives as a male fantasy. Anybody who has ever had the misfortune to encounter one of these women in real life will know of what I speak when I say: run a mile.

She bared her teeth.

> Three members of the audience left before the end of the show. Your unfortunate critic was not one of them, for he was pinned to his seat by the looming deadline of this review. So I can tell you with complete confidence that Hayley Sinclair is a dull, hectoring frump, like one of those 1950s cartoons of housewives beating their husbands with a rolling pin.

She put down the newspaper, spat into the palm of her free hand, and rubbed it in one, slow movement down across her face, smudging her glittering, indigo eye make-up onto her cheeks. She read the rest of the review by heart.

> The only thing I learned during Hayley's tirade was that sugar maple tree sap production is endangered by warming temperatures, which are making harvested maple sap less sweet, and ultimately causing it to lose its taste entirely. Huh.

She smeared the berry lipstick on her mouth in a horizontal swipe of bloody crimson across her face.

> A sap with no taste? If you buy a ticket to this pointless show, that is what you are.

Stuart had his face in his hands, his eyes wide. Lyla leaned over to me.

'Fair enough,' she whispered. 'I cannot *fucking believe* he did that.'

Hayley was speaking again. She described how she'd felt when she met a guy in the Traverse bar after her first ever Fringe show, when she was exhausted but too full of adrenaline to sleep. A guy who was good-looking and funny and kind, someone with whom she could share the feeling of having got through her first show, when she'd been so lonely. And then she described the feeling of finding out that it was all a lie, all a trick.

Trying to set it all down now, I find I can't explain why it had the effect that it did. But people in the audience had hands across their open mouths. Some shielded their eyes. One woman shook her head, her lips making a silent *no*. This wasn't theatre, not really; it was a happening. The audience weren't spectators any more, but a silent, connected web of righteous energy.

It was invigorating in the way that you might feel if you'd just drunk a lot of coffee and alcohol and then started screaming. How could anyone give this woman a one-star review? Hayley was every human who had ever been betrayed, ever been tricked by faith, ever felt the plummet of grief in realising the world is, after all, a dark and lonely place.

I can't retrace her steps on paper. It wouldn't sound right, like trying to dissect a joke that someone else told, a joke that depended on timing and context to be funny at all. It would diminish what it was to be in that room. Because it wasn't just about what she said, or how she looked, but the moment itself and her presence within it. The only way I can put it is this: I felt I'd seen exactly what they each did to one another that night, in so much detail that it was as if I'd been somehow *there*. It was as if the betrayal possessed Hayley and was reborn and replaying on that stage in a giant trauma flashback.

Hayley stood in thick silence, as if even she didn't know what was going to happen next. Then she said, 'Does anyone have a lighter?'

A woman in the front row held up a small pink disposable cigarette lighter. Hayley took it, flicked the wheel and let the spark kiss the corner of the newspaper page which held the review. It caught fast, and the page blackened and curled until Hayley blew out the flame, letting the charred embers from the corner she'd been holding it by flutter down to the stage.

Afterwards, Hayley stood in a spotlight. Half-naked, exposed, incandescent. 'Now it's your turn. What I want is for as many people as possible to hear about this. That's why I'm doing this show. So I'm going to ask the stage manager, Dave, to bring up the house lights. Excuse me, hello.' She was speaking to someone in the front row. 'Which of your friends has a horror story about a man like this? We've all got one, haven't we?'

'Um,' said a terrified, thrilled woman, trembling with adrenaline. 'Probably my friend Greta?'

'Call Greta tonight,' said Hayley. 'And tell her what Alex Lyons did, and who he really is. Tell her she's not alone.'

And then, with the lights up, Hayley saw me. She pointed to me as if her hand was being raised by a puppeteer. 'You,' she said. 'Oh my God. You were there.'

I wasn't too hot any more. I was really, really cold.

'This is his flatmate, ladies and gentlemen.' She almost shrieked it. 'His flatmate, in the audience, among us tonight, come to be part of the show. I swear I didn't arrange this. But this is perfect. She can tell you it's all true. Why did you come here? Did you want to see if I was as shit as he said I was?'

'You left your phone at the flat.' As I stood and produced it from my pocket, holding it out towards her, a wave of reality washed through the audience at the proof I'd presented, crushing any theory they might have had that this was all made up for the sake of the show.

'Why didn't Alex bring it?'

There was a pause. I shrugged. 'Too chicken?'

The audience laughed. It felt good. So this is who I am, I thought. One of the mob. Any grand ideas of my own individuality that I might have harboured, that I could have been capable of going against the crowd, dissolved in that moment. I just didn't want them to hate me. It was heady and seductive, being part of this, buoyed on a rising tide of invincible reprisal.

And, yeah, it felt like maybe Alex deserved it.

Hayley laughed, delighted to find a co-conspirator. 'Come up on stage. Come on, you know him. Tell the group. What's your Alex Lyons experience, what's the worst thing he's ever done to you?'

When someone is on stage, with lights and a microphone, telling you to do something, you just do it. It's the weirdest thing. I didn't even consider not doing as she said. The house lights were turned off as I stepped up onto the stage beside her. Hayley took back her phone. I shaded my eyes against the spotlights with the flat of my hand. The audience was invisible at first, but they took shape behind the lighting rig when I blinked.

This was, actually, a question I could answer. It wasn't even that bad, the thing that Alex had done to me, but it was something I'd always remembered. It hadn't hurt me much at the time. I hadn't known him then, and had been unable to place it within any wider context of what I knew about him. But the more I did get to know him, afterwards, the more it had dwelled in my mind.

'Um. When we first started working together at the paper, there was this one day where I brought in lunch for everybody on the culture desk, so like six or seven people that day, from the sandwich shop round the corner. And then the next day, he brought in lunch for everybody too – except me. I thought he'd forgotten, that maybe it was an accident, but no, he did it on purpose. He said it was because I was new. I had to earn it.'

It felt pathetic to admit something so small, compared to what he'd done to Hayley. But it had stung. And saying it aloud now felt like letting something go. Especially with what Hayley said next.

'What a dick! See?' Hayley said. 'This guy's a joke. He thinks he can get away with being an asshole, just like he goes from show to show, destroying people's reputations without giving a shit about it. And Alex Lyons isn't just one guy. He's every guy. He symbolises this whole business, this whole rotten media that keeps us down and stops us from making art that reaches people. And now, you beautiful people, you can take the Alex Lyons experience on. Please, tell everyone you know, tell the world your own Alex Lyons Experience. We're going to make him famous.'

She lifted my arm above my head as if I were a champion wrestler.

I've never been to a show before where people didn't want to leave. But the closing music kept playing and people were staying, getting another drink at the bar, getting out their phones and calling and texting people they knew. Someone who had the make-up and eyebrows of an influencer was making a video of herself on her phone while crying and pointing to the stage. I'd never seen anything like it. I looked around for Stuart and Lyla, but they'd both disappeared.

I left the theatre, surfacing into the warm twilight of the grey stone streets. A phone buzzed in my pocket, but this time it wasn't Hayley's. It was mine, with a message from Nina on the Features desk. *Holy shit*, it said. *Have you seen this stuff online about Alex?*

Looking back now, this was the first moment I knew that Alex Lyons was living a marked life. Like the subject of a stock obituary lying on file, he was dead already, and he didn't know it.

4

At the flat, sitting on the sofa in the white glare of my laptop, I scrolled through comments and videos and tweets about Alex. There were already dozens, hundreds, more all the time. I didn't even have to look for them. The algorithm told them where to find me and they came recommended for me on every app. I'd tried to call Alex but his phone was switched off. I felt like a lone medieval watchman on the tower as an enemy army approached in the distance.

> Guys I've already seen the show of the Fringe – go see THE ALEX LYONS EXPERIENCE at DeepUnder (venue 742) book now now now

*

> A certain nepo baby in the British media has got a very rude awakening coming for him by the sounds of things on here tonight

*

I'll say one thing about what seems to have happened at a show tonight in Edinburgh and that is that Certain Men in Media have had this reckoning coming for a very long time

*

Wow. WOW. I've never seen a Fringe show before where I GENUINELY didn't know what was going to happen next and if we were about to go storm someone's house or something . . . phew kinda exhilarating actually, anyway go see THE ALEX LYONS EXPERIENCE like yesterday

*

Turns out journalists are truly the worst of humanity as we suspected

*

I haven't seen the Edinburgh show that's apparently already the talk of the festival, but I stand with women and non-binary folks of all gender expressions in the arts in the fight against misogyny that seeks to destroy good art instead of supporting it. *strong arm emoji*

*

Media girlies put your finger down if you have ever been treated like shit by a guy . . . and turns out it was the same POS as this other girl who has made a whole show about it . . . *skull emoji*

*

All together now . . . I cannot fucking BELIEVE he did that . . .

*

As a fellow journo I don't know how he comes back from this to be honest. It's shockingly unprofessional and just not cool. By rights his career should be over, you just don't treat people like that in a professional context – a relationship between a reviewer and a creator is a weird but sacred thing

*

so yeah you should go see the alex lyons experience, I was actually there tonight and I will be getting a ticket to go see it again tomorrow because omfg the TEA

*

besties please tell me who everyone is talking about that did the thing in the show??? *eyes emoji*

*

its alex lyons lol

The front door clicked open and slammed. Alex came into the living room holding a brown paper bag with a spreading grease stain in one corner. He smelled like smoke and kebab.

'I've just sat through a fucking four-hour production of

Richard III, with no interval, in German. I can't even see any more.'

'Alex . . .' I had no idea where to start. 'Have you seen what they're saying about you?'

'Never read the comments.'

'*Alex.* This isn't just *comments.*'

'There's always some noise.'

'*Noise?*'

'When you write the kind of things I write, you get shit. All. The. Time. I need to go to bed so I can get up and write the next fucking review in the morning. My head is killing me. We can't all piss about at quite nice three-star art shows all day.'

'This is different. This is bad, Alex. And fuck off, I'm a journalist too.'

'We're not *journalists*, Sophie. Come on. We're critics, we're not Woodward and Bernstein. You're a *junior culture writer.*' He sat on the arm of the sofa, picking chips out of his paper bag with stained fingers, enjoying being provocative with his low, intense, posh-boy voice, his mouth full. 'When was the last time you broke a story?'

'I think *this* is a story.' But I wasn't sure about any of it, now.

'You're only a journalist when it suits you. That's OK. You have an artistic side, a bit of soul. Fine. But if you want to be a proper critic, you have to care less. We can say whatever we want and get paid for it. That's a huge fucking privilege. But if you obsess over what other people are thinking, you're only going to repeat what other people are saying, and then you'll only produce the blandest possible shit, out of fear.'

'Are you saying what I write is bland?'

'No. No, but when you write something that actually says something, actually *means* something, and then you go looking for what people think about it, you'll just end up hurt, while the people that came gunning for you move on to the next thing in two days. Grow a thicker skin and do the work of contributing to the culture and insisting on high standards, because someone has to. I get this shit every time I write anything. You don't need to save me from it. This isn't new. This is *criticism*. I'm going to bed.'

He took his kebab and he was gone.

He was such a dick. And yet, here I was, second-guessing my own reaction. Maybe Alex's response was the rational one, and I was crazy to be worrying about this at all. Perhaps being a critic did mean being someone who fomented a storm of debate with their opinions in print, and damn the consequences. Maybe I *was* bland. Maybe my problem was that I cared more about people thinking that I was right than about writing.

And I liked thinking of myself as a journalist. I liked those 1930s black-and-white films with fast-talking reporters wearing hats and tailored jackets. I liked that, on Arlo's birth certificate, I got to put down my profession as *Journalist*. I liked that it felt hardboiled and rebellious and came with an expectation of speaking truth to power. My career set me apart from my friends from school and university who had corporate jobs, and when I was probing them about some new boyfriend or tricky situation at work I could say, hey, I'm allowed to ask rude questions, *I'm a reporter*. I liked being in the newsroom and I liked getting breaking news and gossip and injunction details before anyone else. But when it came down to sheer geography of interests, yes, OK, Alex was right. I was more in the art world than the news world. I was only a reporter when it suited me.

It was true, too, that everything Alex wrote for the paper sparked a response. His reviews got more comments and shares than anyone else's. Did he, in fact, go through something similar every week, and it was just that I hadn't seen it up close before, because our interactions had until now only been in the office or at the pub? Here, effectively living together, in a strange city, everything was magnified. Maybe my worries about the outrage pelting towards Alex were just a projection of how I would react to all this – how mortally wounded *I* would be if people were saying those things about me. But they never did, because Alex was a different creature. A more robust person. A better, braver critic.

Journalism is not for the sensitive, but to write anything, you have to be a little sensitive. At least a little interested in hurts and sufferings. That's how you know where to find them. Where on the body to poke around with your knife to expose what's underneath.

Something I like about obits is that, if you pick the right clichés, you bestow a good side on anyone, even the undeserving, without technically lying. Dead people (usually men) who spent their time on Earth being colossal bastards can become *complicated* in their obit. They could have been *no stranger to controversy*, or, my favourite, because it sounds juicily gothic, they could have *wrestled with personal demons*. People (men) who were addicts and abandoned their families can be remembered as having had a *turbulent romantic history* or *a tumultuous home life*. Murderers and dictators, sure, it's harder to repackage, even if you wanted to. But even then, everyone has a version of themselves that's the version they'd want in their obit. The locked Wikipedia article version of them. The version that they could look at and say, well, I guess that's fair. Nobody ever sees themselves as the villain.

It would be hard even for me, though, to package up this particular twenty-four hours in a way that made Alex look good.

I texted Josh with a promise to call again at breakfast time and went to bed. He texted back.

I've had a lovely evening watching Master and Commander. *Speak in the morning x*

I plugged in my phone and set it facing down on the polished wooden nightstand, which looked as though it may have been there since the 1820s. I lay alone on the firm, unfamiliar double bed in my just OK navy pyjamas and turned out the lamp. The darkness amplified the sounds of shouts and breaking glass that drifted up from the pubs and clubs nearby in the streets outside.

I'd been with Josh for six years at this point. Early in our relationship, long before Arlo, we used to drink in pubs near canals in the daytime and wander around Daunt's in Marylebone making fun of each other's taste in books. We went to an occult bookshop in Bloomsbury once and were too scared to make fun of anything there in case it cursed us. We went to the Barbican Conservatory. I took him to Highgate Cemetery and we found George Eliot and Marx. We spent whole weekends lounging around his shared flat in Forest Gate.

Josh wore the roundest glasses you've ever seen and he was coat-hanger-thin, despite eating all the time. He also cycled everywhere. I might have made the mistake, if I were much younger, of equating Josh's effortless thinness with a moral superiority. Now I just think, well, it's not a trait I share. Back then, he had no money for clothes from his PhD stipend and was still wearing the same faded grey t-shirts he'd bought with his undergraduate student loan. He had a rangy intellectual absent-mindedness to him, and when he was eager or nervous or otherwise non-sexually aroused, he pushed up his sleeves to the elbow and did this little throat-clearing thing, which was one of the first things that made him adorable to me.

In Josh, I wanted something deep. I wanted someone who drank good wine and black coffee and read books and had thoughts about them, because this was all that seemed grown-up to me. He asked me what I thought about books and art, too. We almost never thought the same thing. Generally, this was because he never thought anything very concrete, not compared to me. He would tilt his head to one side, and say, well, yes, I suppose, but then, on the other hand, there is this to consider. I would say, but how can you not see it! It's self-evidently true! Why aren't more people getting this! He said he liked leaving space for every possible argument.

Our relationship worked nicely because we cast ourselves in opposing roles. He was the generous, gentle, unassuming, discursive, whimsically open-minded bookish academic; in response, I became the sarcastic, sceptical, media-savvy hack girl with a flip answer to everything. I liked being that version of myself and he liked being that version of him. I'd never met anyone who made me feel that way before: I liked what he brought out in me and what he made me.

I know some of my friends found him boring. Lily from university, who had edited the student paper with me and now worked at a glossy women's magazine, had called him Sensible Josh for the first year of our relationship. My old school friends were less cute about it, but equally unenthusiastic. He could be pleading, when he was sorry, in a way that I found truly unattractive. He desperately wanted people to think he was a sensitive man, and he would never knowingly offend anyone. Sometimes, often, this was infuriating.

But when the newspaper was being insane, and I'd had to work a whole day covering culture news that nobody would care about two weeks down the line, and someone had shouted at me for not filing the copy quick enough, coming home to Josh felt like coming back to a castle no enemy could penetrate.

Until that changed. Anyway, this is how things were.

My phone buzzed with a BBC news alert about something happening in Russia so I picked it up again and swiped away the notification. I read a news story about an Instagram account that tracked the private jet usage of celebrities. It posted every time they took off and when they landed, with a calculation of how much carbon they released into the atmosphere with each trip. It followed their journeys with tiny plane icons gradually exuding a long yellow line behind them, indicating the trail of their route. It was strangely soothing to imagine these celebrities soaring above their own fame, finally alone in the clouds, taking their dogs and cats with them in the cabin as they breezed back and forth across the Atlantic, drinking angelic cocktails, toxifying the sky.

I'd never looked Alex up online, not properly. After what Hayley had said in her show, this seemed like a serious oversight. I had only ever googled people I was potentially dating, or wanted to see more of, not colleagues. LinkedIn was about as far as it went, and I didn't even have an account there. But some of the messages I'd seen on social media that night, about how Alex was a nepo baby, about how this had been coming for a long time, about how he had hurt people – these things kept me awake, like a slight, dull throb of pain somewhere non-specific in my body. I realised, quite suddenly, that I was staying alone in a flat with this guy, and, despite having worked with him for years, there was a lot I didn't know about him. In the last few days, the main two things I'd learned were that he sometimes read Beckett scripts while he ate breakfast, and he took his coffee into the shower. I knew he had a vinyl collection and a Moleskine, and seemed slightly embarrassed about both of these things, even though he also unironically liked them. I opened the browser on my phone. I searched his name.

There was enough information about Alex online that Google served you a little package about him at the top with his name as a kind of headline, with two pictures: his byline picture from the paper and a screenshot of that one time he'd been on TV for a Sky News debate about content warnings in West End shows. Above these was an AI-generated one-line explainer of who he was. It said: *Journalist. Son of Judith Lyons.*

That fact, the son of Judith Lyons thing, was something everyone knew. It was what people online meant when they called him a nepo baby and it was what I thought when I was first introduced to Alex on my first day in the office, too – *Huh, I wonder if he's related to . . .*

I was interested in what it must be like to be the child of a star. My mother was not famous. She was an art therapist specialising in addiction recovery. She died three years before all this. There isn't really ever a good way to bring it up. It's always a bump in the conversation with someone new, because I am still relatively young to have lost a parent. I'm used to it now. These days, if someone mentions mothers, or asks after my parents, or suggests that my mother must love being a grandparent, I say, *my mother died a few years ago.* Sometimes, to spare the other person's feelings, I add the word *unfortunately.* As though she was just unlucky. As though any of us might escape it.

This is growth for me, because in the early days, I just used to say to people, *my mother is dead!* Dead sounds worse than died. I don't know why, it just does. And for a while I felt that I should make it sound as bad as possible.

But then, people's awkwardness in response only felt like another burden. I don't like *passed away.* I like real words for things. She died. She is dead.

As the daughter of a therapist, I know the importance of grief counselling, so I booked the six sessions that were included as part of the Mental Wellness portion of the paper's annual benefits package, which took place over video calling software. I guess it helped. I talked through it all to the extent that I didn't feel the need to talk about it again afterwards. The diagnosis – pancreatic cancer, which is a synonym for 'no hope' – and the rapid decline, and the sudden gaping in the fabric of our little family, which had only ever been the two of us, now leaving only me.

I didn't need counselling to realise that grief would never leave me, and that the rest of my life would only gradually grow around it. So I was prepared when my counsellor, Linda, gently tried to guide me towards these personal revelations. In our final session, Linda said I'd been on a very healthy journey.

'Women are natural grievers,' Linda said on the other side of the screen, her voice occasionally glitching in and out through my headphones. A framed picture of a sea view was visible on the wall behind her. 'Men are trickier. They tend to replace their lost person with an infatuated obsession over someone new, and think they've fixed it. As a counsellor, it can be frustrating.'

I imagined a lot of things were frustrating for a counsellor. Only hearing one side of the story, for one thing. One person's list of gripes, hurts and grievances, their self-doubt, their blinkered view on the world. I wondered if counsellors ever wanted to go and ask their patients' families and friends for another perspective, or if I was missing the point. I'd thanked Linda for her time and felt pleased that I'd impressed her. That I'd ticked that box.

Alex had his own Wikipedia page, but this only consisted of three lines: the paper he worked for, a couple of other publications where he'd written, and that other detail again, that he was the son of Judith Lyons. There was no mention of a father. Wikipedia didn't know Alex's exact date of birth, and put his year of birth at 1989 with his age as 33–34, which was correct (I'd been at his thirty-fourth birthday party in March, held in the same pub near work where we all went for Friday drinks every week, except this time Alex had hired the room upstairs to fill with an extensive supply of women in arts and media, and at about 11 p.m. most of them went on somewhere else and I went home, because I was still on maternity leave then, and had only gone along as a means of reconnecting with my colleagues before starting work again, and the whole thing had been so overwhelming that it left me in a state of dizzy exhaustion).

I'd never added him on Facebook, because that was a thing people had already mostly stopped doing at around the time we met, but I looked now at his partially private profile and saw that we had twenty-two mutual friends. I remembered that, soon after we'd started working together, he'd broken up with a long-term girlfriend called Soraya, which he'd moped about for a while, but I'd never found out much more about what had happened there. The available information revealed that Alex had gone to a private day school in London and then Oxford. This last fact I already knew, because he had told me quite soon after we started working together, and then in the same conversation he'd said the only point of going to such an embarrassing university is so you could mention it occasionally and hate yourself. I'd responded that I'd gone to Cambridge. He'd said, yeah, then you know how it is.

There were a few available pictures. Alex at Glastonbury festival five years ago, wearing neon wristbands and green plastic sunglasses, making a peace sign, his arms around a guy and a girl. Alex two years ago with four friends on a Scottish beach looking moody. Alex last autumn, browsing in a cluttered second-hand bookshop, one hand to his mouth with his fingers curled in thought, and this last one was a photograph so intimate and tenderly observed and possibly taken with an analogue film camera (something about the grain, or the quality of light) that I concluded it must be the work of a girlfriend. Further evidence: it was liked by one person, whose name was India Morris. Her profile was completely locked down.

He had a locked Instagram account that I'd never followed. On Twitter, where I did already follow him, he posted links to his own articles and the occasional pointed political observation. His likes were mostly memes and the odd thirst trap.

I kept going, beyond the first page of Google results, delving deeper into the traces that Alex had left on the internet. I was glad the light was off. Doing this felt invasive. It was as if I were going through the drawers where he kept old clothes or putting my hands in his hair. It reminded me of things I'd written once and posted online without thinking enough about it being there forever – back when blogs were a big deal – and that still probably existed on the internet somewhere, and that I sometimes remembered with an internal downpour of horror and self-loathing when I was brushing my teeth. I worried there might be karma at play here where if I looked too far into Alex's history on the internet, somebody somewhere might, in turn, look too far into mine.

Here in the surviving fragments of Alex's past I found that he had won a national poetry competition as a teenager, for a poem about a blue bird of paradise. It had an unusual rhyme scheme and a surprisingly mature sense of loss for a 16-year-old boy.

As well as the paper, in his ten years in journalism, Alex had written for a theatre magazine and some business-to-business trade publications for the wine industry, which was a surprise. He'd had a jokey blog in 2011 about celebrities wearing badly fitting trousers, on which he had posted four times before abandoning it. There were the archaeological remains of a Tumblr with the same username as his Twitter handle, but this had nothing on it any more. For an exciting moment I thought that this same username, a reference to Virginia Woolf, might also exist as an account on a fanfiction website, but then I realised I was reading it wrong, and that other account actually seemed to belong to a woman in Ohio who was obsessed with *How I Met Your Mother*.

And there I met a dead end. There was a slim, dark blue column of night between the curtains. It was late, now, and the streets were quieter. I still couldn't sleep. Judith Lyons, it occurred to me, was the kind of well-known figure I might be asked to prepare a stock obituary for. We almost certainly already had one on file. I considered asking Brian, the obits editor, about it. In any case, there would be plenty of information about *her* online.

Judith Lyons, the internet told me, had been born in Edinburgh in 1946 and had spent the late 1960s as an ingenue darling of the stage in London, adjacent to the flower child movement, after studying at RADA. Concealing her childhood accent, she had played Juliet and Lady Macbeth and Ophelia at the National Theatre, and on the BBC's televised plays, and then, in the 1980s, as the leading lady roles had fallen away, she had gradually stopped acting, and turned instead to writing and directing. She had adapted the screenplay for, and directed, the definitive film version of *A Midsummer Night's Dream*, drawing on the 1960s and 70s back-to-the-land movement for her version of the fairies of the forest. She, herself, had starred as Titania. The actor who played Oberon had won an Oscar.

In the 1990s she had gone back to theatre, directing plays by Tom Stoppard and Alan Bennett, and only occasionally appearing on stage herself. She had, thirteen years ago, played a female King Lear at the Globe theatre in a landmark production, and been made a dame in the same year. That was when Alex had been at Oxford, before he'd started reviewing theatre. From her list of productions on her Wikipedia page, and on her IMDB, it looked as though she hadn't been connected with anything major for about ten years.

I spent a while trying to find out who Alex's father was. He'd never mentioned him, and Judith Lyons didn't seem to have ever been married, though she was linked to a string of much younger male stars in the late 1990s. There were a lot of photographs of red-carpet appearances of her with handsome young men from this time. (Good for you, Judith.) I scrolled until I was too tired even to put my phone back on the nightstand to charge, and I fell asleep with it in my hand.

I woke to cool blue light and Alex turning the door handle to my bedroom.

'Hi.' His voice was soft, deep and croakily apologetic, underslept, one hand making a tentative shelf in the air, the other holding his phone. His skin was grey. 'Sorry, but when you asked, last night, if I'd seen – what exactly did you mean?'

5

'The messages I've been getting, Soph.' He sat down, heavily, on the end of the bed. 'And – oh God, do you still have her phone? I never met up with you to get it back. Maybe she thinks I've stolen it or something.'

And then I had to tell him. And, this time, he listened, as I sat hugging my knees under the duvet. I told him how I'd seen the posters. I told him how I'd seen the show. I admit, I glossed over some of the detail. I told him how, at first, I'd been worried about Hayley's vulnerability, but how actually it had been like watching this phoenix rising out of something, and to be honest the show had been great, really great, kind of world-changing actually, like a purer kind of performance than I'd seen before, and Alex was, after all, the reason why it had turned into something so good – his constructive criticism had clearly worked wonders, when you thought about it. She'd really taken it all on board. The only downside, as far as Alex was concerned, was that, OK, his critical reputation was potentially destroyed. And, relatedly, everyone thought he was a cunt.

After he had spent ten seconds bent double in a full-body contorted cringe with his fingers raking across his scalp, he shook out his hands and his head.

'She can't do this, though. She's using my name in her show, without my permission. You can't just *do this* to a person. It's against the law. Isn't it?'

'I don't know, Alex. This hasn't happened to me before.'

I had a shower and got dressed, and then I heard him talking to someone in the kitchen on speakerphone. I slipped in as he was making a coffee with the AeroPress, for which he required both hands.

'So it's defamation of character, isn't it, Milo? I know you're a property barrister, but you must have covered some of this on the bar course.' He pre-wet the filter before fitting together the basket and the tube to make the coffee and set a timer on his watch as it brewed. Alex didn't register my presence. I slid two slices of multi-seeded wholemeal bread into the toaster and popped it down, saying nothing.

'Mate,' said the speakerphone. 'Is it true?'

'Is what true?'

'What she's saying you did.'

'Of course it's fucking true. But it's private. Right?'

'Well, it happened to her as well, and she's telling her side of the story. I'm not giving you any professional advice here, but speaking as a friend, I'm not sure there's much you can do.'

'Isn't there a copyright issue? She's using all my words from the piece.'

'It sounds like that would fall under a fair comment defence. I'm actually due in court in about twenty minutes—'

'What about, what's it called – the Trade Descriptions Act? This show is nothing like the show information she's put in the festival programme. It's a completely different thing. A different title, and everything. It's false advertising. Can't we get her on that?'

'And do what, Alex? Get Trading Standards to confiscate her microphone?'

'Can they do that?'

'What remedy do you want? Mate, you're not listening to me. I don't think there's a legal case here. She's going up there on stage and she's telling the truth, right? So, for now, there's nothing you can do about it. I think you just need to take it on the chin. It's like, remember when Edmund Bullen's head was too big to fit into the school cap, and everyone called him "Headmund" for a bit?'

'But everyone still calls him Headmund, and he's thirty-four. Look, I'm not saying we actually *do* any of the legal stuff. You can just write her a cease-and-desist letter threatening to sue her or whatever, and she'll get scared and stop.' The timer on his watch went off and he plunged the coffee into a plain white mug.

'Personally,' I said, 'I don't think that's a good idea.'

'Milo, that's my flatmate. She's my inside man, the one that saw the show. Why not?'

'If you write Hayley an angry letter,' I said, putting my toast on a plate and unscrewing the red gingham lid of a jar of Bonne Maman, 'she'll post it online. No, she'll put it *in the show*.' I pointed my jammy knife at him. 'Anything you give her now is just more material that'll make the whole thing worse. Anything you put in writing, any letter, email, message. Even an apology. You *are* the show, Alex. Anything you do will just fuel it.'

'Sorry, bud,' said speakerphone-Milo. 'Sounds like a shit situation. You still going to Jamie's stag next month?'

Alex tried to buy a ticket for Hayley's show that night, so that he could at least see it in person and know exactly what he was dealing with. Stuart MacAskill's review of the revamped show had gone online that morning, a five-star rave, calling it 'a masterpiece that may permanently alter the British theatre scene and explode the foundations of the performer-critic power dynamic'.

Yes, Stuart had written, the show was short and rough and unfinished. But, he went on, this was

> precisely what makes Sinclair's achievement so exciting. She made the audience feel as if we were at the centre of a drama which is still unfolding, a work still being wrought, with many possible ending points ahead, all of them chilling. As the Ancient Greeks might have felt when gathering at a hecatomb, attending this kind of theatre feels essentially ritualistic, unpredictable, horrifyingly real, somehow inevitable. You can't look, and yet you cannot look away. The only possible response is awe.

The Fringe ticketing app had a little blue clickable calendar on the booking page, and every date for Hayley's show in the week ahead was coloured red. The box office guy on the phone, when Alex called them, after he'd waited on hold for six minutes listening to an eight-bar loop from a pop song that came out a decade ago, confirmed that yes, tonight's performance was sold out, and so were the next eight shows. No, there were no more press tickets available.

'But *I'm* Alex Lyons,' said Alex. 'The show is *about me*.'

The box office person laughed. 'I'd be trying to avoid seeing it if I were you then, pal. Is there anything else I can help you with today?'

Alex hung up.

He was desperate to stop Hayley. I knew he was rattled because he'd given the German *Richard III* production two stars instead of one and said in his review that it was 'relatively compelling', which is the kind of meaningless semi-positive statement that only two days ago he would have ripped it out of me for writing.

I realised there was a part of Alex that couldn't quite believe that nobody was coming to help him out of this, that there was truly nothing he could do, that all this was being thrown at him and the cavalry was not coming to save him. That helplessness, when I saw it in him, pulled at something familiar in me.

Josh rang me and I took the call in the bedroom, though I was reluctant to leave Alex at that moment. The kitchen, on that morning, had the same crisis summit feel that we got in the newsroom in London during moments of national breaking news, when a prime minister resigned or there was a big police incident. When everyone gathered around the big screens suspended from the ceiling that were tuned to the rolling BBC news coverage, and the editor called an urgent conference for the section editors and writers on duty to discuss how to cover it. We all liked being scrambled to cover a major disaster. It was a thrill. (Not that I would admit this to anyone who wasn't a journalist, because it would come out wrong.)

'I saw some stuff about Alex online,' said Josh on the phone. 'What an absolute bellend.'

'Mm,' I said. 'He's freaking out a bit today.'

'I bet. Hope it's not too awkward for you. By the way,' Josh said, so deliberately casual that it put me on alert, 'I ordered a new high chair. I kept tripping over the sticky-out legs on the current one.'

'What? Which one did you buy?'

'A grey one, from Argos. Twenty quid, can't argue with that, I thought.'

'You don't remember the brand? Did it have good reviews?'

'Does it matter, for twenty quid? It's called Little Genius, or something. I don't remember, all kids' stuff has such inane names.'

'Josh, *no*. I've read about those ones. They don't last. And they're hard to clean. If we were going to get a new high chair to replace the one that Sarah was lending us, I wanted it to be that solid wooden one with the steps, the one that *grows with the child*.'

'But didn't you say that one was like two hundred pounds?'

'Yes, but Nina says it lasts them their entire childhood. And it has great reviews online. Why didn't you run this past me?'

'Because I knew you'd say this. And you're not here. I'm the one looking after Arlo while you work for an entire month, and he needed a new high chair, so I bought one.'

'It's not a month. It's just over three weeks. And we'll only have to get rid of it eventually. And I'll be the one who has to list it on Facebook Marketplace.'

'You have to let me make some decisions, sometimes. I'm a parent, too.'

'I know that.'

When I'd first met Josh, through friends at a party, we'd stayed up most of the night talking at my friend Lily's flat after everyone else had passed out or gone home. We talked about our favourite writers, and how nobody ever offered us drugs at parties because we must not look the type, and how we'd both played *Legend of Zelda* games when we were teenagers. He did this dorky thing of waving his hands when he was excited about something and he had amusing hobbies, such as collecting prints of woodcuts from broadside ballads. He also collected antique cigarette lighters, even though he didn't smoke. He showed me a gold one from the 1930s with an intricate monogrammed engraving of the letter S swirled into a pattern of filigree. He asked if I wanted to borrow it. I said I didn't, and he said he was relieved, because he didn't think he could part with it. I made fun of him a little about collecting the lighters. It was the kind of thing an old man might do, and I teased him about that. Why collect something when your hands have no need of it? How could you even learn how to love such a thing, entirely designed for people with different habits from yours?

'I'm the best person to look after them,' he'd said, 'because I'll never use them.'

'But why do you even like them,' I said, 'if you don't use them?'

'It's just funny to me that, as a species, we spent thousands of years figuring out how to make fire, and now we can carry it around in our pocket and we never even think about it.'

I could never do that, I said. I never could mind my own business. I have to use things. I have to know how they feel in my hands. He let me run my finger over the wheel and send up the flame.

The first time I'd introduced Josh to my mother, at a pub near our house, she'd gone all giggly afterwards.

'What?' I said. 'He's sweet!'

'I like him!' she said. 'He looks like Indiana Jones, if Indiana Jones worked in a library.'

And then she'd laughed for ages. She did like Josh a lot, though. 'He's passionate about things, and he's articulate when he talks about them,' she said. 'You don't know how rare that is for adults.' She asked him for book recommendations and often said she was so glad that I had found someone kind. She said it again, as she was dying, in those long evenings where it was just me and her, in the silence left by infinite questions about her life, her childhood, her hopes, her passions, that I couldn't bring myself to ask.

It was always me and her. She and my father had met at art college, and he had become an art teacher in a private school for boys. They had separated when I was very young.

'We're all right just us girls, aren't we Sophie?' she said as she made fruit compote from the raspberries in the garden on Saturday mornings, dancing to the radio.

And we were. She was thoughtful, wry and floatily artistic. I made her laugh.

My dad sent me birthday and Christmas presents and took me out for dinners twice a year, during which he surveyed me with a distant, amused interest. We were more like business partners than close relations. He was always there in the background, even after he married Elaine, who was fine.

My mother was never with anyone else.

He seemed to take my mother's death as the end of his obligation towards me. The dinners had dropped off, though the presents continued. He had met Arlo once and made it clear he thought that he could now check it off his list. I read somewhere that some men only love their children for as long as they love the mother of their children. I tried not to think about that too much.

Josh had gone back to work almost as soon as Arlo was born, teaching at the university where he worked in the English faculty on a contract that was, long after he'd got his PhD, finally approaching something that might soon become permanent. Early modern poetry was his specialism, but there isn't a lot of money in that, which made me, as a journalist in the private sector on a contract with enhanced maternity pay, the breadwinner.

Only, somehow, it had turned out that I wasn't just the breadwinner. I earned most of the money, cooked most of the meals, cleaned most of the clothes, not to mention grew all of the child. Josh earned less than I did, but he worked more hours and his contract was more precarious, and therefore, until I was sent to Edinburgh, his job had always been the priority, even though when I thought about it, I couldn't remember a specific time when we'd actually agreed that.

Maybe that sounds like I resented Josh. And maybe I did. But when he came home in the evenings, and he'd sit marking papers while we watched some sprawling critically acclaimed drama series on TV, for a few hours, I felt warm and safe. On Saturday mornings he'd take Arlo to the swimming pool so I could sleep. He made me a coffee every day before he left for work. Maybe this was just what things had to be like for everyone with small children. Maybe this was temporary.

Still, it was hard. The university had given Josh just the legal minimum of two weeks of paternity leave and we blew through that in a haze of bleeding and tears and silent wonder at Arlo as the new centre of our very small flat.

Josh's parents came to visit one afternoon on day three after Arlo was born and his mother asked, with her hand on my forearm, if I'd noticed that the dishes were piling up a bit, weren't they, and was I coping? And I'd said yes, I was coping fine. She did not wash any of the dishes, or tell Josh to do them. Josh's father had sat on our sofa frowning at YouTube on his phone for two hours and accepting the tea and biscuits that I brought him. My breasts hurt so badly that I cried in our bedroom for the last half hour of their visit while I held a sleeping Arlo, snuggled in the blue-and-green woollen blanket that I'd knitted for him while I was pregnant, knitting being something I'd taught myself to do purely because it was difficult for me to learn and I had to concentrate on it, and when I was concentrating on knitting, I wasn't concentrating on the creeping feeling of doom that had started to curl the edges of my life.

I couldn't call my mother because she was dead.

Josh went back to the university, commuting an hour each way on the train. On that first Monday, in his beanie hat and favourite green teaching jumper, he looked as though he was dressing up in someone else's clothes.

Josh cried a little at the door as Arlo slept on my chest. He kissed my cheek and then Arlo's head, and said he was so sorry he had to go, and he didn't want to, and he couldn't believe how much he was going to miss. And then he cycled to the station, his body unchanged by the emotional earthquake of the last fortnight, and it was just me and Arlo, for hours and hours, alone in the house with the radio on, and a deep silence that no background noise could obscure.

I then became extremely aware that I was the only person available to clean Arlo's little bottom and put milk into his mouth and keep him warm and safe and alive, and either on his back and breathing, or cuddled close to me and making little piglet snorting noises. This all seemed impossible. How could it be that this was really it, all day and all night, all up to me, waking every hour to feed my baby again from my hurting body? A pigeon landed outside the window and looked right at me. Arlo was sick all over my top, and he cried, and I cried. How could it be that nobody was coming? Life really begins like this?

How could it be that my work and my education, all the things I'd taken so much care over so many years to learn, overnight amounted to no useful skills at all? Why had I bothered reading all those books about art and history? They sat on my shelves, laughing at me. Oh ho, said the books. You'll never read one of us again. Those days are gone. Ciao!

By the end of my year on maternity leave, I'd rearranged

my life so that everything pointed towards Arlo. I'd got used to having him at the centre of everything. And now, I had to leave him at nursery so I could go back to the newsroom, delegating smiling at his jolly little face (those cheeks were my mother's) to other women all day, while I put on a skirt and tights and got a skinny mocha to go from the kiosk at the station (the 'skinny' part of the order was a placebo; the double shot was not), to check my pass still opened the silver barriers at the office, to remember how to pretend to be someone who wasn't grieving. Grieving for so many things, now, that I couldn't separate them from one another. Two months later, Graham sent me to report from Edinburgh with Alex, which was a privilege, and an act of trust, and I had to leave Arlo behind again. I told Josh I was doing it, rather than asking him for his opinion. He knew better than to object. If he had, even a tiny bit, I might not have come.

Alex and I both had shows to see that day. I had one exhibition to visit, a graduate art show, and an obituary of a clarinettist to write. Alex had a string of small, hour-long Fringe shows by hopeful new writers, and he was still on edge when he headed out the door to see them. But when I saw him again in the afternoon, back at the flat, before he needed to go out again for a major International Festival show that had transferred from China, he looked unnervingly relaxed.

'I stopped in a bookshop and read some of this book about being publicly shamed.' Alex leaned on the kitchen counter next to his phone, eating a bowl of Rice Krispies, which I hadn't seen someone do at five in the afternoon since I was a student. 'The secret is to wait. It'll blow over.

The news cycle is short. She's told her story – fine. It can't get any worse, can it?'

I told him I admired how philosophical he was being.

'Sure,' he went on. 'Because even if she spends the whole month telling this story, over and over, so what? I just have to brazen it out and keep writing reviews until everyone moves on to the next thing.'

We were going out in the same direction, because I wanted to buy myself dinner, and so we walked for a while in companionable silence. The streets were full of people drifting across the road with blue and orange lanyards around their necks. Alex lit a cigarette. I didn't understand the point in smoking a poetic brand of French cigarettes that were known for the nicely designed blue boxes they'd once had, when all cigarette packets were now sold in the same deliberately off-putting vomit-coloured packaging. But I didn't smoke, so maybe it tasted different or something.

Alex sometimes, as he did now, had the hungry and distracted look of John Lennon in the 70s about him, an aesthetic which my mother, actually, would probably have considered optimal. She was from Liverpool, where she'd been an original flower child, and done the whole art college thing. She considered the Beatles to be *her* band and played them all the time, along with all the folk and country queens of the 1960s and 70s.

I was daydreaming in this way, thinking of her with something that was not entirely sadness, when I saw it. On the corner of Lady Lawson Street, there was a poster that I hadn't seen before, for Hayley's show, on the hoardings at the bottom of the hill. We both stopped. As well as the banner across the poster that proclaimed the show's altered title to be *THE ALEX LYONS EXPERIENCE*, there was a new amendment, in a much larger sticker of unignorable pink. It read:

TONIGHT @ 9PM!
LIVE STREAMED ONLINE DUE TO POPULAR DEMAND!
FEATURING SPECIAL GUEST:
INDIA MORRIS

6

We never agreed out loud that we would watch it together, it was just obvious that we would. So, that night, we logged in to the livestream of Hayley's show at the flat when Alex got back from seeing his play. To make an event of it, we ordered chicken shawarma wraps, chips and dips from a Lebanese place. I bit into my wrap and a translucent orange sauce ran down the side of my hand to my wrist, so I licked it all the way along to stop it from dripping onto my phone. I sat on the floor and leaned my back against the tattered green sofa, and Alex stood near the door, as if keeping his distance from an unpredictable animal. He shifted his weight from foot to foot, biting the nail on his thumb.

Even seen through a laptop screen, and filmed from a single fixed camera, with the stage lighting painting Hayley tangerine, her account of what happened was a tour de force. I ate the dinner mostly to give my hands and eyes something to do that wasn't what I really wanted to do, which was to witness Alex going through the most intense emotional discomfort of his life. In my peripheral vision, he was breathing heavily and then holding his breath, alternating between wrapping his arms around his chest and putting both of his hands on top of his head.

Eventually he had his hands over his eyes, just saying 'Oh God, oh Goddddd', over and over again in a monotone, which reminded me of a Gregorian chant at a choral concert I'd reviewed once in Islington.

'And now,' Hayley said. 'I have a very special guest joining me on stage. Please welcome my new best friend, India Morris!'

'Are we worried about India?'

'We just dated for a little bit,' said Alex. 'There's nothing anybody could complain about. It didn't work out. One of those things.'

She was an actress, too, Alex said as India settled into her seat onstage to applause. She was his most recent ex, the one who'd taken the moody Facebook photo of him in the bookshop. They'd had a situationship for a few months last autumn until he'd ghosted her because, he said, 'She couldn't keep up. It would have been cruel to let it go on any longer.'

India told Hayley that she was in Edinburgh that summer because she had a part in a new play about a sci-fi dystopia where AI takes over a town in Suffolk. India played the AI. She, like me, had seen the posters for Hayley's show, recognised Alex's name, and bought a ticket. And she had spoken to Hayley after the show, and said that she, too, had a story to tell.

India was tall, maybe almost as tall as Alex, with straight, dark hair. She was thirty years old, and, in a black dress with batwing sleeves, looked like an elevated teen goth.

The story she told, on stage, started with how India and Alex had met on an app. Alex's picture had shown him looking off to the right with a half-smile, and on his profile he'd mentioned authors he liked: Hanya Yanagihara, Sally Rooney, Chimamanda Ngozi Adichie. And then, almost as an afterthought, Truman Capote. Hayley nodded with her eyes closed in recognition while India was saying these names, like, *yeah, yup, checks out.*

Alex and India had been seeing each other for a few weeks before he'd come to a show that she was in. This was a turning point. He didn't review it, but afterwards he'd made her feel, subtly, without ever saying it outright, as if she wasn't a very good actress. As if there were an invisible league of talent for which she didn't quite qualify. When Alex looked at India after that, India said it was always as if he were looking slightly to the right of where she really was, not meeting her eye.

'One time,' India said, with her long legs crossed, leaning forwards and holding the microphone, opposite Hayley. 'He said, it's not as though you'd do Ibsen, is it? It's not like you could do Stoppard. He said that, for some actresses, the ceiling of their career might be a soap opera, and that's where I should aim.'

'That's not a bad thing!' Alex said from behind me, seemingly involuntarily, bursting through his hands.

'Stoppard's heavy going.' I dipped a lukewarm chip into a cardboard pot of muhammara. 'Did you mean it as a compliment?'

'No, but I didn't think she'd realise that.'

'And then, just before Christmas,' said India. 'He wrote an article for his Hot Ticket column thing that he has, listing the best and worst shows currently on in London.

And he put mine in there, under the worst column, with just one line about it, and he said it was to be avoided at all costs. And then he just ghosted me.'

'It's almost like a foreshadowing,' said Hayley. 'Like, an escalation of behaviour. Like they say about sex criminals starting out with indecent exposure.'

India and Hayley talked about Alex, what he was like, did little impressions of the way he smoked his cigarettes. They were sisterly and conspiratorial and funny about him.

Undoubtedly, this was bad for Alex. The problem with India contributing her own story to Hayley's show was that it started to make Alex look not just like a critic who'd once made some awful transgression and treated one person badly. It started to make him look predatory, like someone with a pattern. It started to make redemption seem impossible. It actually started to gross me out, too, even though, instinctively, I still felt as though Alex and I were on the same team, bound by the same commitment to a paper with an office four hundred miles away, linked by Graham as our line manager and invitations to the same Christmas party. Was it too much to call it gang loyalty? Just by being a critic at all, in the same line of work as Alex, I felt like an accomplice. Sides were being taken, and I fell naturally on his.

When the standing ovation was over, Hayley signed off with a promise that the show would be live online every night for the rest of the month. Alex sat next to me on the sofa. He was staring at the laptop screen, which had now turned black and was displaying a message in small white text saying: *Live stream has ended. Please close this window.*

*

I kept him company as he smoked on the street outside. It was busy with people going to late shows. Six American teenagers and their teacher, all in matching polo shirts with the name of their school on the back, stood in a circle doing vocal warm-up exercises. In the other direction, two drag queens, both over six feet tall and at least ten years older than us, one wearing a gigantic purple feather head-dress and the other in turquoise PVC heels, toppled towards us, taking it in turns to swig vodka from a bottle.

'Cheer up, sweetheart.' The queen in the headdress winked at a miserable Alex as they passed. 'It's the festival!' They turned the corner, laughing.

'How many stars,' I said, leaning against the rectangle of intercom buttons in the doorway that smelled of urine, 'would you give her show now?'

'Three? One? I don't know any more. This isn't *theatre*, is it?'

Alex knew that what he'd done was wrong. He said as much. But, at the same time, his behaviour, his rattled frustration, told me that there was a feedback loop going in his brain telling him that, while it was wrong, it wasn't *that* wrong. All that had happened was that two people had met at a bar and had sex. It was, in many ways, a happy story. She wasn't blackout drunk. She hadn't said no. He hadn't done anything to her that she hadn't *wanted* him to do. The sex was good, even. It was something that had probably also happened between a hundred other people that same night in Edinburgh alone. Alex was the only one being punished for it.

And after all, Hayley had been the one, in the Traverse bar, who'd asked him where he was going next. She'd leaned into him when he'd kissed her. She was the one who'd said she wanted another drink, but she didn't want to pay festival bar prices. And yeah, OK, he was the one who suggested they just pick up something from the Sainsburys Local to drink at his place, which was only round the corner. But she had said, that sounds good, and she had selected and bought the gin and a bottle of tonic and discovered a single, shrivelled lime in the fruit and veg aisle, and posed with it for the security cameras at the self-checkout.

At the flat, she was talking and joking and touching his clothes and his hair. She was the one who'd sat close to him on the sofa, while they had the whole endless flat to themselves, while I was out at my show. She was the one who'd put her hands on the back of his head as he licked her clit, and said, yeah, keep doing *that*.

OK, so she'd consented. But she didn't have all the relevant information about the person she was with. Alex was not stupid. He could acknowledge that, if Hayley had known about his contempt, known what he'd written about her show, known what he was – come on – *deliberately keeping from her*, she would never have gone anywhere with him. If she'd had all the information, none of it would have happened.

'But how is that different from any other relationship that doesn't work out?' Alex stared down the road in the direction the drag queens had gone, in the direction of the Sainsburys where Hayley had bought the gin. The lights from the pub on the corner were brightening as the night deepened. 'Every break-up happens because the other person gradually realises that you were awful all along. The only difference is that she discovered I'm awful all at once, on day two.'

That reminded me of something my friend Zara had said to me once, when we were renting a flat together when I first moved to London. It was a tiny, damp, third-floor ex-LA flat in Leyton which we rented from an Austrian woman. When I told Zara I'd got the job at the paper, she'd said, 'With every job I've ever had, if I'd known beforehand exactly what that job entailed, I never would have taken it. But still, congratulations.'

Soon after that, the ceiling of the flat fell in where the damp plaster in the bedroom had disintegrated, and I moved in with Josh.

I told Alex about Zara's philosophy. Alex agreed that it also applied to relationships. If you had all the information, up front, about everyone you were considering sleeping with – a slideshow of all their worst moments, a clip of the most skeevy porn to which they'd ever masturbated, the most embarrassing anatomical problem in their search history, their most unreasonable political belief, that terrible thing they'd screamed at their mother – would you still sleep with them? Probably not. Every new fuck is a calculated risk.

'But then,' I said. 'You didn't have all the information about her, either.'

'That's true,' said Alex. 'I've never even googled her.'

I got out my phone. There actually wasn't much on the internet about Hayley Sinclair, not from before the last 24 hours. She was a few years younger than us, and apparently more adept at keeping her private self hidden online. In any case, there were other people with the same name, who were clearly not her: an English rugby player, an accountant in Perth. The Hayley that we wanted was not to be found on Facebook or Twitter. She had a brief write-up on the website of her agency, a small company without anyone famous on their roster, which said:

Hayley studied English at the University of Bristol before going on to the Royal Central School of Speech and Drama, where she gained an MFA in Advanced Theatre Practice. She is based in London.

Performance credits include: Angela in *Blue Remembered Hills* (Bush Theatre), Belle in *La Belle et La Bête* (Charing Cross Theatre), Duchess of Malfi in *The Duchess of Malfi* (Watford Palace Theatre), Rita in *The Sex Business* (The Other Palace), Annabelle in *Pendulum Baby* (Royal Court), Ensemble in *Pandemic! The Musical* (Maltings Arts Theatre).

She is a passionate sustainability activist and this year is the co-writer, creator and performer of a new solo show, *Climate Emergence-She*, for the Edinburgh Festival Fringe in association with True North Stage.

Next to the profile were two headshots. One serious face in black-and-white, and one laughing face in colour. In both of them, Hayley's skin was clear and perfect, her eyes supernaturally enhanced. The agency page linked to her Spotlight profile, where her listed skills included a playing age of 20–30, an 'expansive, sexy' vocal character, an alto singing range, and the accents English-RP, American-California, American-New York, American-Standard (Native), Australian, Cockney.

The only other thing of note that we found was a short interview with Hayley from July in a London newspaper, profiling *Climate Emergence-She* as part of a 'What's On at the Edinburgh Festival' round-up. This feature was the reason that Hayley's show had come to the attention of Graham at the paper, when he'd been putting together the list of shows and events for me and Alex to review, and said we should cover something contemporary, something about feminism and the climate. Hayley's interviewer for the piece was Ethan Harlowe, who had been an intern with us at the paper two years ago. It was a short Q&A and I read it aloud from my phone while Alex ground the end of his cigarette under his Doc Martens.

What do you hope people will take away from the show?

I've put my heart and soul into this show, which was co-written by my friend Marie. Marie is an actress, but she has a chronic condition that's stopped her working. She feels passionately about getting this message out there, so I want to do it for her. I've never performed my own writing before, but a lot of people have put a lot of faith in this show, and funding too, which is fantastic. I also decided to make it a critique of white male supremacy, which Marie and I have been talking about for a long time. I'd like to do another show about feminism one day. I have a lot I'd like to explore there. But for now, I just hope that people fall in love with our show and our cause, which is the endangered natural world, because we've worked so hard on it. It's definitely the most significant moment in my career so far.

Alex asked if we could stop reading about Hayley now.

The next morning, Paul Ellis called Alex. Paul was our most senior editor in London, except for the editor of the paper as a whole. He was above Graham and stayed out of commissioning, so if he called, someone was either about to be made redundant or to be given some particularly unpleasant brief. For example, ghost-writing an article by a cabinet minister. It worried me that he'd remembered we existed.

Paul was a white man of fifty who had begun his career as a hip-hop critic for a cult music magazine, and had undertaken this vocation happily until he discovered that managerial editing roles at national newspapers paid much more. He still, however, considered himself an expert on hip-hop. He wore suits, except on Fridays, when he wore jeans and a grey marl hoodie. ('I love how Paul keeps it real,' Alex said one time, in front of him.)

After my job interview with Graham and Paul, Paul had been the one to offer me the junior culture writer role, my first full-time gig at the paper. Paul had said I was a nice writer but to stop trying to be funny. I'd thanked him, and then filed my copy to Graham whenever possible.

Paul was not angry with Alex. How could he be, when Alex's review of Hayley's show had got over a million hits online, and thousands of comments, and a record number of subscriber conversions for a theatre review? No, Paul was ringing because he'd heard, while driving his Tesla to the office, a teaser for *Woman's Hour* on Radio 4, in which Hayley would be appearing for a discussion of 'the ethics of men reviewing women, following a sensational backlash to a theatre review by the critic Alex Lyons'.

Alex, Paul said, needed to reclaim the narrative for the paper.

'He gave me a choice,' said Alex, as we walked together through Princes Street Gardens towards a Caffe Nero. 'Option A: go and see her new show and review it again, ideally giving it five stars. I said, look, Paul, that's no choice at all. I don't believe in censorship, and I stand by what I wrote. And anyway, she's not going to let me anywhere near the auditorium now, is she? Then he gave me option B. Which is, convince Hayley to agree to an interview, where I go to her with my sackcloth and my ashes and my Dictaphone, and say I'm so sorry for besmirching your honour, please tell me more about your pain. And then we all shake hands, and have a good laugh, and they snap a glossy picture of her looking like a girlboss for the front cover of the Saturday magazine.'

'Of course,' I said. 'God, don't they realise that'll just make everything worse? Why would she even agree to it? She must hate us all now.'

'Paul had all his usual psycho reasons.' He did a little impression of Paul's manic excitement. '"It'll drive engagement and subscribers, Alex. This is *our* story! We can't let anyone else take it over!" It's all about the bottom line for him. Good-quality criticism means nothing, it's all just monetised content, traffic and clickbait. And all this shit obviously looks like a very promising little war. He said if I did it, it could send us all stratospheric. I said, "Up to a point, Lord Copper," but I guess he hasn't read *Scoop* because he thought I'd gone insane and told me to pull myself together.'

'So you're getting the cover?' I'd never had the magazine cover. 'Did Paul say if he'd seen any of my art reviews? Is he happy with them?'

'Weirdly, we didn't get on to chatting about your career. Can we focus on me? In fact, I doubt I'm getting the cover, because, to show that I was willing, I called the agency we found last night, and turns out Hayley's not with them anymore. As of yesterday, she has a new agent.'

It turned out that Hayley's new agent was Lyla Talbot. He would not be reaching out to her about the interview; my hunch had been right after all. Lyla and Alex had indeed slept together once or twice after she'd left the paper, in circumstances that he said he'd rather not go into right now.

7

The next morning at 11 a.m., Alex hooked up with a French-Canadian comedian named Elise that he met on an app. He went to her place. After they'd had sex, he bought a book of collected Tennyson poems on his way back to the flat. He felt better.

Online, someone had put together a supercut of Hayley delivering sass in her show and looking hot. I watched it on a loop three or four times. While Alex was out, I'd checked Hayley's website again. She had put a contact form on a new, designated page:

Send in your own one-star review of notorious asshole Alex Lyons and be part of our movement!

The show was now different every time, becoming more elaborate with each performance, and we watched them all. She'd hired a set designer who'd recently graduated from art college and supplied sparkly costumes, music, and scenery in brightly coloured abstract shapes.

*

In the most recent performance, she had installed some small pyrotechnics. She would burn things, in an aluminium dustbin on stage: more copies of Alex's review; but also other newspapers and magazines that contained bad reviews of different Fringe shows, sent to her by the people they were about; small things that terrible exes had left at people's houses and never reclaimed; clothes they'd been wearing when certain things had happened that meant they couldn't ever face wearing them again.

And, as well as telling her own story, she incorporated into the show a dossier of messages, voice notes and videos from other women giving their accounts of what Alex himself had done to them.

And so, during each new show over the course of that week, through onstage speakers and video projections and screenshots, Hayley introduced her audience to the following women:

Sasha, a theatre agent who'd been seeing Alex for a few weeks when they'd bumped into his mother at Waterloo station and, instead of introducing Sasha as his girlfriend, Alex had pretended for twenty solid minutes that Sasha was his personal trainer. After that, he'd never spoken to her again. ('That was me being kind,' Alex said. 'I spared her from having to get to know my mother. Nobody ever recovers from that.')

Jasmine, older, with a tongue piercing, whom Alex had taken home after seeing a show she'd directed. He'd said to her, while they were still naked and out of breath in his bed, that he didn't fancy her, so he hoped she wasn't looking for anything serious. ('What, should I have led her on? We were both adults. I was being honest.')

Cara and Nilam, two more actresses, who had discovered that Alex had been sleeping with them both while they were both appearing in the ensemble of the same boutique musical. ('They became friends as a result of that. And I actually went to see the show again a few weeks later, and I think their bond really improved the cohesion of the piece.')

Florrie Drummond, a children's TV presenter, had sent Alex the nudes he'd requested from her, and then, when he'd ghosted her straight afterwards, lived in such constant terror that he would distribute them and ruin her career that she eventually gave up presenting and took a new job in behind-the-scenes TV production. ('But I never sent them to anyone,' said Alex. 'She didn't even ask me to delete them. She's angry about something I didn't even do!')

There were anonymous accounts too, sent from burner email addresses. An actress who was feeling low after an unsuccessful audition had gone out and got way too drunk and met Alex at a bar. She knew his name from his reviews. She gave him a blow job in a Soho alley. After that, she realised she'd lost her phone and wallet at some point in the evening, so after their encounter she accepted a crumpled twenty from him for the cab home. Once she got home, she stood in the shower for a long time.

There was a singer whose fiancé had recently killed himself. She sought out Alex online. He was a friend of a friend. She messaged Alex and told him about her grief. She said she needed to be with someone. She needed to feel something. She said she wanted someone to degrade her.

OK, he wrote back. *Now?*

They'd taken pills together and stayed up all night. Months later, she could not believe he had agreed to that request, made from the depths of her despair, loss and self-loathing. Remembering that night still made her feel sick.

('It's not like I feel good about these memories either. But this is what modern relationships are like. These women wanted me to do these things. I'm not responsible for the sad things in their lives that made them seek me out. I gave them what they were looking for.')

He couldn't meet my eye after that particular set of stories, though. I watched his hands, gripping his bottle of beer. I imagined the grip tightening around someone's neck. I saw the small flash of his incisors as he tipped the bottle back against his lips. I imagined them biting. I considered whether I was afraid, or disgusted, or neither. Most of all I struggled to picture it.

But I could believe it. I was old enough to believe it of anyone.

Miranda's story was, I think, worse. Alex had barely thought about Miranda since he was eighteen years old, and he didn't enjoy thinking about her again now. Miranda had been one of only twenty girls who had joined his expensive all-boys school for their co-educational sixth form. In the first week of the first term, the boys had convened, in secret, a 'Pull the Pig' competition, in which they voted to designate the least attractive new girl, and agreed to each chip in five pounds to a kitty that would be awarded to the first of the boys who succeeded in having sex with her. Miranda, who had an overbite and frizzy hair and played the cornet, and was taking A Levels in chemistry, maths and music, was declared the target.

Alex was the victor, succeeding after a three-week campaign. It happened at Miranda's house, in her single bed with a purple Groovy Chick duvet cover, while her parents were away at a wedding in Somerset. It had been, for Miranda, the first time. Alex had told everyone at school about it in order to collect his winnings of £515, which he had spent on an ancient car in which to learn to drive. Miranda was known as 'Lyons' Pig' for the rest of her time in sixth form. ('I didn't come up with that name. And actually I told the lads to stop saying it,' said Alex. 'And teenage boys are just. You know.')

Miranda said in her email to Hayley that while doing her A Levels she'd stopped eating, stopped going to parties, stopped trying to make friends. For a while, she abandoned her hopes of being a full-time musician. But, after a lot of work on her self-esteem at music college, she eventually joined a professional concert orchestra. At thirty-four, she was married with two young children, teaching music at an all-girls school. Still, she had never forgotten what Alex had done to her.

I wondered what my exes would say in a show about me. I doubted whether I'd made as much of an impression on mankind as Alex clearly had on these women. My romantic history was a long way from his. The first porn I watched was at the house of a boy in my year called Niall. There were six of us from school, all of us about fourteen, drinking homemade lemonade in Niall's garage on a Sunday afternoon. He had a big square computer set up on his father's old office desk in the corner. The porn was called Milf Hunter. All of us girls squealed with thrilled disgust, clutching each other as we watched a guy with a beard and a patterned shirt, apparently the Milf Hunter himself, approaching three older women around a pool that I assumed, for some reason, was in Miami.

The women all had waist-length dead straight hair, dyed either black or brass, nothing in between, and nails spiky and long with white ends. Their skin was varnished with a deep tan under scrappy little bikini tops and bottoms that arched up their thighs in a permanent hoik. At the Milf Hunter's approach, they all started alternatively kissing each other and sucking on a dildo as if it were made out of something insanely delicious, and then the Milf Hunter fucked them all in a feat of choreography as much as anything else.

Niall was about to show us another video of a woman in Thailand popping ping pong balls out of her vagina when I said I had to go home. Now, I think, I'm lucky that I reached the relatively advanced age of fourteen before I saw any of it. It seems kind of quaint to look back on now. Nobody got choked, anyway. I've read all the articles about children watching brutalising porn on their phones at school at the age of nine and I'm just as terrified about it as everyone else.

The first boy I tried to have sex with was Luke, who had an interest in art-house cinema, by which he meant the film *Mulholland Drive*. We were sixteen and watched it in his bedroom while his parents were downstairs. We'd been officially dating for a month, which felt like a really long time, and I guess it was, if all you're doing is kissing and walking up and down the high street of your small town together after school.

He was so nervous that he couldn't get hard. Shortly after that, at the suggestion of his best friend Mikey, he gave up watching porn for Lent, which he found very difficult, but which meant that, by Easter, he was risen.

By that point, though, I'd moved on to another boy at

school, Johnny, who said he masturbated ten times a day. I didn't know whether that was more or less than the average. A boy called Chris claimed to enjoy danger wanks, where he started wanking in his bedroom, then shouted for his mother, and tried to orgasm before she reached the top of the stairs. The boys all talked about edging.

I didn't know what to believe about boys.

Alex couldn't look away from the livestream. On the night of Miranda's appearance, he couldn't eat his pasta salad from the supermarket either. He stabbed at it with the bamboo fork, making figures of eight in the pesto dressing as he smeared it up the sides of the clear plastic bowl.

'There's something pornographic about this. Look, there she goes,' he said, as Hayley walked offstage at the end of the show. 'The Ghost of Christmas Yet to Come, pointing at my own name on my grave.'

Alex thought, or hoped, that Hayley's show would have a brief flare of cultural attention before burning out. He was wrong. With every day that Hayley performed her sold-out show in the week after Alex's review, her online audience grew, and so did the conversation around it. Before seven days had passed, she had been a guest on *Newsnight* and *Loose Women* and the *Today* programme on Radio 4. There was a news story in all the papers, even one in ours, though our paper buried it low down on the page, as if hoping people wouldn't read it. The piece was written, I thought very even-handedly and non-sensationally, by our colleague, Nina. ('Fucking traitorous Nina!' said Alex.)

Nina had sent me a message the day before. *Hey you, how's bonnie Scotland? They've asked me to do a story about*

Alex for the news pages, sigh. Crazy times! Is it all true, do you think?? Are you OK being up there alone with him? x

Well, he's not denying it . . . I'd replied. *But it seems like it's complicated. I'm OK, really x*

Yeah? she'd replied. *So you're taking his side?*

I didn't reply. I didn't tell Alex about it, either.

Alex still hadn't fixed up his own interview with Hayley. In truth, he wasn't even trying. Paul asked Alex daily if there were any updates, and Alex said he was working on it, and even Paul understood that it might not be immediate, but it would be worth waiting for. Paul really wanted Alex to be the one to interview her. He wanted a dual-purpose scoop and act of penance.

I heard Hayley's interview on *Woman's Hour*, purely by chance. I'd missed the beginning, and when I tuned in, sitting at the kitchen table while Alex was out at a show, Hayley was talking in her careful, husky voice about how she doesn't feel she has as much of a connection to America any more, not since the death of her mother, years ago.

'Jeez,' I said aloud to the empty room. I dunked a biscuit into my tea. 'Does everyone have a dead parent?' The room didn't answer.

Still, it was one of those things about Hayley that teased out an instinctive sympathy in me. Not for the first time, I could see another world where I'd ended up on her side instead of Alex's. She sounded as if she was absorbing every painful thing in her life and taking energy from it. I envied her that.

Hayley was talking about her upbringing in the United States. She mentioned she grew up poor, but didn't dwell on it except to say that the day she'd got her British

Citizenship she'd cried because she'd never have to worry about healthcare again. That seemed a little extreme to me, but I don't really understand how it works over there.

'But can I put it to you,' the interviewer was saying, perhaps sensing a need to change the subject from Hayley's self-mythologising, 'that some people may wonder if the scale of this response is really fair? You could have achieved the same effect, setting the record straight, and calling out bad treatment, by writing an article, maybe. Even a blog post. And then you could have carried on with the show you originally brought to the festival, which sounds as if it also had an important message at the heart of it? Why not do that?'

Hayley didn't hesitate before her response. 'Because look at all the other times women have done just that – spoken up politely when they've been abused and treated badly by men in positions of power. And what have they achieved? What's changed? Nothing. The same injustices keep happening. It's time to try something different. That's what I'm doing here. That's my project.'

The accusations against Alex evolved over the course of the week into extensive media discussions about his state of mind. Was he just a pathetic, sexist, sexually incontinent Jack Kerouac wannabe, or did he have a diagnosable narcissistic personality disorder? Should he be imprisoned, or medicated? Was he a beast or a man? Was he the embodiment of all male vice, a symbol for all men, everywhere, and here we were, finally and with Hayley as an avenging angel, approaching the reckoning that men deserved? If Alex could dish it out, why shouldn't he take it? Journalists were supposed to hold people to account, but who was there to hold *them* to account when they treated people badly?

It wasn't fair, Alex said. It wasn't as if he was some fat old sleaze with his hand on the thigh of a terrified secretary, he said. He hadn't broken the law, he said. Women had always seemed to enjoy having sex with him. Why was that suddenly wrong?

More and more each night, Hayley's show became a detailed biography of Alex's life. He was the villain in a story where she was the main character. She talked about his mother, and printed out pages and pages of his reviews from the internet and pointed out where he'd made factual errors or just been plain rude, sexist or unfair. It wasn't just a character assassination. It felt like an exorcism.

Alex had to accept that his predicament had cut through from just being a focus of Edinburgh gossip when, in the House of Commons, which had been recalled during the summer recess for another issue entirely, the Leader of the Opposition made a joke about needing to leave the chamber.

'I've got to be home in time to watch *The Alex Lyons Experience* tonight,' he said to a chorus of braying honourable members. 'Mr Lyons appears to be the only person in the country less popular than the prime minister!'

Alex received more manic calls from Paul Ellis. Alex told him that he was still working on getting the interview with Hayley for the paper. In reality, he was drinking a lot of niche craft beers, with the kind of high alcohol percentages you usually only see on spirit bottles, and smoking his lungs into dust. His eyes were red. His hair was greasy. He was still seeing shows and churning out reviews. Somehow, his reviews became even more mean-spirited, his voice more vicious with every piece he filed. Every show he saw was pointless, infuriating, an insult to the tradition of theatre. Even shows that other critics raved about, he said were a load of gash.

Alex? Graham's email response to that review was tentative. *I hope you don't mind, but instead of "a load of gash" in this paragraph, could we say, "completely without merit"?*

Fine, Alex wrote back. *I don't care.*

Still, Alex felt that there was a reasonable explanation for every one of the stories that formed part of Hayley's show. Yes, taken together, they looked bad. Individually, however, Alex said there were two sides to every encounter. And maybe that was true. About some of the events, he even said that he'd remembered them with real fondness, nostalgia, warmth to the women involved, up until now. Now everything was tainted. But with each new story, each new scorned woman arriving to make her accusation, part of Alex still believed, despite the stress that the experience was putting his body under, that this too would pass, that it would dissolve into popular culture and be dismissed as one summer of madness, and that the people who really knew him, his colleagues and his friends, would understand the truth: that Alex was, at the heart of it all, just a normal guy with normal desires who'd been unfairly exposed.

These women, Alex said, were deliberately removing the important context of all these situations so that they would seem virtuous, and he would seem like a monster. This was turning into a PR exercise for them, at his expense. He ought to write about this, he said. In fact, he ought to be in Parliament, talking about this. None of this was fair. He was the person who was wronged here. His dignified silence was costing him his reputation.

Then, over his next cigarette, he would decide that actually it was definitely best that he should say nothing at all, because he wasn't the kind of guy to be bullied into doing anything, and anyway, I was right that anything he said would only give Hayley more ammunition against him.

And then Lavinia appeared on Hayley's show. Lavinia's name, when it materialised on Hayley's website one morning, was the first moment that I saw something in Alex's face that I could recognise as self-doubt.

'Oh, fucking hell,' he said to his open laptop while I was picking bits of cereal out of the plughole in the kitchen sink, something I've always found to be an oddly satisfying task. He did this guttural sort of groan thing and his face tightened into a grimace. 'But it was so long ago!'

'What?' I said, taking off my rubber gloves. 'Who is it?'

Lavinia was Milo's little sister.

When we watched the show, it became clear why he was so worried. When Alex and Milo had both been 21, and Lavinia had just turned 17, Milo's family had invited Alex to join them on their annual two-week family holiday to their home in Tuscany. Milo had always been happily ignorant about what had really happened on the last day of that holiday, when Milo and his parents had taken a day trip to Pienza, and Lavinia stayed at the villa because she wanted one more swim in the pool, and Alex stayed behind with her, because he said he needed to catch up on some reading for his final year at university.

In the stillness of late morning, Alex had seen Lavinia wearing only her daisy-patterned swimsuit, walking past where he was reading on a rug under the orange trees beside the stone path down to the pool, her skin honeyed by the sun. The villa was quiet and entirely their own. He put down his battered black paperback of *Vanity Fair* and touched her hand. He told her that she was very pretty.

And Alex asked Lavinia, who was at boarding school and had never had a serious boyfriend before, but who'd known Alex since she'd been a child, if she wanted to lie down beside him in the shade. And, when she did, a little nervously, Alex kissed her neck and her collarbone, and, as her body responded to his touch, he gently undid the strings of her bikini, and had sex with her right there under the orange trees.

('But that was really nice,' Alex said to me.)

Almost as soon as their plane landed back at Heathrow, Alex told Lavinia that he couldn't ever speak to her again.

('OK,' said Alex. 'That was bad.')

Alex remained friends with Milo for the next thirteen years, without ever mentioning any of this. He hardly ever visited Milo's parents' house after that, and on the few occasions when he did, if Lavinia was there, he greeted her with offhand indifference. Milo didn't know about it at all, until Lavinia, who was now a thumpingly successful entertainment lawyer and did a good line in ruthless corporate sass, sent a voice note to Hayley. Hayley played it through the PA system for her show, with all of Lavinia's carefully restrained anger made audible. Hayley also made the transcript available on her website. This is how it concluded:

> Alex was someone I'd known since I was eight or nine years old. Although I'd had a privileged upbringing in many ways, it was also quite sheltered. I looked up to my only sibling, my older brother, Milo, and his friends,

with a devotion that bordered on heroism. They were so funny, so cool, so clever and well-read. They seemed to know everything about the world and to react to it all in exactly the right way, with irony and erudition and humour. They were the men that I thought *should* be in the world, the men I wanted to surround myself with. They could be silly and annoying sometimes, and they spent an incomprehensible amount of time at our house playing darts and table football and smoking roll-ups at the bottom of the garden, but Alex, in particular, had always been kind to me. He remembered surprising details about me: the names of my friends, the music I liked. I counted him as my friend, too, almost as much as Milo's. And yes, I'd probably had something like a crush on him for a long time.

Because he spent so much time with our family, I trusted completely that Alex cared for me. And I was so happy for those few minutes when I realised that he could see me, really see me, and that he wanted to be with me, too. But, after that time in Italy, when he left me hurting, and confused, I felt used. It was as if all I'd been to Alex was the fulfilling of one short moment, part of a romanticised vignette that he'd found superficially, ephemerally appealing to construct, before moving on to get another kick somewhere else.

I've thought about this a lot over the years since it happened.

At first, I assumed that Alex was maybe just embarrassed, or even ashamed. But over time, I realised that he never cared about me at all. At seventeen, I'd thought that, of all the people I might be able to be vulnerable with, to risk something of myself with, that Alex would be safe and considerate, because he truly knew me. Learning that I was wrong about something so fundamental turned out to be among the most upsetting and the bleakest moments of my adolescence.

After that, for a long time, I struggled to trust men, and, in relationships, was terrified of getting too close to anyone in case they cast me aside as casually as Alex had done. Now, in the context of all his other behaviour, and the cruelty of his writing as a critic, I have to conclude that he probably cares about nothing. And I have grown to become a stronger person only in spite of Alex, not because of him.

Milo sent him a text: *You're a fucking piece of shit.*

WEEK ONE

Saturday, 5 August

8

Somehow, only a week had passed since Hayley's first show. Alex woke from a dream in which he repeatedly slapped Hayley across the face during sex. This made him feel very uncomfortable when he woke up with a boner because it made him wonder if he really might be sick in the head.

This was the kind of thing he told me now. Sometimes, when he spoke, it was as if he had forgotten he was talking to anyone at all. It just spilled out of him, as if there was so much to say that it brimmed over and out of his mouth as he was making endless cups of black coffee. Or even while he was writing his reviews, hammering away at his laptop as he ranted. It was amazing the way he could split his brain like that and be writing one thing while saying something completely different. Often, I didn't say anything back. I just let him speak.

There were some people who wrote in to Hayley's show who had never had a direct personal encounter with Alex, but who had suffered as a result of his bad reviews. Alex was just as indignant about these. What about the five-star reviews he occasionally handed out? What about the grateful actors who'd been able to afford to buy a house because of the ticket sales that Alex's reviews had helped to generate? Didn't that cancel it out? Where were they?

None of them, if they existed, contributed. Instead, Hayley heard about a one-star review of a production of *Macbeth* that had been so excoriating about the lead actor, whose name was Daniel, that he had given up his acting dream and retrained as a social worker and trauma healing advocate.

Hasan, a puppeteer, had blamed the breakdown of his marriage on the stress of Alex's one-star review.

An actress called Dreda, a single mother of very young children, had borrowed money to pay for the childcare for her show and got into unmanageable amounts of debt for her first big break. She was singled out for particular and personal criticism by Alex in his one-star review of the original romantic musical in which she was the star. She told Hayley that she had considered taking her own life, when it seemed her career was really over, and it was only the fact that it was a Saturday and she had nobody else to take care of her children the next day which stopped her.

The stories about Alex's sex life were the ones that stoked the social media fires. They were what kept people talking. But the stories of the people Alex had reviewed were the ones that troubled me most. Dreda's account haunted me. I imagined her reading the paper, alone at home after the children were asleep. I imagined how helpless she must have felt to see her reputation, her promise, her passion, put in the hands of some cocky, privileged white boy in a newspaper, and shattered.

It made me wonder if Alex had really grown up understanding the sacrifices that performers made to be on stage. The risks they took. Even I hadn't known the stakes until I'd heard these stories, not really.

I imagined the disappointment that must have curdled within Alex's mother, despite her outward support, when her son had decided to do *this* with his life. She hadn't made any public comments about any of this, I realised with a start. I didn't even think she'd called. Alex barely talked about her.

But I also knew, from knowing Alex the way that I now did, the power he must have felt the first time he wrote something about the actors and directors who so desperately wanted his approval. Maybe there had never been any possible way for him to gain the admiration and attention of his mother and her friends, because all their attention and admiration and worry was, already, terminally turned on themselves. Theatre people wanted critics like Alex to love them simply because they wanted everyone to love them. And when Alex held back his love, choking it in qualifiers and nit-picking and cool dismissal, they must have wanted his approval even more.

I looked at Alex over his breakfast bowl of cereal, hunched over his phone, hair across his eyes, his face a crumpled, unreadable frown. I wondered if the tide of retaliation against Alex's whole being was starting to make sense to him. Surely, each cut was losing him blood.

How enormous a thing it must be to face the sum total of your flaws, and find that they were worse than you imagined, and obvious to everyone in the world except you. Maybe, like trying to look at the sun, it wasn't quite possible yet for Alex to look at the truth about himself without experiencing so much pain that he then immediately had to look away again, dazzled by the brightness of his own cruelty.

The briefing emails that our editors were sending to Alex got more curt every day. He had the feeling they were talking about him at the daily conference and not telling him, yet, what they planned to do about him.

His friends, who'd started off by sending amused messages when they'd first seen his name connected with Hayley's show, were fading away as more details of Alex's transgressions were revealed. He heard the loud silence of their disgust. He didn't have it in him to reply to Milo at all.

At the bus stop I saw three identical new posters of Hayley, looking amazing in a backless black dress, to promote an appearance at a festival cabaret night run by a TV network.

I stayed up late every night with Alex, drinking and listening as he talked it through again and again, telling me about his childhood, his exes, his dreams. I was getting less and less sleep. Stuart messaged me to ask if I was free for a drink at the Pleasance bar, and I made a mental note to reply, but I kept forgetting to respond to messages these days, and I left him on read.

I wrote my reviews in a hurry and when I was alone I looked forward to whenever Alex came back from his shows, fresh with more things to tell me, more indignities and torments to relate. He was at the centre of his own national scandal and I was directly adjacent to it. He never asked me anything about me or my life, any of my own mistakes. The mistakes were all his, each more terrible and fascinating than the last.

'To be honest,' I said one warm evening, when we had the windows open, because I'd made soup and there was condensation on the glass from the cooking, and the candle I'd lit on the table flickered in the air. 'I like all these women. They seem kind of great.'

'Yeah, well. I liked them once, too.'

What's more, though, I believed them. Not that this should make a difference, but they were the kind of women it was easy to believe. They were articulate, creative, self-aware, emotionally intelligent people. I wanted to be friends with all of them. They reminded me of some of my best friends, Lily and Zara, friends who hadn't had their own children yet, women I loved, but who lived with a wild freedom that now seemed unreachable to me. They were still there, still nearby, but their lives were lived at a different pace from mine, with different background music. It was a kind of dislocation. I missed being with women like that. I wanted to hear more of their stories.

Instead, I was stuck in the paper's dingy, draughty, empty flat, just me and Alex, day after day, while Hayley's show became brighter and more sparkling and more powerful every night. The more stories that came out about Alex, the more I wondered why my own experience of Alex's cruelty had been so small, and so chaste. He didn't buy me a sandwich that one time. That was the sum total of his transgression against me. Had there ever been any indication he might have done anything else to me? Was I just the kind of girl you didn't buy lunch, and that was it? I remembered again what Nina had said, about everyone having a bit of an Alex crush. Could I admit to that? Something of Alex was, it was true, lodged in my brain, and couldn't be prised out. He had the strange ability to make you feel as if you were the only other person who was in on a joke, the only other person who understood some fundamental truth about the world that has escaped other people, and there was something addictive about that.

And I was, physically, the closest person to him now. I slept within the same walls. I kept my shampoo and conditioner bottles on the shelf in the shower next to his herb-scented body wash. We ate together. Each morning we poured milk into our coffees from the same four-pint bottle in the fridge. Proximity was a kind of intimacy.

Maybe that was the simple explanation for my deepening fascination with Alex's life. Maybe it was just that I was a journalist, and he had become a story. And now, surely, I saw him more closely, more clearly, than anyone else did. That was the extent of the attraction, I told myself: reportage.

My mother had thought it was hilarious when I got my first magazine internship. She called me her Girl Friday. She said it was the perfect career for me, a vocation where I could be sharp and cynical, not ponderous like her, but still think about paintings and art all the time, the most precious thing we shared. She bought me a trilby hat that she found in a charity shop and said she was glad I wasn't doing politics or news, but cultural reporting, and art specifically. 'Real news,' she called it. 'The news of being alive.'

Graham messaged me asking if Alex was all right. *I think so*, I replied, glancing up at Alex, who sat across from me at the kitchen table, eating his soup and looking obsessively through his phone. *I mean, he's brought all this on himself, hasn't he?*

The Lavinia story hit Alex pretty hard, though. It had reminded him, Alex said, of the sanctuary he'd found as a teenager with Milo's family, and how he'd ruined it. Lavinia had got it wrong in her version of what happened, he said. Alex had cared about her. He'd also, however, horrified himself by desecrating something that he'd considered sacred.

Growing up in the shadow of fame, Alex told me late one night in the flat after too many beers, he'd never felt a sense of kinship with his generation. He didn't have a normal experience of growing up. He'd always been the son of Judith Lyons, connected to her reputation. Even in the news stories about him now, her name was mentioned alongside his as if it were an inextricable part of it: *Alex Lyons, son of the actress Dame Judith Lyons . . .*

Milo's family were different. They were rich, like Judith was, except much more so. Both of Milo's parents were lawyers, and they expected that their children would inevitably become lawyers too, because this was a family where the dinner table was a forum for debate, and a sense of right and wrong, and persuasion, were important.

Milo's father, Julian, a commercial barrister, understood performance and audience in a different way from Judith. He talked a lot about how he'd *trodden the boards in his time*. He meant that he'd been in student plays at

Cambridge, where he'd read English before doing a law conversion and the bar course in London. He called his own son 'a lovely boy, but dim', both to Milo's face and behind his back, which Alex thought was unfair, though it was said in a fond sort of way. Julian seemed to look forward to talking to Alex about literature. He lent him some books while Alex was preparing for his Oxford interview.

Milo's home was stable and intelligent and built on reason. It was a square house in Hampstead painted in neutrals and bought with commercial law money, which I'm pretty sure is more money than I've ever seen. (People always think journalists are rich. Actually, the only rich ones are almost always the ones, like Alex, who had money to begin with. Though admittedly there are plenty of those.)

Alex's own house, on the other hand, weathered the surges and lulls of a life in the arts. The Lyons's slim Camden townhouse, bought by Judith in the 1980s in a state of poor repair and not well-maintained since, had a white frontage of peeling paint and a blue plaque, commemorating a nineteenth-century travel writer, between the first-floor arched windows. It was a busy interchange for theatrical comings and goings. Inside, there was striped blue-and-white wallpaper in the hall and murky-coloured walls in the living room. Judith had once bought two big tins of paint in different shades, one a pale yellowish brown and one light pink, and she and Alex had mixed them together using a thick twig from the old quince tree in the garden, until they had made an original new colour. The colour wasn't exactly lovely, but it was guaranteed to be different from the colour of anyone else's walls. The painted walls were covered over, in any case, by eclectic framed pictures. The old carpet on the stairs was frayed.

Here, nothing was more important than the next show. Judith Lyons travelled a lot, but when she was home, she invited guests for dinner most evenings, or else took them out to the Greek restaurant round the corner, where the waitresses pretended not to recognise megastars.

Before he was a teenager, Alex's school work, and seeing his friends, had to fit around his mother's rehearsal schedules. He stayed late after prep school whenever she didn't pick him up on time because she really had to finish blocking a scene. He read a lot of books sitting on the wall outside his school. Any troubles that he might have shared with her about his friends or his fears had to come second to the last-minute chaotic panics that filled the house before the euphoria of a first night. Rehearsals took priority over everything. How important could Alex's maths homework possibly be, when the curtain was about to go up on the biggest new show of the season?

On those nights, there were marked-up scripts and overflowing ashtrays scattered all over the house, sheet music piled on top of the piano, storyboards and tiny set models and enormous bunches of flowers sent from everywhere and set down on every surface, stuffed into vases so huge and heavy they could kill a man.

Opening nights and premieres, those blissful glories of limelight and attention and applause, were followed by the despondency of gaps in work, where his mother's life became suddenly meaningless to her, and she was convinced she would never work again.

Until the next script arrived on the doormat, or the

next artistic director dropped round for a whisky sour, or the next eminent producer phoned to tell her that he'd just had a really great idea.

Alex's early life followed this intense repeated rhythm of preparation, climax and release. And Judith lived, always, with an awareness of anticipated reception and response, an insatiable obsession with audience as a creature with teeth, who was easily spooked and must be appeased. One of Alex's godparents bought him a hardback Folio Society edition of *One Thousand and One Nights* for his twelfth birthday, and when he read about Scheherazade he found her familiar.

His mother's friends were never lawyers or politicians or CEOs. They didn't open bank statements or talk about kitchen appliances. They talked about poetry and physical transcendence and they swore a lot. They saw themselves as outsiders, even while attracting a lot of money and attention.

Alex watched his mother talking to the media and listened to her bringing out her sumptuous performative conversational style on TV and radio. He heard her tell the same anecdotes, the ones that always went down well, and came to know the exact moments people would gasp and laugh. (He'd roll his eyes and look down at his hands during those.) He saw the concentration in her face as she scoured the papers for reviews. He felt the reflected triumph of a rave write-up, and the occasional, infuriating anguish of a three-star that *read like a four*. He noted that she never got one-star reviews, or even two-star ones. She was just that good. He saw how carefully she arranged her clothes and jewellery to look casual and artistic. He was born knowing that the performance never really ended. Everything the Lyons family did was part of the show.

'And there's nothing more tedious than hearing actors talk about the craft of acting,' Alex told me. 'They turn their most weirdo, specific personal failings into some pseudo-profound generalisation on humanity. And they talk so loudly while they're doing it, too, as if they're treating you to exclusive insight into their magnificent art, and you should be grateful. And they're all sweetie and darling to each other's faces, but you should hear the shit actors say about each other behind their backs! They're the worst for it, far worse than any critic. Actors are the bitchiest people alive.'

Alex met Milo Harwood when they were both twelve years old, in the same form at their private North London day school. The first time he went to Milo's house, he was fascinated to discover that, in this family, there was a new form of currency. This was argument. The Harwood family didn't act out rehearsed stories, paced to telegraph the jokes and turn the mood on a hairpin bend from jolly to poignant. Instead, at dinner, the Harwoods took up a moral or legal position that was new to them and they argued it, improvising until they really believed it.

Milo had asked Alex if he wanted to stay over one Friday night after school. Alex kicked off his PE trainers next to Milo's on the patterned tiles of the hallway floor. All the rooms were white with framed black-and-white photographs of abstract scenes. There was a lavishness of clear surfaces. The words that came into Alex's head when he walked in were *pristine* and *angular*.

'Help yourself to anything in the cupboards, boys.' Milo's

mother, Vicky, a solicitor, athletic and distracted in a white shirt and camel-coloured trousers, emerged briefly from her study in a breeze of something coconutty and clean. 'I just have to hop on another call.'

She disappeared again. Alex could hear her voice through the door, authoritative and serious on the phone. They loaded up on Jaffa Cakes and Mini Cheddars and Lucozade. There was a snug room off the kitchen devoted to Milo's PlayStation 2, a giant TV, and a white leather sofa that sweated against Alex's body. They played *Tony Hawk's Skateboarding* on the PlayStation until dinner. Lavinia, whom everyone still called Livvy at this point in her childhood, must have been about eight. He remembered all this in photorealistic detail, to the extent that I wondered if he was embellishing the memory to make a better story in the telling. He made an audience of me.

'It's nothing special, just pasta. I've snuck in some of the nice tomatoes from the market.' Vicky spooned spaghetti out of a big white bowl. Nothing in Alex's house matched or was unchipped. 'I hope that's OK with you, Alex? We always just have a relaxed dinner on Fridays.'

It wasn't Alex's idea of relaxed. There was a wine glass beside every place setting, including Livvy's, though hers was filled with apple juice. Vicky poured sparkling water for Milo and Alex. Milo, who was cheery and gregarious at school, lowered his eyes and acknowledged his heap of pasta with a gruff monosyllable.

Alex didn't know whether to call Milo's mother Vicky, as she'd introduced herself, or the more formal Mrs Harwood, so he avoided addressing her directly. He cleared his throat and adjusted the top button on his school shirt.

'This is great, thanks. At our house on Fridays it's usually beans on toast, if my mum's in rehearsals.'

'Life in the theatre!' Julian Harwood unfurled a pressed blue linen napkin from its silver napkin ring and put it on his lap. Alex copied him. It seemed the right thing to do. 'Milo, I saw something in the paper that seemed like your cup of tea. I wonder what Alex thinks? The National Lottery, the columnist said, in a rather offhand way, is a necessary tax on the nation's stupidity.'

'Gracious.' Vicky sipped her chilled Muscadet. That bottle, at least, was familiar to Alex. His mother's friends drank it sometimes. Judith preferred harder stuff. 'What's a *necessary* tax?'

'You need taxes to pay for schools and hospitals,' said Livvy.

'But monetary scarcity is an illusion, perpetuated by tax,' said Milo. Milo? This was a boy who usually smelled of Wotsits and wiped his nose on his forearm, yet here he was speaking with considered ease and using long words, with a surer sense of himself than Alex had seen before.

'But does the lottery do the same thing?' said Julian. 'Alex, what do you think?'

Alex felt a new kind of spotlight fall on him, and he did what all good actors do when this happens and their lines desert them. He improvised. 'I guess it's more like a kind of drama?'

The contrast between Alex's stuttering and Milo's unexpected fluency was unpleasant. Alex tried to access a similar level of confidence to his friend. 'I just mean, the way they make the machine spin the coloured balls on a Saturday night. The celebrities pressing the button, and the balls getting released one by one. Talking about the numbers as if they have their own histories and personalities. I know the money is real, but it might as well not be, because almost nobody will ever win it. And if you don't, it's not stupid to be entertained by the dream of winning. I mean, like, it's just a show.'

Julian laughed. '*Panem et circenses*, with a bonus ball?'

'Trust the thespian,' said Vicky. 'Oh, blast! I left the garlic bread in the oven.'

Blast, Alex thought. His own mother would have gone for a stronger word.

The debate went on into dessert, a chocolate tart from the deli.

There was adrenaline running through Alex's body. He'd loved being put on the spot like that. He liked that he'd made them laugh, and that he'd contributed a new thought, the clay of it still wet. It was refreshing to be talking about something around a dinner table that wasn't anxiety over whether some actor didn't get a part because it had gone to that other actor who always got those parts, or that a brilliant film wasn't getting made because of insane financial reasons, or that a writer still hadn't finished the treatment they'd sworn would be a fully drafted script by Friday.

It felt, to the twelve-year-old Alex, as if his brain were expanding in all directions, like the universe, as he minted new and provocative pathways through politics, gender, money, in the time it took him to twist a lump of spaghetti around his fork.

Honestly, it sounded like hell to me. Pretentious, insufferable. But Alex got really into it. Maybe petrol should be illegal, he said. Maybe cigarettes should be free, but only on prescription. Maybe men shouldn't have the vote! Alex liked taking that last idea for a stroll, arguing himself into obsolescence. Maybe, as Livvy suggested, the eating of ice cream should be compulsory on Wednesdays. It would supercharge the dairy industry, she said.

The Harwoods weren't saying what they really believed. They were just playing devil's advocate, working through what could, with the right argument, be something that *someone* believed.

The next morning, after sleeping on a mattress on the floor of Milo's bedroom full of Warhammer figures and posters of skateboarders and short-skirted female tennis players, Alex discovered that the Harwoods bought all the broadsheet newspapers every Saturday. They spread them out over the kitchen table and pointed out interesting stories to one another – even from the business section – over breakfast.

Julian Harwood took out the theatre reviews for Alex. It was the first time Alex had read them from the other side, as a newspaper reader, instead of as someone from team theatre.

Being with Milo's family filled up something in Alex that he hadn't previously felt as an emptiness. But now he knew the emptiness was there, and had defined the edges to it, it became impossible to ignore.

In time, separately, the teenage Alex discovered that sex offered a similar sense of peace, a sense of acceptance. Yes, it was a version of performance too: the physical sensations were all real, but the emotions? Well, that depended. That was part of the appeal.

He remained almost equally obsessed with arguments

and with sex. Because, for Alex, the thrill of a strongly held opinion, well-expressed, was *physical*. And, by the time he was sixteen, he'd learned that when he was experiencing anything that temporarily focused his body and mind down to a set of neurological responses – sex, arguments, cigarettes, drugs – *that* was when he felt he finally got close to knowing who he really was. There was temporary physical transcendence in opinion, argument, words. There was another way of living. Infinite other ways. The Harwoods had given him that.

After Lavinia, his sanctuary was gone. Everything about them was tainted for him. He could still be friends with Milo, but he couldn't face Milo's house, his family, the pure goodness of what they'd offered him and what he'd poisoned. After that summer holiday, he had to search for something new and more powerful to quench his overheated brain with meaning and hope. He started writing for Cherwell, the student paper, when the new Oxford term of his final year began a few weeks later. He never wanted to see Lavinia again, even though this pained him. He didn't want to make her life any worse than he already had.

'Does that make sense?' Alex downed the last of the beer and clinked the bottle next to the four others on the living room floor.

It didn't really make sense, not outside of twisted Alex logic. But I was getting used to twisted Alex logic. Trapped in Edinburgh with him, I began to feel like his minder, or his officially appointed carer. Sometimes, I was the only person who knew for sure he was still alive at the end of every day. As the noise grew around Hayley's show, I was definitely the only person who saw, in Alex's face, a tiny flickering of fear, at first only visible as a barely perceptible interruption to his arrogance, like a power cut that dims the lights for just a hundredth of a second.

9

I heard her name on the radio in a café while I was writing up a piece first thing in the morning. *'From One Star to *the* Star: The Unstoppable Rise of Hayley Sinclair. We speak to Hayley next about being a woman on a mission to change the cultural scene to be a better place for women and a fairer place for performers.'*

The segment was only three minutes long, but that was enough to get across her presence as an edgily adorable current darling of the arts scene. She was light, self-deprecating, funny. There were pictures of her everywhere online. She was a gift for photographs on socials, her colouring fair and her clothes grungy in a way that felt reminiscent of a 90s punk aesthetic. In the photographs I saw of her, I looked for evidence of the pain and humiliation she must feel after what Alex had done to her. I couldn't see it. She looked strong to me.

She had that edge of American-ness that a certain kind of British boy goes nuts over. There was something essentially polished about her, perhaps because she sounded more like the people we see on TV and in movies in this country than like people we meet in real life. And there was something unusually clean about her teeth and her nails that made the slapdashness of the rest of her, of her hair, skin and clothes, feel deliberate. She was quick to laugh, I'd seen in the interviews, and when she did she leaned forwards in a way that both mocked you and included you. She was without obvious class markers in a way that I now realised I found baffling, which immediately made me ashamed of how often I must assign these markers to other people. There was a looseness to her, a messiness and a drive of chaotic focus, that I think, if I were being flip, I might call the American dream. She was living someone's dream now, anyway. She was the golden shiny object of the moment. The protagonist.

She was confident enough to find talking easy, no matter her audience. I envied her that. She never seemed to dry up in any of the interviews for which she was booked. Her speech was unhesitating. She had a face vibrant with conviction and a gift for maintaining eye contact way past the point it was comfortable, her eyes lit with determination.

During the day, I still had my own shows to go to. It was more than a week since Alex's review of Hayley's show, but it felt as though a year had passed since I'd left London. I wondered how much Arlo would have changed by the time the festival was over. Would he have learned new words? Would his walking, running and climbing have become more daring? Would he still remember me?

I distracted myself by looking again through the art

festival programme and the list of exhibitions and installations I was scheduled to review over the next few days. This was difficult because, for so many of the exhibitions, I wished I could take my mother with me to see them. When my mother had been at art college, she had exhibited her paintings. But she'd never had the instinct, she said, for devoting a career to it. Later, she incorporated art into her therapeutic practice. She said it was amazing what beauty, and what darkness, people produced with their hands when they couldn't find the words for what had happened to them.

I went to an exhibition of 1970s feminist protest art with her when I was eighteen. It was an exhibition full of film footage of women screaming and painting things in their own menstrual blood and photographing themselves having orgasms and I was both exhilarated and a little terrified. I was young enough, then, to be hopeful that feminism had fixed everything already and there was no work left to do. And I wasn't sure I liked these women who seemed to want to fill up the world with ugly fury. They were monstrous to me.

They were monstrous, though, in a way that I wanted to touch and understand. Something of Hayley reminded me of those artists. She was so beautiful, and she glowed with that same ugliness: the beautiful ugliness of a truth that you don't want to hear.

I'd learned in school about Mary Richardson, the Canadian suffragette who came to the UK and slashed the Velazquez painting of the naked body of the *Rokeby Venus* in the National Gallery in London with a meat cleaver, in protest at political violence against women. Our history teacher, a wry and short-haired woman whom I liked a lot, presented Mary Richardson as a hero, and I'd agreed. I loved the whole concept of what Richardson had done: taken a man's vision of a female body and turned it into a work of art that said something for women.

Later, I read that Mary Richardson had gone on to become a prominent fascist. This upset me. I'd been to visit the National Gallery and seen the repaired *Rokeby Venus*. You couldn't tell where the slashes had been. I didn't even think it was a very good painting. I preferred Botticelli's *Venus and Mars*, in the same gallery. I loved everything about that one, the way strength and vulnerability were meshed so closely together that you couldn't tell them apart.

That morning, there was a performance art show on the Southside where the artist, whose name was Ryan Delingpole, sat in a barber's chair in a former lecture theatre with a white towel around his neck. Ryan, in an exploration of intimacy and transgression, invited ticketholders to lick his face.

When I arrived, two men were already licking Ryan's face. This was good news for me, because while Ryan's face was big enough for two people to lick it at the same time, it was not big enough for three, and so, with Ryan's licking availability filled, I could just watch. Ryan had impressive stubble along his jaw, and I worried about the potential abrasive effect on the lickers' tongues. But they were really getting into it, licking and licking, like a cat at its paws, and all three of the men had their eyes closed, licking and licking and being licked, and it was actually kind of meditative, cosy, and even soothing, the licking and licking, just me watching these three men with my notepad, in the quiet of the space, and time dissolved until there was only licking, and then a bell rang and the box office staff turned up the lights and showed us out.

'Thank you,' I said to the usher, clicking the lid on my pen.

From there, I walked to the Modern Art Two gallery on the north side of the city, where the streets were green and overhung with trees. It was an exhibition of the history of theatre costume, with pieces on loan from the V&A, and more from collections around the world. There was a Japanese Surihaku robe, which I read in the catalogue had been worn for Noh performances in the eighteenth century, and which was decorated all over with gold and silver *Kikyō* blossoms in the shape of stars that made me think of the decorated ceiling of my childhood bedroom. In another room there was a wall of Venetian masks, chequered in black and red, and lustrous replicas of the red and blue costumes worn in Renaissance revenge tragedies. Beside a doorway, there was a stuffed, beige, massively oversized phallus, which, I learned from a dry information board next to it, may have been like the ones used in the comedies of Ancient Greece.

In a dim side room, a white digital clock projected onto the wall counted down from thirty seconds. I sat on an uncomfortable bench, alone in the dark. When the clock reached zero, a film began to play. It was archive footage, the subtitles said, of an interview with a noted Shakespearean stage actor and Oscar-winning film star of the 1980s, Peter Ogilvie. His face was familiar, and I'd heard the name before. He was talking about how the costume becomes the character. The footage was poor quality, filmed a long time ago and only partially restored, and Peter Ogilvie's face flickered in and out of vision as his voice rumbled around luxurious diction. The projection had a ghostly translucency on the wall.

'You must take care only to wear elements of the costume when you are really playing the character,' he said. 'His shoes, his watch, his underwear: all must be quite different from your own. Otherwise, you find the character leaking out into your everyday life. One can become too close to a character. When you start to hear *him* speaking, instead of you, as you address your friends over some everyday trifle, that's when you have to look out.'

He laughed a rattly smoker's laugh. My phone vibrated, and I was irritated when Josh's name flashed up – I was at *work* – before remembering that I hadn't phoned him for our regular breakfast-time check-in, and then I was flooded with guilt and love, suddenly longing for Arlo's dark, serious eyes.

'I'm so sorry I didn't call.' I stood in the corner of a room full of mannequins robed in commedia dell'arte costumes, but thankfully empty of people, except for the curator, a mousy and young-looking guy in big glasses, who stood nervously in the doorway, pretending not to watch me. 'Work's been crazy.' I folded my arms across my body in an act of self-protection and faced the corner away from the curator, curving my body around my phone.

'How's Alex?'

'He's been this bizarre mixture of angry and wounded, like a bull backed into a corner, and Hayley's like this matador, flapping her cape at him. I'm at an exhibition right now, that's why I'm whispering.' I wanted to tell him more about Alex and Hayley. I'd spent so much time absorbing Alex's side of the story, it was all I could think about.

'It's not been easy here, either. I'm having a nightmare getting this funding application in. It never ends. Are we still OK for me and Arlo to come up on the eighteenth?'

I thought I heard the sound of cannon fire and cello music in the background. Surely he couldn't be watching *Master and Commander* again. He watched it whenever he was depressed and listless and wanted to feel hope again. But I couldn't judge. I did the same with *Pride and Prejudice*.

'I'm not sure, I'm having to take on more stuff now that Alex is in this insane spiral.' I felt a tug inside me towards something, but the direction felt more temporal than geographical, like a pull backwards rather than across space. Had there been a time before this when things were better? I struggled to remember how things had been before my mother got ill.

'OK, let's talk about it later then. I need to book the tickets or work out what to do with Arlo if we can't come up. It's just, it's tough trying to balance work with looking after him and keeping up with the laundry. I can't believe single parents do this all the time. It's hard, you know?'

'Yeah, I do know, actually.' I really did. 'What's Arlo doing now?'

'I just dropped him off with Mum. She's been loving spending time with him. They've been at the splash park.'

'He's at your parents' place?'

'I'd never get this work done otherwise. Mum's keen to help out.'

'Really? She wasn't keen to help when I was on maternity leave.'

'You were at home then. Sophie, I know it's difficult, but please don't do that thing of punishing me for still having a mother.'

'I'm not. Jesus, that's not what this is about. I love that Arlo still has a grandmother. That's important to me, as I have said many times. I'm happy they're spending so much time together.'

'Good. And we'll see you when we come up? It'd be unreasonable of them not to give you one weekend off in a whole month.'

'Yes, though I'll still need to work. It's just how it is. I can't help it. And it's not a month, it's just over three weeks. Please don't get annoyed about me having a job to do.' My voice was getting louder than I wanted it. The curator had shuffled out of view. Two more journalists walked past and tried not to look curious as they ducked into the anteroom to watch Peter Ogilvie's film.

'I'm not. I do understand. I want you to be able to work, it's important to me too.' His tone was conciliatory, and I briefly softened, but then he continued: 'And hey, at least you're getting a full night's sleep. I mean, I'm assuming. Given that you're apparently sharing a flat with a sex addict.'

'What does that mean? You don't need to worry about me and Alex.'

'God, Soph. I'm not worried about you and Alex.'

'Sure. I don't think he's interested in moody mums who still can't fit in their old jeans, anyway.'

'Ha! No, you're not exactly his type, are you?'

He really laughed. A bit too much. It was the first time I'd heard Josh laugh since I'd left for Edinburgh. The only time he'd laughed, and it wasn't at my jokes, but at *me*, and how undeniably, hilariously unfuckable I was. I was the same age as Alex. We worked in close proximity, and now slept in the same flat, just the two of us. But as far as Josh was concerned, to Alex I might as well be an overstuffed armchair.

After we hung up, I walked around to the end of the exhibition, where there was a deep, rich blue and yellow star-embroidered cape designed to be worn by Oberon in an RSC production of *A Midsummer Night's Dream*. The colours reminded me of Van Gogh: something about the bleeding combination of indigo, royal blue, purple, and yellow, with flecks of aquamarine.

My mother once took me, when I was nine, to see the Van Gogh paintings at the Musée D'Orsay in Paris, a stop-off when we'd driven to the south of France on holiday when I was a child. She told me she'd loved Van Gogh since she was a student, because he's an artist whose mental health has been so speculated about, which she thought was interesting. But when she saw his paintings in person, she told me how struck she'd been to see something other than Van Gogh's own mind in all their captured wildness. She'd seen something of her own mind there, too. It had pulled her in.

I thought of Alex's memory of his first experience of theatre and tried to map it onto how my mother had shared her love of art with me. Were they the same memory, formed in two different ways? I remembered standing next to my mother in Paris in front of *Starry Night Over the Rhône*. It's not the more famous of Van Gogh's starry night paintings. That one's in New York. This one is quieter, more reflective. A view of the river from the quay. The Great Bear constellation in the sky. Two lovers in the foreground. And we stood there, us two, letting it settle on both of us together for the first time, like moonlight.

'I wish I could paint as gorgeously as that,' said my mother. She took a sketchbook on holiday. She did watercolours instead of taking photographs.

That night, on our hotel balcony, my mother stayed up late and painted the view of the city. She put the Great Bear in the sky. It didn't feel as though painting was a world from which I was excluded. It felt more like a way of seeing that I shared with her, and that would be mine to keep, even when she was gone. As if I'd inherited the view from her eyes, as well as the colour of them. Her name was Elizabeth.

Walking through Edinburgh, I kept glimpsing Hayley in the distance, walking down the street with purpose, drinking out of an enormous reusable cup, or wearing sunglasses and coolly looking through her phone. Whenever I saw her, other people around me had usually seen her first. You could tell by the fizz of excitement in them, and how they tried not to look directly at her.

When I got back to the flat from the costume exhibition, there was new blue graffiti on the pavement outside the door:

HELLO ALEX

It was written the right way up for someone, presumably Alex, to read as they walked out of the flat. I didn't like that the people who hated Alex knew where he was staying. Obviously Hayley knew where Alex was, but she wouldn't do something like this, would she? It was probably one of her flying monkeys. I shouldn't think of them like that. She was in the right, wasn't she? Still, it was an escalation, and it made me feel under surveillance, guilty by association.

With my key in the lock, I had the feeling of being watched. As I turned to look behind me, down the street, a guy in a puffer jacket was walking slowly away. He had a camera with a long grey lens slung over his shoulder.

So we'd reached the point where Alex had paps waiting for him. This is what it must be like to be a pop star, I thought, grimly. Except the photographers didn't want me. They wanted Alex. Ideally, they wanted him looking dishevelled and shifty enough to caption the picture with a phrase like 'SEX BEAST: Alex Lyons leaves his flat in Edinburgh looking concerned'. I know, because I'd written picture captions like that once, back when I was working late-night news desk shifts. (I'm not proud of it.)

At the kitchen table, I'd filed my reviews for the day – four stars for the licking; five for the costumes – and I was writing an updated stock obit for a minor member of a 1960s guitar band, who was not yet dead, but I was on his case.

The landline phone on the kitchen counter, a grey brick from a previous age which neither Alex nor I had ever used, now had a flashing red light, indicating a new voicemail message. I assumed that would probably be another paper, someone that didn't have Alex's mobile number, calling for a quote. I ignored it and looked at some of the online reaction to Alex's most recent negative reviews.

*

Delighted to announce I've got a one-star review from Alex Lyons. Thrilled to be pissing off all the right cunts!

*

No bc how embarrassing would it actually be to get a GOOD review from Alex Lyons of all people right now, I would simply die

A short profile of Alex was running that day on an American news and culture website. *Alex Lyons: British Media's Biggest Sleazeball?* It was mostly a round-up of tweets, but it jumped on the fact that Hayley was American and it positioned her show as some kind of UK versus USA showdown. There was also a long piece in a rival UK paper, linking Hayley's show to other stories about exploitation in the arts over the last five years, making Alex seem like part of a malevolent trend. In the comment pages of a different paper, one of the highest paid columnists on Fleet Street was really letting Alex have it. Alex was giving journalism a bad name, she said. Newspaper arts desks had for too long been full of rats like him, and it was time to call in the pest control.

Had Alex ever wanted to be famous? I still wasn't sure. He'd chosen a career path that never promised him fame, though it did guarantee a steady supply of attention in a less obvious way. For Alex, I think that becoming a critic partially meant becoming a professional spectator, more important than the average audience member. His opinions, rather than his person, were amplified and illuminated.

What was it about watching his mother's life that had

made him think fame wasn't for him? I had asked him, the night before, if he'd ever seriously considered becoming an actor.

Yes, he told me. When he was seventeen. He'd heard about a production of *Equus* with a reputable production company in a small theatre in East London that was casting with an open call. You just had to email them a picture of yourself. He skived off school to get the bus to the audition by mid-morning. He'd printed off the script they'd emailed him when he'd got in contact with the producer under a false name.

Waiting outside the door to the rehearsal space for the auditions, in an anonymous office building in Camden, he wrung his bundle of script between his hands, messy with yellow highlighter. His sweat smudged the ink. He wanted a cigarette. He thought longingly of the pack in the inner pocket of the school backpack over his shoulder, calculating if there was time for a smoke before someone came out to get him. There wasn't.

'Alex Harwood?' That meant him. The assistant director, a woman in her thirties with punky hair and combat trousers who moved with the choreographed precision of a dancer, came out to meet him.

He nodded and tried to breathe through his nerves. The director, Greg Kennedy, was a man Alex hadn't met before, which was the main reason he'd chosen this particular production to try for. Kennedy looked bored when Alex came in.

Alex acted out the prepared scene opposite the assistant director, Jen. He thought it went OK, but the director was looking down at his notes on the table for most of it. When the scene had finished, there was a disappointed silence.

'Would you take some notes?' Kennedy said, in a way that wasn't a question.

'Of course,' said Alex. His voice broke a little. He swallowed.

'Can you try it again, and give it more?'

OK, so he was one of *those* directors. Alex let his irritation flare into his next attempt at the scene. He gave the lines more attack, projected his voice more, put more into his gestures.

'Thank you,' said Kennedy. 'That's all.'

'That's all?' said Alex. 'Are there any more notes, or anything?'

Greg Kennedy took off his glasses and put them on the desk. He looked steadily and critically at Alex, as if seeing him for the first time since Alex had arrived.

'You're not quite what we're looking for, I'm afraid.'

'Is that the polite version?' said Alex, who thought he knew how this went.

'Yes, it's the polite version.' Greg Kennedy didn't break Alex's gaze. 'But you seem like a straightforward sort of person, and I've worked with a lot of young actors over the years, so I'll be straightforward with you, if you like. Over my career I've developed a quick sense of actors' strengths, and whether they've got that something, that presence that's going to set the stage on fire. Or whether they're most likely looking forward only to a career of begging for scrap parts in small-bit productions. And I have to tell you, Mr Harwood, it's a tough business, and it's not for everyone. Full of hardship and disappointment. It's a kindness, telling you now, while you're young. It's important to be clear. You must only be an actor if there's really no other option for you. Otherwise? Find another career.'

When Alex got back to his empty house, he slammed his schoolbag into his bedroom wall and stared at his fists for a long time. He was glad he hadn't told his mother he was going. She'd said he could be an actor if he wanted, but he'd needed to find out for himself if it was even possible. Now he knew, for certain, that she'd been wrong. And if she was wrong about that, she might be wrong about a lot of other things, too.

It wasn't necessarily that Alex thought Greg Kennedy had been entirely correct about Alex's ability or potential. Alex wanted me to know that. No, what shocked Alex most wasn't what Kennedy said, but Alex's own despair at hearing it. This honest summary of Alex's lack of theatrical talent, heard for the first time in his life, and coming from someone who had no idea of his experience or connection in the business, sunk him. If anything, Alex was grateful to Greg Kennedy, even while allowing himself the luxury of also hating his guts. Because Alex already knew, from observing the process in his mother and her friends for his whole life, that being an actor meant humiliation. You really have to love the good parts to be able to tolerate the bad moments, the many rejections, the only occasional successes. And here was his first real rejection, his first bad moment, and it had floored him. There was no getting up again. He hated the way he felt. He never wanted to feel that way again.

The day after the audition, Alex got a phone call to his mobile from an unknown number.

'Hi Alex, I'm so sorry about yesterday.' It was Jen, the assistant director. 'What Greg said to you was out of line. It's been a really long week. Anyway, I had a word with the producer afterwards and we both loved your performance. We'd like to offer you the part, if you'd still consider taking it. Do you have an agent?'

'Um, yeah. Of course. Wow.'

'Great. And is that under the name Alex Lyons?'

Alex's hand gripped the phone more tightly. 'How did you get my name?'

'Oh, the producer saw your polaroid this morning and mentioned that she recognised you. I bet your mother's thrilled to have another actor in the family!'

'Thanks,' said Alex. 'But I've actually changed my mind. Sorry, please don't consider me for the role any more. I'm sure the show will be much better with someone else.'

He hung up before she could convince him otherwise. He didn't trust himself not to accept under duress. That night, he'd gone to a friend's house party with the sole intention of going to bed with some girl, any girl. At that, at least, he'd succeeded.

Alex had grown up watching fans queuing up behind railings to see his mother in person. She had been draped in richly coloured, robe-like clothes, looking amazing and twinkling and exactly how the people who watched her films wanted her to look. He had seen the letters from Judith's fans arriving at their house, the crazy ones already filtered out by her agent, so she only received the ones that were loving, interesting, or politely requesting a signed photograph.

He had seen how men desired her. They didn't realise that they desired a character, not a woman. Or perhaps they did, but the ineffable impossibility of her was part of the appeal.

He saw the way that reporters, usually men, arrived at

the Lyons house with their notebooks full of questions, and he saw how they softened when she looked them right in the eye, said their name, made them a cup of tea, sympathised with them about how hard their job must be, and he saw them close their notebooks but leave their little silver voice recorders running with the red light on as they fell under her influence. He hated these men. He wanted them to get the hell out of his house.

He also knew he saw more clearly than they did. He could speak more elegantly, more cuttingly than they could. He'd spent enough time among artifice that he'd learned damn well how to tell the truth. He'd decided long ago that if he were ever to become a journalist, he told me, he would be better than any of those that had dogged his mother. He'd make sure of it.

Being a critic meant that Alex, unlike his mother, almost never directly interacted with anyone who liked his work. He presumed they must exist, otherwise the paper wouldn't still be paying him. Sometimes, he received handwritten letters sent to the office in spidery handwriting from very elderly people who wanted to tell him he was right or wrong about something, or, surprisingly often, to tell him a story about a time that they remembered seeing Laurence Olivier on stage. That was about as good as it got. He got letters and comments all the time from people telling him that he was not as talented as his mother, and that he only had a job because of her. This, he said, didn't bother him as much as I'd thought it might. He said he didn't much care if his surname was the reason he got his first internship in newspapers, his first interview, his first byline. He'd never asked any of his editors if his name had been the thing that first opened a media door to him, because he *knew* he was a good writer. Alex felt that newspapers were lucky to have him, name or not, and that was the end of it.

The carelessness of this way of thinking astonished me.

He didn't know if there was somebody who bought the paper every week just to turn straight to his theatre reviews, see what he thought and laugh at his jokes. Though maybe there was. Yes, he hoped there was.

I didn't tell him that this is what I did when I read the paper. I always turned to his reviews first. They were always funny, always surprising. It wouldn't have been a useful sort of flattery for me to say so, anyway. I was a peer, not a fan. The only real attention that Alex ever got in person for his work came from his colleagues, which, for him, didn't count. Any benign attention in the newsroom usually came from Graham, who emailed us every day in Edinburgh, though even Graham was sparing with praise.

'The really fucked-up thing is that the closest thing I have ever had to an actual father is probably Graham,' said Alex as he was heating up some lunch.

I knew what he meant. Once, a work experience kid called Jamie, who was on the desk for two weeks at twenty-two and fresh out of Oxford, and played the flute to grade eight and derived a lot of his self-worth from that fact, had burst into tears when he'd been tasked with the senior editors' coffee run. He had never made, bought or drunk a cup of coffee in his life. Graham, who had not been to university at all but learned the journalism trade after getting a job as a tea boy on his local paper when he left school at sixteen, took Jamie out to lunch and told him that he was doing really well.

When I was newly pregnant with Arlo, and secretly navigating the complex maternity leave application system on the HR intranet portal during my lunch breaks to make sure I would qualify for enough money to buy food when the baby came, Graham asked me if I was OK, because I looked a bit pale. That's how he became the first person at the paper that I told. Telling any of my female colleagues would have felt embarrassing, for some reason. Unfeminist somehow. None of the women my age at the paper had children. Children were for the columnists on six figures. Confessing to being pregnant seemed like going to see the headteacher of my school to admit to something that would lead to the whole class getting a detention. I felt like an inconvenience in waiting.

'Oh, Sophie,' said Graham, in a corner of the newsroom that was the quietest place in the building. 'Brilliant news. Made my day. You're going to be a great mum. And your mother, I'm sure she'd be so proud, if she were here.' He put a hand on my shoulder and looked at the ground to hide the fact that he was trying not to cry. I hugged him. I was more grateful to him than I could say.

Graham went out on his own lunch break and he bought me a bunch of daffodils to put on my desk.

'How come Sophie gets daffodils and I don't?' Alex asked as I was putting them in a plastic tumbler of water I'd got from the cooler.

'Because she's a better journalist than you,' said Graham. He tapped Alex lightly and affectionately on the head with a rolled-up copy of that day's paper. 'Do some fucking work.'

This was back when Alex was in the office every day, writing up features or news stories. It was only a few weeks later that he got the promotion that meant he could be a critic full time, and swan in and out of the newsroom as he pleased.

Paul sent an ominous email to Alex to suggest they have 'a quick chat' on the phone over the next few days. Alex sent me a screenshot of the email as I sat at the kitchen table, my shoulders aching. I crunched my neck from side to side. I should do more exercise. I just spent every night hunched in an armchair at the flat. I considered doing some yoga from a YouTube video. My mother used to do yoga once a week with two of her best friends, and when I was a teenager they all used to tumble back to our house together after their class at the community hall.

I'd sit at the kitchen table with my homework and a cup of tea, tutting at them as they came in, as if they were the wild children and I was the fusty parent, eavesdropping as they spilled over each other on the sofa. Suddenly I missed those nights very badly.

'Bloody yoga,' said one of them, a police officer whose name was Meryl, one time over the usual bottle of post-yoga wine. 'What I actually need is therapy, don't I, Liz?'

'You're terrible,' cackled their friend Suzanne, a chemistry teacher at my school. 'You're so mad you'd send your therapist to the psych ward. At least yoga makes you shut up for forty-five minutes.'

They all killed themselves laughing at that. 'Not if I had a therapist like Liz,' said Meryl. 'The most patient woman in the world.'

'Oh, I don't know. I'm just as messed up as everyone else,' said my mother. 'If not more so.'

This fascinated me. But I never asked what she'd meant

by it. And now I never could. At the funeral, Suzanne organised all the flowers without me having to ask her, and Meryl got very drunk and sobbed noisily into my shoulder after everyone else had gone, and I loved them both for it.

The door buzzer rang. With Alex still out, I answered the intercom. Through it came an urgent trill.

'Darling, is that you?'

10

I've interviewed enough famous people – artists, dancers, some actors – not to be easily starstruck any more, but even so, Dame Judith Lyons sweeping into my flat with an enormous vase full of flowers was a *moment* for me. I'd seen her in period dramas when I was a little girl. To me, she occupied a nonspecific cultural memory of bonnets and bodices. In person she was smaller, daintier than on screen, but also more concentrated and vivid. Her face held weariness and subtleties that cameras couldn't translate.

She heaved the vase onto the kitchen table. It was festooned with nodding orange and purple flowers and was huge, heavy, and extremely ugly. It had a bizarrely lumpy shape, a thick bottom, a pitted and gnarled texture, and was overall an unusual feat of ceramic art, with lurid hand-painted scenes on the sides in clashing shades of maroon, green and yellow. The small handles at the top didn't look capable of supporting its immense weight. It must have been at least four feet high. I'd no idea how she got it all the way up the stairs to the flat. It looked very much like one of the most important pieces at the major ceramics exhibition I'd reviewed days before. But it couldn't be the same one. It must be a reproduction.

Even offstage, Judith had stage presence. Her fingers and wrists were gilded with nuggety rings and heavy resin bangles. Pendants of gold and pearl hung from her ears. A chain of pieces of sea glass was linked around her neck, and yet she bore all this weight lightly. Her clothes were in layers of flowing fabrics of red and turquoise, not unlike the Renaissance theatre robes I'd seen at the exhibition. She smelled smoky and floral, a combination that made me think of standing outside gallery openings on winter evenings. Within seconds of her arrival, the whole flat smelled of her. She had short, dark-dyed hair in a pixie crop around her pale face, and eyes that were unnervingly like Alex's. They had that same attentive ease. She called me darling with a native tongue.

'Thank you for letting me in, darling. I did tell Alex what time I'd be coming. I saw it all on the bloody news. Is there tea? Can I be a pest and ask you to make it for me? Rosehip, if you've got it. Probably too early for something more interesting. I loved your feature about Gwen John, by the way.'

God, she'd read my pieces. Maybe Alex had even mentioned me to her. She reapplied something the colour of blood orange to her lips and rubbed it in with her little finger while looking in a small compact mirror from her handbag. She was expansive, but with an edge to her that I wouldn't quite call nerves. It was something more like complete self-awareness. She occupied the whole of the ragged green armchair in the corner of the kitchen, her face lit from one side by cool window daylight, like a Vermeer. For the first time since I'd arrived in Edinburgh, the flat seemed not vast and empty, but brimming over. That must be what they paid her for. I'd have felt as if I were her audience, except for the fact she'd read my writing, and I'd seen her films, and this brought us into a strange kind of relationship where we both knew each other's voices without ever having met before. I eyed the vase, but it didn't feel like something I could ask about.

'I sometimes forget people actually read the paper. I'm really sorry. I don't think we have any rosehip.' I half-opened the cupboard to check for the tea that I knew wasn't there, softly horrified at not having rosehip tea to serve to a national treasure. I wasn't sure I'd ever even seen any for sale anywhere, which now seemed catastrophically unsophisticated of me. 'I did find some chamomile yesterday, inside this tin with a picture of a Highland stag on it?'

'You're sweet. I've just had a nightmare in Dubrovnik, so I'll choke anything down. And of course people read the fucking paper, darling, don't do yourself down. I saw your review of that god-awful exhibition at the Serpentine last month, too – 'New Directions in the Abstract', or some bollocks – you gave it three stars but I could tell you hated it, didn't you?'

'It wasn't completely my bag, no.' I made the tea, and some for myself, because, I suppose, I wanted to drink whatever Dame Judith was drinking. She shared Alex's disarming habit of perceiving and remembering slightly more about you than was normal. It was true, I hadn't liked that exhibition much: post-Pollock splodges and splats were not my thing. At the same time, I'd worried that I was missing something obviously powerful that other people would think it inept of me not to have mentioned. So, in the end, I wrote that the colours and shapes were *dreamlike* and *ambivalently alluring*. And then put three stars on it. In this case, three stars meant, sure, if you like this sort of thing. But I'd been glad to get out of the silent gallery into the green park around it, which was alive and crawling with the start of summer.

Judith said she was in Edinburgh for the weekend, to see some of the International Festival shows. She was staying with Murray in East Lothian. She said *Murray* as if I should know who that was. She was distracted, and troubled, playing with the rings on her fingers and looking out of the window.

'How *is* he, darling?'

I wasn't sure how much she knew about the Alex situation. I didn't know if he'd told her about it himself, or if she'd just seen the fallout. I wanted her to know that I did care.

'None of us saw this coming,' I said. 'The Alex thing.'

'I *am* worried about him.' She leaned towards me in the armchair over her tea, clacking her painted pink nails on the mug, speaking with a combination of low voice and intense eye contact uncannily like the way Alex talked. 'He's a sweet boy. And so like his father – but he just keeps carrying on with these actresses. It's all very Freudian. And the thing is, darling, they're only out for themselves. But there we are.'

Alex came home at that moment, holding a bottle of raspberry Lucozade and his Moleskine. He was unsurprised to see his mother and hugged her as she surrounded him in perfume and drapery. He called her Judith, which suggested the kind of grown-up family relationship that I would have thought was very cool when I was a teenager, but which now looked more like keeping something at a distance.

'Have you been terrifying some poor sods on the continent? And what the hell is that?' He nodded at the vase. His usual easiness had a little more roughness when he was speaking to his mother. He pushed his hair back off his face a lot.

'Darling, I was just saying to Sophie, I've come from one circus to another. And everyone's taking you so seriously! All life and death! The thing is, a bit of trouble is such marvellous publicity. Will you look after this wonderful vase for me? It's a gift from the artist, but I'm flying tomorrow night and it's not exactly hand luggage. I'll pick it up on my way back through.'

I looked at the vase through narrowed eyes. A piece by an artist of international fame, worth an uncountable amount. And the artist had just *given* it to Judith, for her to stuff flowers into.

'I don't need the publicity. I liked not being talked about,' said Alex, leaning on the kitchen counter with his sleeves rolled up. 'At least, I liked it better when they talked about my writing, instead of about my . . .' Alex sipped his Lucozade, deciding what words to use, 'private life.'

'It happens to the best of men, just look at Murray. *He* doesn't listen to what anyone says about him. Doesn't even read the papers any more. On his third husband, and *he's* just left him for some Los Angeles rent boy. Murray says he can't let it faze him. He just gets on with it, and he's doing OK, really he is. He's even bought a

Coravin, which I thought was a bit drastic. Plays a lot of piano these days. He has the most extraordinary light baritone. Do you remember him in *Hay Fever*?'

'All right,' said Alex, and his voice sounded quieter than usual in comparison with Judith's stagey resonance. 'You're going to scare the horses in a minute.'

'Sophie's tough as boots, aren't you, darling? I can tell she's a hardened old media maven, not one of your Bambi ingenues. I bet she's heard a lot fucking worse. And I bet she can't stand her own mother, either.'

A little conversational wasp sting. She kept talking.

'I've booked Timberyard for one o'clock,' Judith went on, 'and I've got some stories to tell you about Croatia that'll make you do that hideous nose-wrinkling thing you do when you disapprove. Is that what you're wearing? Don't you have an iron here? Well, come on.'

Judith took Alex out for lunch at Timberyard, a nice restaurant that had once been a theatrical props and costume store, as it said on the website. Alex told me later that everything was served with a seafoam *jus*.

While they were gone, I couldn't concentrate on work. I got an Instagram notification telling me that Josh had posted a photo, which he hadn't done for weeks. It was of him and Arlo and one of the other mums from our NCT class, Laura, and her fourteen-month-old daughter, Rosa, with ice cream cones at the park. *Babies in the sun,* said Josh's caption, with a sun emoji.

It wasn't exactly jealousy. What was Josh supposed to do while I was away? The other dads had work, and it wouldn't be fair for Josh to stay at home on his own, even if his mother was helping with childcare. And it wasn't as though he was going to shag anyone in a park full of toddlers.

And yet, and yet. The old sickness tugged at my navel.

Four years ago, Josh slept with one of his students. I'd thought that academia's self-validating affairs with students only happened to professors on the other side of sixty. Josh was a thirty-year-old adjunct, and Coralie was nineteen, and it still happened. It wasn't illegal, but nonetheless it felt so excruciating, so out of date. So nineties. When I found out – when I saw the blurred picture on her Instagram, with his arm around her, her with her great hair and loose patterned trousers and a tight sleeveless top, and I realised – I felt the cringe before I felt the betrayal. She was of the generation that hardly put anything on their Instagram grid, so even though it was months after the fact, it wasn't hard to find. The caption to the image was the emoji of a heart on fire.

He was supervising Coralie's dissertation on Milton. Josh said, when he was explaining to me – or excusing, briefly, before I told him I didn't want to hear any more – that it started because she'd waged a campaign to get his attention. It was gratifying, he said. Academia really grinds you down and is very low on praise or recognition, as a career. He said he had felt unwanted.

I'd thought that was pretty weak, and I told him so. He was sitting on the sofa in our flat and I was standing by the door. I could have left without hearing his side of things. I almost did.

And then he said how sorry he was. He started to cry. He was so completely sorry, he didn't even recognise himself, and there was no excuse for what he'd done. He wouldn't minimise it or explain it away. He said I had every right to feel however I wanted to feel. He was devastated that he'd hurt me. But, he said, he wanted to be really clear that he had not been the one to put any pressure on Coralie, from a position of power, to do anything.

He told me it had just been a couple of times. After his English Faculty Christmas party, to which I'd been invited but hadn't gone because I'd had to be on overnight duty at work after Alex swapped shifts with me at the last minute.

Josh and Coralie had gone back to her shared student flat to drink cheap wine with her friends, and it had happened there. And then again, in much the same way, after the faculty summer party in the gardens of the senate building when I was at work putting the Glastonbury coverage online. Both times I'd been working overnight at the newsroom.

Sex once is a mistake, but twice with the same person, with a distance of time in between, is an affair. I hadn't crystallised the difference before, but when I was confronted with it, I knew it instantly and instinctively. After the second time, he said Coralie hadn't contacted him again, and Josh had avoided her as much as possible.

Superficially, I'd forgiven him. After that one conversation, I hadn't ever wanted to talk about it again. It had felt as though to talk about it would give it more weight. Privately, I'd kept his betrayal inside me long afterwards, like the stone of an olive in my mouth that I hadn't yet spat out. Something protective. A talisman.

It was the kind of thing that people do forgive. I'd seen enough married journalists at the paper taking cocaine and shagging someone from the commercial team to know that affairs happen.

And it was years ago. But, in the flat in Edinburgh that August, time was collapsing. Looking at the new Instagram post of Josh with Laura, it felt as though it was happening again. He'd chosen someone else over me while I wasn't there. A better mother figure, this time. Someone who prioritised being at home with her child.

He'd told me the Coralie thing was nothing except sex, and anyway I was working a lot at the time and we didn't see each other much, even though we were nominally living together. I hadn't wanted to hear any more.

I was thirty then, and I wanted children, and I was very afraid of not having them. In that six-week course of grief counselling, I'd told the therapist that part of the reason for having Arlo with Josh was that I couldn't stand the thought of having a child with someone my mother had never met. Josh had known my mother. He had made her laugh. He gave my life a connection back to her that I didn't have it in me to sever.

We weren't married. We still aren't. There was never a vow that was broken, only an understanding. And I deliberately kept that emotional wound from healing. I fed the pain of it with constant background attention. It was an insurance policy. If I ever needed to end the relationship, that one old sin could be the reason why. I would never be trapped. There would always be a blameless path for my escape.

And then we'd had Arlo. And even though we'd planned for him to be there, when it happened, everything became a lot more complicated than I'd thought it would be. The escape path was overgrown and lost.

*

Alex came back to the flat alone.

'She's invited me to go to East Lothian tomorrow with Murray Maclean.'

'Murray *Maclean!*' I did know *that* Murray, the veteran Scottish character actor who'd turned down a knighthood because he believed in Scottish independence and was now more famous for his role in a hit American TV show. I'd updated his obit to add that in, just after I came back from maternity leave. 'Are you going?'

'It would be good to get out of Edinburgh. You're invited too, by the way.'

'Bloody hell, no I'm not. That's just a thing people say to be polite.'

'No, she means it. Don't make me go on my own. You might want to come anyway. Murray's got Egon Schieles on every wall. I tried to find pictures of them online once, but they're not mentioned in any catalogues anywhere. Murray won't say where he got them. My mother says they're Nazi loot. You don't have to come if you don't want. But we'd get some space away from the freaks writing love notes on the pavement outside. And that disgusting vase. Come on, please? You've got the day off from shows tomorrow, haven't you?'

11

I told him I'd go. But first, that night, was the Summerhall media party. I applied a red lipstick in the hall mirror, frowning at how the colour was too dark, now, for my skin, which was older and paler than it had been when I'd chosen that shade three years ago. How long are you supposed to keep a lipstick for? I hadn't worn this one, or any others, since Arlo was born. The once-sharp top of the colour was rounded over from how often I'd pressed it to my lips. But that was before.

I was checking to make sure I had my keys and my phone before leaving when Alex emerged from his room wearing all black and a leather jacket, looking like the frontman of a minor indie band.

'You're coming?' Watching him with one eye, I wiped some of the lipstick off with my little finger.

'Course I'm coming. I go every year. Should I not go, just because people are calling me a cunt on the internet?' He looked in the mirror beside me, pinching his fingers at his hair, making it stick out in a slightly more direct upward direction from his scalp. 'You look nice,' he said. 'Are you walking?'

Going to the party would prove, Alex said on the way, that all the chaos was just an internet thing, and real life was something different, full of normal people who didn't actually care. He still wanted to go with me instead of arriving there on his own, though. I wondered if that meant part of him worried that he might be wrong.

Summerhall was a venue right in the middle of Edinburgh, a sprawling converted university complex with a grand stone entrance, built in the nineteenth century as a warren of lecture theatres, offices and meeting rooms. Its fabric, in a state of terminal decay and romantic artsy crumble, was covered over for the festival with a veneer of colourful posters, bunting, flags and paintings. The annual festival media party was organised by one of the Scottish arts magazines, held for enough years in a row that it had gained a feeling of heritage, even if it was mostly just an excuse for journalists and performers to get drunk together. The magazine that started it wasn't even printed any more. It only existed online.

I'd been to the media party years ago, before I'd met Alex, when I'd worked in Edinburgh. It was then, and remained, invitation-only.

It wasn't really a normal party, but a whole festival in itself. Performers from that year's festival – mostly comedians and musicians and cabaret acts – were invited to do scaled-down versions of their shows in all the different rooms, while the journalists got drunk and watched them. Performers hoped that they would be able to convince some of the journalists at the party who liked what they saw to come to their actual full show, and to review it, or otherwise give them some sort of press coverage. The party was therefore a kind of theatrical red-light district. A mosaic of performances designed to entice. There was also a lot of free booze. And karaoke.

Going into the party, I had the strange feeling of no time having passed since I last attended it, despite everything that had happened during the years since. Eight years, in fact, during which time I'd joined the paper, met Josh, become a mother. The last time I was here, I'd drunk too much and ended up making out with the bassist in a friend's band. The party was precisely how I remembered it. There was even the same branding on the banners and the decor, the same alcohol companies sponsoring it, the same desperation of people begging you to see the thing they'd made and tell them it was good. The only thing that had changed across the years was me.

Before the whole Hayley thing, Alex would have been greeted on entry by flattering acquaintances from journalism and theatre. This was the kind of party that would once have welcomed Alex into its heart. He would have been one of the people that every performer knew by name and wanted to bring to their shows.

That night, however, nobody acknowledged his presence. They recognised him, sure, and then looked away. One guy made a face like a clenched-teeth emoji. Before the party, I'd thought Alex might disappear to be with better, cooler people than me as soon as we'd got inside, but he stayed close.

'Fucking hell,' he said. 'I need a drink.'

He walked to the bar next to me. I felt like his minder again, or maybe more like his security guard. He seemed newly, strangely vulnerable. I noticed that I felt more confident because of his diminishment. There was a power in being his only option. His last patch of stable ground. I felt the strength of myself in that.

Because it was one thing for Alex to have been on the receiving end of a social media backlash, but it was another to go headfirst into the physical reality of ostracism. Yes, this was confirmation, if we needed it, that Alex was a pariah. I think he only stayed at the party after those first few minutes of rejection out of stubbornness. Now, he was an outsider. His ticket was a formality, something that couldn't be technically rescinded, but it granted him entry in only the most literal way. It let him into the building, but not, any more, into that life.

I considered, for the first time, if it was a risk to be seen with him like this. But then, I reasoned, everyone already knew I worked with him. They might even wonder, if they knew my name and job title at all, if I were a victim, too. And maybe it was something of my own stubbornness that made me stay with him. I told myself it was loyalty.

This thought was interrupted by the sight of Lyla Talbot, talking with enthusiasm to some people I didn't recognise, one of whom was in a lime-green three-piece suit. She saw me, smiled and mouthed a *hello*, then saw Alex, widened her eyes, and turned back to the people she was with.

Alex picked up his pace. There were so many people we had to get past to get to the bar and get some drinks, which I now felt was the most urgent task. Everyone there seemed at least ten years younger than us. They were dressed as if they were a slightly different species, in a style which had emerged and displaced my own without me noticing. I wore a navy jumpsuit and lipstick and heels, and when I arrived I realised that I was dressed as if I were wearing a costume from long ago, in these clothes I'd owned for five years. When I used to go out all the time, girls wore jeans and a nice top. Now, they were wearing plain-coloured cropped tank tops and fun bottoms, glittery skirts or patterned trousers or palazzo pants. My clothes, my body, were out of date. Everything had switched upside down at some point and now I was the wrong way round from everyone else. Alex's eyes lingered on the exposed waist of a girl with a navel piercing.

There were people older than me here, too, but they also lived a life that I didn't know, a life of artistic suspension, not structured by reproduction. They did not have the faces of people who knew the daytime CBeebies schedule or the expected developmental milestones of a one-year-old. If they had children, they had bohemian children who spent their lives dancing in the front row at rock gigs, missing their health visitor appointments.

A comedian with a microphone and long hair was up on a podium in the middle of the central courtyard as we passed. He didn't recognise Alex, or maybe just didn't see him, because he was saying in a rapid Australian accent, 'What I don't understand about this Alex Lyons guy is that he's so obviously so fucking cringe, why did any woman want to sleep with him when they could have found a perfectly good rat on the street that would give them a better time?'

The bar at Summerhall is called the Royal Dick. That's its real name, but as Alex walked through the doorway it all seemed so on-the-nose, like another way the world was mocking him. The doorway was crammed with people we had to push past. The bar was in a room of dark blue-green walls and exposed pipework, framed architectural drawings of Summerhall on browned paper and cabinets of antique glassware and old veterinary tools. It used to be a vet school, and on the opposite wall was mounted a line of horse skulls, femurs and pelvic bones. A tall window to the courtyard was covered with origami birds in orange and pink and yellow paper. Alex queued at the bar and got us each one of the free cocktails that was included with our ticket and we sat together in the corner seats.

Above the heads of the crowd was a projection on one wall, a showreel of highlights from acts at this year's festival playing with the sound off. It showed a woman dressed as a peacock, doing a fan dance with an exuberant feathered tail of turquoise and black. Then there was a choir of jumping teenagers in matching outfits. Then a juggler on a unicycle wearing fetish gear, with an old-fashioned jester's hat on his head. Over the top, pop tracks played by an unseen DJ bled into one another.

Alex had an espresso martini, which he said he chose for the caffeine. He ordered me something lurid and orange which came with a free pair of matching orange plastic sunglasses.

'Oh, fuck,' said Alex. 'It's her.'

Hayley entered the room in the middle of a cloud of female acolytes. Someone, a dark-haired woman in her forties, put her hands on Hayley's shoulders. She was drunk enough to lean into Hayley's face and say, with feeling, 'Hayley Sinclair. You are *such an impressive woman.*'

I asked Alex if he was going to say anything to her.

'No. Obviously not. What should I say?'

I suggested it might be a chance to say sorry.

'What for? What should I even be sorry for, now?

Everything I've done, she's turned into the best thing that could ever have happened for her career. If anything, I should say you're welcome.'

'Are we just going to sit here all night bitching about it?'

'Maybe I *should* say something to her. I should ask her why she's trying to ruin my life. I should.'

'I don't think that's a good idea.'

The video projection on the wall changed. It flickered into a familiar face, the face of Peter Ogilvie, that Shakespearean actor from the costume exhibition, but it was a clip of a stage performance, not the same archive video interview I'd seen at the gallery. That meant he must actually be at the festival this year. Weird – I'd presumed he was dead. He was wearing one of the costumes from the exhibition, floor-length maroon robes of a Shakespearean king. His mouth opened and closed in silent soliloquy, his face first frowning in fury, then cracking into laughter. The image cropped tight around his mouth.

'Christ.' Alex's eye was drawn to it, too. He nodded at it. 'That's the last thing I need.'

The music had got louder without me realising, and I wasn't sure I'd heard him properly. But now he was watching Hayley, who was still at the bar, her laughter punctuating the low vibration of the beat. She was ethereal, her hair catching the blue and red light. Someone else tapped Hayley on the shoulder and she was absorbed into another conversation in which she was the star.

'Do you want another one?' she asked a friend. 'Mine was eight quid, would you believe it. Anyway, it's my round.'

There was a gap in the queue of women speaking to

her. I could have gone up to talk to her and filled it. She had a shine to her entire body that I found fascinating. Since I'd been in the audience at her show, she seemed to have grown taller. Her skin was juicy and supple, like a recently watered plant, and she moved with a clean, brash grace that emphasised the slight shabbiness of the room. She picked up her new drink, a glass of white wine, and turned from the bar as she was putting her debit card back into her bag. And that's when she saw Alex.

All the possible ways she could react flickered in her face. Her friends noticed her noticing something and followed her gaze, and their eyes fell on us too, but they didn't know who we were, not straight away. Hayley looked as if she was about to say something.

Alex stood up – 'I'm just going to get this over with,' he said to me – and moved towards Hayley. He spoke before she could, saying, 'All right, do you think we should—' and he was smiling, turning on the Alex charm now, the cheeky-boy Alex, the flirty Alex, the whole act, as if she wouldn't know that act for exactly what it was.

He touched her arm. And this was like lighting a fuse, and the explosion was Hayley throwing her drink in his face. Then immediately she turned away from him, facing the bar with her gasping, impressed friends. 'Stay away from her, you creep,' one of them spat. It had all been so quiet, so decisive, so sudden, and it humiliated Alex as thoroughly as it soaked his hair.

The only response from the other people in the bar was very British: raised eyebrows and the awkward turning of backs as Alex stood still, dripping, for one second, two seconds, of stunned hatred.

He blinked and wiped the wine out of his eyes, shaking

it off his hands. He came back to our table and grabbed his phone, and I asked him if he was OK, but he headed towards the door out into the courtyard without saying anything. I called his name, but he shook his head and kept walking. He patted a pocket for his cigarettes, clocked the *No Smoking* sign, swore, and was lost in the crowd.

He'd left the remaining half of his espresso martini on the table. Not knowing what else to do, I downed it. It had a sickly, smooth bitterness after the sharp zest of the orange spritz monstrosity that I'd been drinking. The combination made me feel worse. Hayley's friends were laughing together now.

I went to follow Alex, but he seemed to have really gone, and I couldn't see anyone else I recognised. How could it be so easy to bump into someone I knew in the street during the festival, but here, at a party full of journalists, so far there wasn't a single face I knew? I tried to walk through the party with purpose. Stuart MacAskill must be here. I messaged him – *Hey, are you at Summerhall? x* – but there wasn't enough signal, and so my message remained unsent, a tiny grey clock icon next to it instead of double ticks.

I walked through crowds of people younger and cooler than me, through the grand deteriorating building, designed for education but now, falling apart, filled up with performance, aching and dying and full of life. I pierced through the crowd with my shoulder, gripping my bag close to my waist. A large man eased himself past me, pressing his open sweaty palm into the small of my back as he did so.

Since my mother died, I'd felt the nearness of death, which writing obits only sharpened. It was like dark coloured ink on wet paper, bleeding into everything. Sometimes, waiting for death felt like waiting for a difficult phone call scheduled for some time in the afternoon. The whole morning spent in the foreshadow of it, unable to settle to anything. Not worth starting anything new, now.

Arlo had recently learned to say 'Moon'. It broke my heart, because to him, now that he had the word for it, everything might be the moon. He pointed at anything that glowed and said, *Moon*. The round nightlight beside his cot. His own pale face in the mirror. An abandoned white football under the rained-on shrubs at the park. *Moon!*

The version of myself that walked through Summerhall, not knowing if each staircase was one I'd been up before, picking up drinks from unmanned trays and stands, looking for people I might know, was someone I wasn't sure I recognised. She was both someone new and someone I used to be.

I remembered the first time I'd interviewed a writer. It was a poet that I'd liked, and I'd taken my voice recorder to meet her in her local pub, asking her anything I wanted. She'd been a bit tipsy and indiscreet and we had a great time, because she was just thrilled that she was going to be in the paper, and so was I. Soon after that, I remembered interviewing a comedian called John something, and expecting him to be chilled out and fun like he was on stage, so I asked him some cheeky questions, but he turned out to be grumpy and obstructive, and I left feeling confused and self-conscious. I remembered interviewing a pop singer on the up, who was dressed in red leather and amazing boots, and she was sweet and open, but her management team were hovering nearby, and they intimidated me so much that I didn't ask her anything interesting and dropped all my notes on the way out. I'd learned something from all these encounters. I'd gradually learned how to be a journalist in my own way.

And I remembered the first cultural news byline I'd had in the paper, a story about the artist who had just won the Turner Prize. My mother cut it out of the paper and put it on the fridge. She took a photo of it in situ to send to me. The cutting had stayed on the fridge until after she'd died, until I had to take it down when I was emptying her house.

In the blue-and-green changing light of the party, two drinks down, I felt newly indulgent and protective of the Sophie who had written features on subjects she knew nothing about, and used words that she wasn't confident in the meaning of but wanted to put in anyway just to feel herself typing them. She was twenty-four and knew nothing about anything. She was still there. She was still me.

I accepted a free glass of some kind of well-diluted cocktail from a waiter in a bright pink top. I looked down at my own clothes. I was in costume as a younger version of me, surrounded by the ghosts of my old ambition. Watching the others move through the party was like watching a phantasmagoria of other possible versions of myself. Which one of them was the kind of journalist I could be if I were braver? Which of them could interview a celebrity and approach them not with deference, but with a verbal magnifying glass, enlarging the part of them they didn't want the world to see, and trying to find out the answer not to the question, *who are you*, but to the question, *why are you like this?*

That's what I'd been trying to work out with Alex.

Why was he like this? How did a person get to their mid-thirties on a wave of perfect propulsion towards exactly where they wanted to be, only to find out they'd been wrong all that time? I wanted to be near him in the same way that, standing on a cliff, you want to look over the edge.

I remembered hearing that actors in crowd scenes are supposed to not say real sentences, but *rhubarb rhubarb rhubarb* over and over again, so it comes across on stage as general hubbub without the risk of them accidentally saying something more interesting than the script and stealing the audience's ear. It felt as though the people at this party, too, were not really talking, but just saying *rhubarb rhubarb Alex*. People said his name in the middle of their conversations and tuned me in to them as I walked past.

'This Alex Lyons thing is so insane,' someone said.

'I wasn't surprised. Find me a critic that isn't an arsehole.'

'I knew he was an arsehole. It's just kind of satisfying to find out that he's a perv as well.'

Why was he like this? A vile critic and a shit boyfriend. Did one trait cause the other? Which was worse? I was at another bar now, and this one was decorated in a rough attempt at the Hawaiian with a fringe of yellow plastic grass and a pile of plastic coconuts. There was an interactive customer feedback device propped up on the bar. *Tell us what you think of our service*, it said, and underneath that there were two buttons you could press: an angry red face or a smiling green one. Excellent or worthless, nothing in between. Review your experience, share your thoughts, recommend us to your friends, swipe left, swipe right, leave a comment, have an opinion.

The barman asked what I was having. I ordered something containing rum and drank it out of a fake coconut.

'Best show I've seen at the Fringe is hands down, balls out, *The Alex Lyons Experience*,' said a boy who looked about twenty, wearing a straw hat and a pair of the free orange sunglasses they were giving out.

'Totally,' said a skinny girl in cut-off denim hotpants. 'It's not even like a show, it's like a *ceremony*. I've been three times. She's amazing. He's so gross.'

The problem with being a critic is that, eventually, you realise you aren't saying anything any more. You're just some idiot responsible for filling a space in the paper with words, the only point of which is to be printed next to some advertising. And reviews are often just advertising, too. Critics pretend that isn't true, but it is.

I was starting to understand why Alex gave out so many one-star reviews. Yes, they were mean. But at least they weren't PR.

'Fair criticism doesn't exist,' he'd said to me in the newsroom once. 'Life isn't fair, so why should I be?'

Thirty years ago, when I was a small child, if adults wanted to find a plumber or a boyfriend they did it through the people they knew. An introduction or a recommendation from a trusted friend was enough to say something or someone was worthwhile, without you having to spend a day researching it.

Personal recommendation has been replaced with consensus. We used to know a person really well, and we decided based on what we knew of them whether we would like the things they liked, too. Now, people don't even want newspaper critics any more. We don't know the anonymous people on the internet making any of the recommendations we're looking for, so we rely on there being hundreds of people rating everything, a critical mass of approval, a thousand faceless reviews on Amazon or Goodreads or Trustpilot.

I took a glass of free wine from a tray beside the pile of coconuts and somehow bumped into the girl standing next to me, which made her knock into the bar in turn, and together we tipped over the remaining wine glasses on the counter. 'Oh shit,' she said, laughing in horror. My arm was soaked.

'Are you all right, Sophie?' Stuart MacAskill had appeared behind me. Where had he come from? He put a hand on my sweating back. 'Can I get you some water?'

'Stuart! Stuart. This is a really important question.' I hugged him, spilling a little of my wine over his shoulder. 'Would you buy a toaster that had five stars? But then what if *you're* the person who *liked* a two-star toaster that nobody else wanted? What if that one was the perfect toaster for you? What if *you* would give that toaster five stars?'

'OK, honey.' Stuart put his hands on my shoulders and steered me away from the bar. Stuart had a pink streak of chalk paint in his hair and was wearing a loose tank top that showed arms he'd been working hard on. 'Do you want to come and sit down with me for a minute?'

'Why do we even need other people to vet our opinions for us in advance? God forbid we make up our own mind about something and then change it later.' I couldn't stop this stuff coming out of my mouth. In my own ranting, I heard the voice of Alex. His cocky, derisive tone. I felt clammy and sick, the espresso martini and the orange thing and the rum and all the wine curdling in my stomach.

I waved Stuart away and went back out into the courtyard, where I found a stand with a big glass keg full of water and one of those tiny fake taps on the side of it, made of plastic and painted in peeling silver, and you turn it and it almost comes off in your hand, so you have to humour it as it trickles slowly into a paper cup. I stood there in the cool air, occasionally losing my balance, until I'd had several cups of water. I felt better, or at least not like I was about to be sick any more.

The night had darkened and cleared and there was a crescent in the sky among the stars. Tilting back my head, I stared at it for a while. *Moon!*

I wandered back inside, into a half-filled theatre room where a cabaret was happening. In the pool of a lonely blue spotlight on the stage, a sad Pierrot with a beautiful voice was just finishing a set where he sang slow operatic versions of Y2K pop songs, transposed into a minor key. I took a seat during hearty applause as he bowed after his last song and retired into the wings.

The next act was a band called Down Home Mountain. The lead singer had blonde dreadlocks, and sang bluegrass covers to her banjo while wearing a cocked bowler hat with a feather in it. The audience thinned out, but I'd had enough to drink that her performance really spoke to me, and this woman finger-picking her way through a song about how much she missed the landscape of her childhood was devastatingly profound. I loved her, I loved the Pierrot, I loved the festival, and suddenly everyone in this mad, gothic city in the moonlight was flawed and perfect and beautiful.

I needed a wee now, though. I found the toilets and my vision rippled.

When I came out of the toilets, I turned the wrong way and went down a corridor past a grey door with a sign printed out on A4 paper that said:

ARTISTS' PREP AREA, NOT FOR PARTY BUSINESS!
NO FUN HERE!

Out of curiosity, I opened the door. It was bigger than I expected inside, not like a cupboard at all, but like a disused school classroom, with stacked-up chairs turning it into a maze, and piles of coats and old mattresses on the floor.

And sitting on one of the mattresses was Alex.

His hair was still wet and his eyes were red. He had his wrist to his nose as if he'd just done a line. He looked up at me with a slack, open-mouthed half-grin.

'I've been looking for you,' I said. I plonked myself down beside him. 'Why are there so many young people at this party? There should be a party where people in their thirties and forties can get as drunk as they want, and everyone wears a badge that has their salary ballpark on it, so you don't find yourself accidentally being intimidated by a teenage crypto millionaire.'

'I used to be an angry young man,' said Alex. 'When did I become just an angry man?'

The room swirled. I leaned on his shoulder and inclined my head so that my ear was on his collar. I shut my eyes. He smelled of smoke and cotton and wine. He tilted his head back against mine, just for a couple of seconds. His hair, wet from Hayley's drink, was cool against my forehead. This was the closest his face had ever been to me.

He lifted his head away. He put his hand on my cheek, and the smell of smoke was even stronger now. I didn't pull away from him. He smelled of when I was a teenager at a house party, cheap and alive.

Someone opened the door. It was a girl with pink hair, and I guess she was looking for the toilets or something. 'Oop, sorry,' she said, putting a hand over her giggling mouth, and shut the door again.

'Fuck.' Alex pulled away from me and sat up. 'Do you think she recognised me? Oh shit. Look at you.'

'What is that supposed to mean?'

'You're drunk, and I'm doing this to you.'

'You're not doing anything to me—'

'Oh my God. You'll be straight on to Hayley, won't you? Fuck.' He looked terrified. Both his hands were on his forehead. 'And I can't even blame you.'

'No! It's not like that, we're just having fun.'

'You're the only person who's been kind to me all through this.' He was recoiling from me now, backing away towards the wall as if he'd just discovered my body was covered in insects. 'And this is how I treat you. I was supposed to be your friend. Fuck, this is their entire point. This is exactly it.'

'I *am* your friend.'

'Can we, like, just be cool about this? Can I say sorry? Can we go and get another drink?'

I swallowed. My lips were thick against my teeth. 'Of course.'

'Please don't cry.'

'I'm not.' I pressed my palms against my eyes. 'I just need another drink.'

'Sure. Yeah. Let's do that. OK.'

How could I say anything else? It was me. I was Alex's come-to-Jesus moment. He bought me another ridiculous cocktail at the bar, and I chose the one with the stupidest name on the menu, so I could force myself to laugh at it, to be fine, like it was no big deal. I made him give me one of his cigarettes to smoke in the smoking area. We were the only people in there who weren't vaping.

'I've been thinking of vaping more, actually,' said Alex, fast and animated. 'Not instead of smoking. As well as.'

I told him that sounded healthy. He lit up for me. I hadn't smoked since I was a student. I dragged heavy on the hurting rasp of it, pulling the small buzz into my brain. After that, I bought us some chips to share from a food van in the courtyard and I was glad when they tasted like ash, too.

Alex and I were friends. Nothing had really happened. This was probably what cool art girls did all the time and never thought about it afterwards. We had another drink, my round this time, and he had a whisky and I just had a Coke. We drank in a depressing, sexless silence. Then Alex left. He said he'd see me later. I didn't ask where he was going.

I could leave, too, and go back to the flat, except that this presented two equally unappealing possibilities: that Alex would be there, or that he wouldn't. It was a better idea to stay out for as long as possible. I got another drink, another orange spritz, in an attempt to take me back to the beginning of the evening rather than wallowing at the end of it.

My brain was grasping, in a tipsy tic of repeatedly echoing internal monologue, towards the sickening fact that I'd just been turned down by the one person in the country who was famous for having sex with absolutely anybody, no matter who they were, no matter how inappropriate the situation, no matter how much he didn't even *like* them. The poster boy for indiscriminate sexual trawling. The man with no moral compass. British media's most notorious fuckboy.

It wasn't as if I'd imagined any possible romantic future with Alex. I'm not an idiot. I wasn't heartbroken. It was just that all our frank, late-night conversations about some of the most raw moments in his life had seemed to lead us here.

There was more. To Alex, I was a writer. A peer. I was not someone grieving or mothering or otherwise to be pitied. I'd thought he would recognise this, the warmth of it.

I pressed my fist into my abdomen as far as it would go. The guilt hadn't hit yet. There was no room for it, what with all the shame. I hadn't thought about Josh at all. Worse, I hadn't thought about Arlo. There was only a slideshow of self-pity, thinking about how alone I was, cut off from the younger person I'd almost become again. The girl I'd almost got back, for a second there, for a one-night-only reprisal of my old self, a few glimmering moments of emotional mirage. A bud had bloomed in the darkness of my head. And then reality saw it, smiled, and plucked it out.

12

Back in my bed at the flat, I held the light of my phone to my face. Josh had sent me a video from when he'd been giving Arlo a bath earlier that night. In the video, Arlo was splashing and blowing kisses towards the camera and holding up a small red boat in one hand and a purple sponge shaped like an octopus in the other. Josh didn't need to tell Arlo to smile for the video. He was already accustomed to smiling at phones. Josh sent a written message underneath the video. It said, *Someone misses you!*

  I hated myself a lot then. I started to imagine, as a consoling thought, a future of just me and Arlo, somewhere else. We'd rent a small flat with white walls. I would never be able to afford two bedrooms in London on my own, so Arlo could have the one bedroom of this imaginary flat, and I would sleep on the sofa every night. It would be cosy. Josh would be happier without me, anyway, and he could see Arlo at weekends.

  What was I doing? Alex had saved me from my worst

impulses. He'd given me a chance to put that humiliating encounter down to drink, and, even better, to blame Alex for it. Nobody would have a hard time believing that it was all Alex's fault. It was, if anything, harder to believe that I'd been the one to touch him first. If that girl hadn't opened the door, would he still have stopped?

Alex was right, too, that I could go to Hayley the next day and tell her about it if I wanted. Some new material for her show, hot and fresh. I could go to her and say, *He's still doing it. I was drunk and lonely and I trusted him as a senior colleague, and guess what he did to me? This very weekend! After you'd already called him out, and after everyone knew what he was! The gall of him!*

But here's the really shameful truth of it: I still wanted to be Alex's friend. I wondered if I was like one of those people who understands in a rational sense that wild animals, like wolves and bears, are dangerous, undiscerning predators that are stronger and faster than humans, but who walks into the Canadian forests anyway, thinking that maybe I was different, and the bears would know to be gentle with me, their claws remaining retracted behind soft, indulgent paws.

Even I would have called me a pick-me, the way I'd acted. I'd thought I was Alex's only option, but even then, he didn't pick me. I was that unpickable.

I sent Josh a voice note back. I told him I missed him and Arlo, too, and things were crazy, but he'd never guess whose house I was going to for lunch. Murray Maclean. Yes, that one. I promised I'd try to steal something tiny from his house, like a pebble from the driveway or a cork from a wine bottle. I said I'd call as soon as I got back afterwards. I sent them both all my love. I recorded a video of myself blowing kisses for Arlo.

Josh sent a voice note right back. 'We can't wait to see you on the eighteenth. I just really miss you. So, yeah. That's all. I just wanted to say it out loud.'

I didn't reply straight away.

I was still going to Murray's house. Not going would make things seem like a bigger deal than they were. In the morning, Alex and I were as carefully normal as possible. Alex even made me a coffee, and was actually quite cheerful, more cheerful than he'd been in days. I'd had a panic about what to wear and eventually gone for a floral sun dress and trainers. And a jumper and a jacket, partly in case it was cold, and partly in case I regretted the dress more generally. I didn't have breakfast because I still felt a bit sick.

Alex drove us both to Murray's house in a rented car. On the way, we talked a little too loudly about work and the people in the newsroom in London. We put on a great performance of being friends who were chill about everything. The coffee had helped, but I still had that queasy kind of hangover that made my bones feel limp and soft, and it felt as if I might dissolve into the car seat if I stopped concentrating on looking straight ahead. The longer I was in the car, the worse it got.

A pap shot had appeared on a rival paper's website that morning. In the picture, Alex was smoking a cigarette and looking directly into the camera with one eyebrow raised. He looked tired, but overall still pretty cool.

I teased him about it. 'I reckon you staged that pap shot. Told them where you'd be and when. You don't look grumpy enough in it for it to be real.'

'If I had, I'd have worn a nicer dress and given it the full Princess Diana. Did I tell you about the wildflower meadow that Murray's got? I'll show you when we get there. It goes right down to the river.'

I would have been humiliated to have photos of me in the street put online and in the paper like that, but Alex wasn't. He looked unbothered and unapologetic in the pictures, which only made people online angrier.

His mention of the meadow made me think of a painting my mother had once done of a wildflower meadow in Cambridgeshire. I wasn't sure what had happened to it. I suddenly wished I could look at it.

We arrived at the house of Murray Maclean, parked on the gravel just inside the electronic gates, and walked along a mown path between tall grasses towards an old, grand building that squatted like a great toad in the countryside. It was huge and square and stone, with a name engraved in slate on the wall outside: Seil House.

We were let in at the big front door by someone who acted like a butler, except he looked about twenty-three and was wearing a pressed white linen shirt with an open collar, as if he'd just got in from a beach in California. This threw me into a state of awkward paralysis, because, probably, I had more in common with this person, in age and in life circumstances, than I had with the people I was there to see. I let him take my jacket (and possibly, by the way he was looking at it, burn it) and smiled at him with an expression that I hoped conveyed a sense of camaraderie. He smiled back with blank, professional affability. His teeth were a lot better than mine.

'My name's Reuben,' said Reuben, as if this were the most delightful piece of news ever. I wondered if I was supposed to tip him, but I didn't have cash. 'Murray's expecting you, just down the hall and on the right. If you need anything at all, you let me know, guys, OK? I'll be right with you.' He disappeared through a door I hadn't noticed up to that point.

'He's new,' said Alex. 'Maybe Murray's signed up for some kind of twink subscription.'

The house was clean to a standard I'd never seen outside hotels and it smelled of florals and spices. There were three glass jugs of late summer flowers in the hall, their sprays of orange petals nodding down to the floor. This was not a house that a toddler had ever been inside.

The rooms were so spacious and ornate that they would look odd if they didn't have sculptures in, so they did have sculptures in. One in the hallway was a Henry Moore, I registered with an inward blink of panic, wishing I'd worn shoes that were not white trainers. Yes, they were my most expensive white trainers, but come now. They weren't Henry Moore in the hallway trainers.

'What the hell's that supposed to be?' Alex said to the statue.

'Evocative,' I said.

'Don't start reviewing it, nobody's paying you. I don't see the point of statues. Nobody ever built a statue of a critic.'

'I've heard that before. I can never remember who said it.'

'Fuck knows,' said Alex. 'Someone talking bollocks.'

'You've found the Henry Moore,' said Reuben, who had reappeared behind my shoulder with a tray of drinks. 'It's one of my favourite pieces in the house. Please, do go in.'

Without touching either of us, he shepherded us into

the room where Murray was, though the room was so big that I didn't see Murray at first. This was a room big enough to hold two grand pianos, one at either end. Between them there was a long table of dark wood with carved legs. It could probably seat twenty. What do you even call a room containing all those things? A drawing room, a ballroom? A run of twelve-foot-high sash windows looked out onto a long lawn that sloped down to a river that ran horizontally as a slick of brownish grey under the low summer cloud, with a line of trees behind and a path that disappeared into them. A heron opened out from the trees like an umbrella, making a silent clatter towards the sky, then hinged itself invisibly away.

Murray rose from a striped armchair beside the window and made a welcoming 'Ah!' noise that wasn't really a word. He was smaller and slighter than he looked in films, and he didn't have Judith's vitality, the quality that made her the centrepiece of every room she entered. Reuben set down the tray and excused himself with a cheerful deference. Alex kissed Murray on both cheeks and so did I. Alex helped himself to a drink of something fizzy from Reuben's tray.

The room was full of things, and all Murray's possessions were from places that I didn't know you could buy things from. 'Wonderful boutique in Yemen,' Murray said as I admired a garnet-coloured rug, and 'Got it off a drug dealer in Lisbon,' as he poured Beaujolais from a twisted blue-and-green glass carafe. 'I am a terrible magpie, you see.' It was uncanny to hear his voice in real life, a voice I knew from BBC dramas, Christmas supermarket adverts, and, lately, that HBO series about the rich WASPy criminals. You know the one. I only got as far as episode three.

'Mind if I smoke, Murray?' Alex was already lighting up. 'Sophie's gagging to see your Schieles. Is Judith here?'

'She's been in the pool all morning. Wrinkly as a walnut.' He looked as if he were thinking about something else, and leaned towards Alex's ear, confidentially. 'Listen, son, it's—'

'Darlings!' Judith emerged from, presumably, the pool, with her long arms outstretched, jangling with bracelets and fabrics, her hair wet and tousled, water-smudged kohl framing her eyes. Her cheeks were reddened and fresh. She spoke as if it were her house as much as Murray's. 'You made it. Sweethearts, come and sit, and tell me the news about everything. Journalists, yes! Tell us the news! Murray, have you got drinks or not?'

We sat in armchairs made from striped fabrics that my skin had never touched before, rough but luxurious, as if challenging you to find them uncomfortable, the kind of fabric that you knew was good quality, because otherwise there was no explanation for why it would be here. Reuben left a tray of small things to eat that each looked like an amuse bouche from a restaurant. One of the stoneware plates held only a scatter of thin, curled shavings of parmesan, translucent as rose petals, each one the size of a Pringle. I didn't know you could just eat parmesan on its own. In my house, parmesan was a dust.

'Glorious parmesan,' said Judith, so I had some. It tasted of salt. 'So good to see you again, Sophie. I'm delighted you've come all this way.'

'Oh, it's just lovely to see you again, Judith,' I said, and cringed inwardly at saying her name out loud. Was it OK for me to call her Judith? It felt weird to call her by the same name that Alex did, but I'd said it now.

'Thank God Alex made it all the way here without swerving off the A1 into some Jezebel's den of iniquity!' She laughed, as if to signal this was the kind of thing we could all joke about, but Alex looked sour, his hands in his pockets. Her remark landed awkwardly into silence until Murray started saying something to Alex about a wrongheaded casting decision in a West End show, which Murray objected to seemingly entirely on the basis that he should have been cast instead. Luckily, Alex had a lot to say on the matter.

But there was a tension between Judith and Murray. He kept looking at her meaningfully and she was not meeting his eye.

A breeze mussed the white linen curtains and a bee bumbled past the open French doors to a paved area and a walled garden draped with vines and studded with fertile fruit trees. The sight of the orchard, of grapes upon grapes, figs and apples and medlars and mellowing pears all growing in a cool Scottish summer, tree branches twisting and drooping with the weight of them all, made the entire house seem thousands of miles away from Edinburgh, not forty-five minutes in the car.

Alex was doing a good job of acting as if nothing had happened between him and me the night before, to the extent that it almost made me wonder if anything really had. I'd been worried that this was the opening of some major chasm, but maybe this kind of thing happened to him so often he was able to put it out of his mind with ease. His hair curled around his ear and at the nape of his neck. He twisted one of the curls at the back around his finger as he talked to Murray about the next show at the National that Murray was about to start rehearsing. In profile, Alex looked like a bust of a Roman emperor. I noticed for the first time how crooked his teeth were. His eyelids were puffy, and his lips were quite thin. He cracked on with a plate of fat green olives with a sense of familiarity.

We sat down to lunch. Through the windows, in the distance, a herd of deer grazed in the field beyond, like a charm. The Egon Schieles on the walls danced under the dappled light like a gallery of enchanted skeletons.

'I like the self-portrait on the end, there,' I said.

'I'm fond of him,' said Murray, with shy pride. 'Especially that to-hell-with-you expression on his face. It gives me a bit of zip when I'm eating my porridge. Reuben informs me it's significant for some historical reason or another, but, well. You're the art expert.'

'Oh, I don't know, I just love the sort of jangly shapes,' I said. This was a fully idiotic thing to say. I kept talking. 'I mean, Schiele always has this contorted mode of draughtsmanship that's beautiful and disturbing at the same time, doesn't he?'

'What the fuck does that mean?' Alex got up and went to stand beside the pictures. He leaned right towards them, his nose almost touching the paint. 'It's creepy, that's what you mean.' I looked from the portrait, with its tall hair and wired eyes and angular jaw and shoulders, its sexual pose and the glare of its eyes, as if challenging you either to a fight or to the best night of your life, and back to Alex.

'Right, creepy,' I said. Dishes of lobster arrived and I spent the rest of the meal trying not to look at the pictures.

*

Judith asked me about my parents, and whether they were journalists too, and I said no, and then she made a very sorrowful face when I told her about my mother being dead, and she silently placed a hand on my forearm in a way that was genuinely quite reassuring. It was remarkable how she managed to arrange her face and body to feel appropriate for any situation. I suppose that's why she's so famous. She was performing, and it was all for me. Why? Did she do it all the time, even with no audience? Even alone?

I once wrote a feature about BDSM subcultures when I'd been working for the Edinburgh magazine and interviewed one of the local dominatrices. (I know that word looks wrong, but I promise it's the correct plural. I had a colourful discussion with the sub-editor about it at the time.) This dominatrix (singular) worked under the name Ms Vyvyan Burns, and she told me about how BDSM is a performance for the benefit of the submissives, but that doesn't mean that the subs have no control. It's actually the subs who have control of everything, and a good dom knows that they're really the one in service. Passivity is power, because a passive person can become active at any moment. They're all potential. The dominatrix, on the other hand, has nowhere more extreme to go. They need their sub, their audience, their victim, to make any sense at all.

'Caught at North Berwick this morning,' said Murray, cracking open the claw of his lobster. 'Can't get better anywhere in the world.' He was showing off to me, too. It was flattering and a lot of pressure at the same time. He was endearingly unsure of himself for someone so well known, and I liked him. He was self-conscious, thoughtful, eager to please. I found all this appealing.

Alex tore apart his lobster. Judith took hers to pieces with a delicate precision. The innards of mine slithered out of the shell all at once, slick and wet as a newborn. The flesh tasted of lemon and cream. Alex's hands were covered with lumpy white entrails. He licked his fingers.

'The maddening thing about all this fuss, Alex,' Murray was saying, quite jovially, 'is that much worse things used to happen in theatre all the time and nobody minded. Honestly, I blame women's lib. No, Judith, I'm not saying women don't deserve all the rights they've got. It's just the tone of the thing. Everything they're accusing you of, boy – good grief, if this were 1972, nobody would bat an eyelid.'

'We were talking about it this morning,' said Judith. 'It really is peanuts compared to what men used to get up to back then.'

'And those of us who remember the days when being gay was actually *dangerous*,' Murray continued, 'can't stand this sort of hysterical modern puritanism. These days, people go *looking* for outrage. And women are in charge of everything now anyway. Not that I'm complaining about *that*.'

'Well,' I said, my voice high and pained, not wanting to have to change my opinion of Murray after liking him so much. 'Would we really say that's true?'

'Alex's case demonstrates the point. Don't you think, Jude?'

'I think it's all just fucking showbusiness, darling,' said Judith. 'There's nowhere on Earth hotter than a spotlight. But after a while, it always dies down, and nobody wants you any more. Believe me.' She downed the dregs of her wine and poured herself another glass. She rested her chin on her hand. Her face, her slightly pouting smile, was as carefully arranged as if she were posing for a photograph, though nobody was taking one.

'This lobster is divine,' she said, putting her knife and fork together.

'Do you only write about art at the paper, Sophie?' said Murray. 'Or theatre, too?'

'Odds and sods. Art mostly,' I said. I was conscious of Alex watching me. 'Oh, and the obituaries.'

'Anyone we know?' said Judith. 'Who's died recently, Murray?'

'Jonathan,' said Murray.

'Oh, did you do Jonathan? Poor Jonathan. I thought that one was very *juste*.'

They were talking about this ancient actor. When the news broke that he was dead, we had to check the news wires three times because the editor said he was sure the guy had already died five years previously. 'That one wasn't me, no—'

'You must have to write them so quickly after the sad news arrives.'

'Well, we usually write them when people are still alive. Especially if they're of a certain age. Or have been ill.'

'How macabre!'

'She's probably got both of you on file,' said Alex. 'Look at her! You have, haven't you?'

'No, no,' I said. But guiltily, involuntarily, I glanced at Murray. He looked appalled. See, this is the problem with telling people you do obits. They start looking at you as if you're wearing the full scythe-and-cloak get-up, about to tap them on the shoulder and beckon them to the beyond. 'I may have written a rough version of yours,

Murray. But it's not – it's not a diagnosis. And it's not final.' Alex was delighted, and Judith laughed too, and I felt a desperate surge of belonging.

'How long's Murray's obit, Soph? One sentence? Two?'

'Don't be so vicious, Alex,' said Murray. 'It doesn't suit you half as well as you think.'

'The boy's like his father, I fear,' said Judith. 'Past saving.'

Alex rolled his eyes and Murray went to open another bottle of wine, struggling with the cork and then popping it inelegantly into his chest.

'How about we spend about as much time talking about my dad,' said Alex, 'as he does thinking about me.' His grin was unnatural, brave and unhappy.

'Speaking of which, has Pete spoken to you about all – this?' said Judith.

'He sent me one of his incomprehensible emails that was all about him and how he's featured in some exhibition about theatre costume. Why?'

Oh. How could I have missed that connection? Peter Ogilvie was Alex's father. He'd never talked about it.

'He *rang* from hospital, darling. He was all upset. Saying if he'd been around more, if he'd taken you to football practice, all the old songs. Pissed as a fart. Typical Pete, somehow managing to get sloshed even on the NHS. He agreed with me, though, that we shouldn't intervene. Mummy and Daddy rushing into the press to scoop up their little prince! You can look after yourself, can't you, Alex? Do you know, Sophie, I'm not sure Alex was ever really a child, not truly. I could always speak to him just the same way I spoke to anyone, about sex and work and whatever. And he was a remarkable boy. So wise. You should have seen him when we had people round. A performer!'

Bring The House Down

'Pete's in hospital?' Alex's face was hard to read.

Judith was pouring herself some water from a jug. Her hand trembled a little, just enough that the jug nudged the side of her glass and a glug of water splashed over the edge and onto the table. 'Fuck,' she said.

'Are you going to tell him or not, Jude?' said Murray.

And now I saw, all at once, what the weird atmosphere was about. Murray was looking at Judith with a pained urging that she was completely ignoring. I thought we'd been invited here out of support, and that Alex had come because this was his last refuge, the last place, outside of the flat, where everyone didn't hate him. Now I saw the design of the event for what it really was. I recognised, from when my own mother was dying, what I saw now in the faces of these two strangers. The spell of the house was broken.

'It's hard to find the words,' said Judith. She looked at me, desperately.

'The words for what?' said Alex. He pushed the earthly remains of his lobster around on his plate. 'What's the fucker done now?'

Judith said nothing. I wanted to scream. Couldn't he see? Didn't he know?

Murray's face was red. He had both his palms flat on the table and looked as if he couldn't decide whether to stand up or sit down. His forehead was pained. 'Pete doesn't deserve for you to hate him, Alex.'

'I know what he deserves.'

'I'm sorry about all this, Sophie,' said Judith. 'Can I get you another drink? Murray, get Sophie another drink.'

'Oh, I'm fine, really—'

'Stop fucking worrying about Sophie,' said Alex. 'For

once, could you worry about me? What aren't you telling me this time?'

'Don't talk to your mother like that, son.'

'Oh Alex, not this again, please, darling. I've given you everything I possibly could.' Judith was on the verge of tears.

'You've burdened me with things I never asked for.'

This felt unreal, like being inside a play, and the whole thing was so awkward I wanted to crawl under the table.

'You don't know how abnormal you are.' Alex spoke with heat and impatience. 'You think your work excuses everything. You spend so much time pretending to be other people that you forget how to be a real human being. And everyone just loves you for it. Nobody ever calls you out on all your extravagant bullshit. Or if they do, you don't listen.'

'I think we all need some fresh air,' said Murray. 'Why don't you go have a smoke, Alex.' Murray fumbled in his pockets for a cigarette and a lighter to give to Alex, but found nothing. 'Go for a walk.'

Alex stood, pushing back his chair sharply, and left. Without him, there was a terrible pause. I wondered if Judith would go after him, or Murray. They didn't move.

'Thank you so much for lunch,' I said. 'I should . . .'

'Oh, yes,' said Judith, relieved. 'Please do.' I headed in the direction Alex had gone.

I went outside into the dewy silence of the East Lothian countryside. Alex wasn't there. At the bottom of the garden, towards the river, I found the opening to a bridlepath through a kissing gate and, as I was figuring out how the iron latch worked, I saw Alex up ahead on the path beyond.

I caught up with him and asked if he was OK.

'Never go back to the places you felt safe as a child,' he said. 'You realise how unsafe you really were. But then, maybe it's irresistible. Remember that meadow I was telling you about?' He pointed back down the path behind us. 'It's over there.'

I followed his gaze, thinking buttercups or poppies or even just long grass, but couldn't see anything that looked meadowish at all. 'Behind the tennis court?'

'It is the tennis court, now. And the pavilion next to it. There was also this little fishing hut where I used to come and sit sometimes, just to be by the water. I'm going to see if that's still there, at least.'

We walked for a few minutes down the path along the river. It was quite secluded down there through the trees. The path sloped steeply towards the water, which was high up the banks for summer, and running a fast current. It wouldn't be dark for hours yet, but the clouds were low enough in the sky to cast a general dimness, and the thick summer leaves on the trees swished loudly in the wind.

The stone fishing hut was still there, set in a clearing of the trees. The hut looked more ornamental than functional, pretty but neglected, with white windows on either side of a door from which blue paint was flaking off in long ribbons. It had a chimney in the middle of the roof. There was a tall poplar on one side, and a wooden wheelbarrow on the other, which was painted red.

I peered through the window, but it was too dark and dusty to see much. Alex tried the door of the hut, but it was locked, so we just looked down to the river, which met the grassy bank with a little stony beach. My hangover was all gone now. I sat on the dry ground and the air smelled of warm leaves.

'From here on down that path it's just the river, on and on.' Alex sat beside me and lit up a cigarette. 'Parents,' he said.

'Parents,' I agreed.

'She couldn't even – I did think about calling him when all this Hayley shit started. But it's too late now.' His eyes were flat as paint.

There was a rippling on the surface of the river. 'Is that an otter?'

'An otter? What the fuck, Sophie? No, it's not a fucking otter. It's a rock. Christ.'

We really didn't have very much in common. 'No, it is an otter. Look, it's got a fish.'

'Oh,' he leaned forwards to get a better look. Whatever it was dove out of sight. 'Huh. Fuck, I need to talk about something else that isn't me. Tell me about you. What have you done that you wouldn't ever want anyone digging up?'

'Stop interviewing me.' It was new and uncomfortable, him turning his interest around on me, though yes, I liked it a little bit.

He laughed, put out his cigarette in the earth and left it there. I felt very alone, very remote. Around the carefully maintained clearing were the kinds of woods that might have had bears living in them once, in some prehistoric Scotland three thousand years ago. Now it was all just midges and squirrels, otters and rocks and owls. I felt the same shift in my perception of danger when I'd first googled Alex, when I'd realised I didn't really know him at all, didn't know the full extent of what he'd done, couldn't imagine the nights he'd spent hurting people by making their lives worse in infinite indelible ways.

I closed my eyes for one second and during that fraction of time I had this bizarre image come into my mind of a magician's assistant from the days of music hall and variety shows, a woman in sparkling clothes who would step into a black box onstage and be stuck all through with long, glinting knives, and the man would be the one plunging them in, and she would emerge at the end to applause, unpenetrated, unwounded, miraculously intact despite all the violence that everyone had seen done to her, and this was the act.

'I'm sorry about last night,' I said, all in a rush and jumble of abasement, to break the moment apart, and he looked right at me then.

'No,' he said. 'No, you were – it's all right.' He picked up my hand, consolingly, almost like a nurse at a deathbed, and squeezed it, holding it in his lap. The splintering of an invisible line. He seemed so sad, looking at me with his face so near to mine, his body very close. And this was it, this was the moment: he kissed me, and this time he didn't stop it and neither did I.

The rocky ground dug into my back as Alex's weight pushed against me. The angles of his body re-aligned in my mind now that I knew how they felt as well as how they looked. I was dead sober and it was all entirely unlike Summerhall. It wasn't a thrill. It was just wretched, as if nothing mattered any more. I thought about when I was at university, a time in freshers' week when I'd slept with the first person who'd laughed at something I'd said since I arrived, which set the tone for three years of fitting my body into the shapes that I thought other people wanted them to be.

I thought about Lavinia under the Italian trees. I thought about that girl who'd asked Alex to degrade her and I thought I understood her. I wanted that, too. I wanted him and maybe I even wanted it to hurt. His hand slipping up my dress between my legs and his face in my neck, so intentional, so sure, all gave me this sick feeling of anticipatory, unstoppable regret, like drinking several glasses too many, or staying up four hours too late. It had that same miserable excess.

A mad, distant part of my mind was thinking, *so this is what all those impressive, creative women were talking about – the famous Alex Lyons! What's it like? You're about to find out, Sophie! This is gonzo journalism, bitch!* And deeper than all this, I felt a murmur of internal vindication: I'd been wrong. He wanted me after all.

And then he pulled away from me.

He didn't say anything. He shook his head. I thought I would cry, but I didn't, although my eyes were sore. It was Alex who buried his face in his arms, and he made this awful sound in his throat of half-choked despair.

Neither of us said anything as we put ourselves back together in a grim awkwardness of not looking, not wanting to see. It was all so absurd.

We walked back towards the house in silence and stood for a minute in the garden while Alex smoked the last of a cigarette and blew the smoke up into the dim sky. He flicked the end sparking towards the roses.

I started walking towards the door to the house, but Alex didn't follow.

'Shouldn't we go back in?' I said. 'Say goodbye?'
'No thanks. We shouldn't have come here at all.'
'My jacket's still in there.'

Alex shrugged. I couldn't go back in there alone. I just couldn't. I mentally wrote off the jacket. I had another denim one anyway. We headed back to the car together, any sheen of friendship rubbed away.

In the passenger seat, I picked tiny leaves out of my jumper and put the radio on. It was an interview with some actor going on about the difference between stage and screen, and Alex said 'Fuck that' and switched it to BBC 6 Music, which was playing a throwback indie rock song I hadn't heard since I was about fifteen, and Alex turned the volume up. He sometimes glanced at me, worried, as he drove, but I said nothing, and mostly he kept his attention on the road on the way back to Edinburgh, and I stared at my hands in my lap, my skin slimy and uncomfortable, and I started shivering, actually shivering, as if wet all over, raw with self-loathing.

13

When we got back to the flat, I locked myself in the bathroom and vomited. I didn't know whether the vomit was my delayed hangover or a physical manifestation of something more existential. I get like that sometimes. I threw up during an exam once at school, and had to run to the toilets, pursued by my French teacher. When things overwhelm me, it comes out in my body: rashes, shivers and eruptions. Centuries ago, they would have thought I was possessed by demons.

I sat on the cold tiles of the bathroom floor with my back against the door and hugged my knees. All along the side of the bathtub was a line of black mould. The shower dripped. I thought of how I'd showered in it that morning, taking my turn after Alex, and how the room had been still full of the steam from the hot water that had run across his body. I thought I might throw up again.

My mind ticked back and forth between two prevailing thoughts: the first was a storm of self-hatred and shame. The second was a sense of a debt repaid. I understood it now, for what it was, the dread that had lived in me for those last few weeks: the dread of what I might be capable of doing, how I might destroy my own life. It swelled inside me, smug and triumphant, and I was like a boa constrictor with a rat in its belly, a rat swallowed whole but still just about alive, still able to tear the snake apart from the inside.

I still thought I might cry. Still no tears came. Only shaking and weakness, as if I had a fever. I dug out my phone from my pocket and tried to write a message to Josh. It was my instinct to tell him, but what possible words could I use? I could call him, but how could I? Did I owe it to him to tell him at all? I asked myself this last question with a flash of anger. He hadn't told me, after all, when he'd done this and worse to me.

The problem was that I didn't know what I wanted him to do with the information. I didn't know whether I wanted this to be the end of the relationship, or whether I wanted it to continue in some other form. I didn't know anything at all, except that I missed Arlo desperately, and now I seemed unbearably distant from him. If Arlo had been there with me, right then, I would have taken him in my arms and walked out the door and kept going until both of us were safe, somewhere far away, me and the only certain love I had left. As it was, I felt ripped from my son unjustly, even though it had been my own decision to come here.

But my baby was, I tried to reason, going to be here, with me, in a few days. Josh and Arlo were coming up to Edinburgh. I'd tell Josh then, maybe.

Or maybe I wouldn't. Maybe this was how things had to be now: the two of us living separately but in parallel for the sake of our small child, occupying a space of waiting until he was old enough to understand that his parents had in fact savaged each other's lives long ago. I put my phone away without sending Josh anything.

The next few days passed in a kind of dream. It was as if Alex and I had gone back in time and were simply colleagues again. We talked about work with a deliberate professionalism. Mostly, though, we avoided each other. It was weird and uncomfortable. There was a wound where there had not been one before. I thought again about Lavinia, and about how Alex had said he'd blurred together elements of his life that should never have been mixed, desecrated what had once been sacred.

I spent a lot of time between shows wandering around the city, standing in bookshops as if they might contain the answer. Sometimes my mind seemed to block out what had happened with Alex, as if I were moving mentally through a maze full of dead ends, and I couldn't even really remember it had happened at all. Other times, the images of it burned in vivid colours behind my eyes, my body filled up again with all the sensations from beside the river, my face contorted at the memory as if I had a mouth full of ulcers and lemons, goosebumps across my skin, sometimes even a physical full-body shudder of recalled desire.

I felt guilty. Of course I felt guilty. But also, but also. There was something else, too. My life had rippled into the lives of other people. I felt large and heavy and consequential.

On the Monday morning, Alex and I were both back on call from the flat in Edinburgh. Alex was in the armchair in the living room, highlighting lines in a photocopied bundle of Brecht and drinking black coffee from a small cup with a perfect half-moon of crema on top. He looked Parisian, almost feminine. A cigarette end was cooling in an ashtray he'd taken from a beer garden. He'd lasted until this point without smoking in the flat, but was past caring about that now.

I was finishing a piece of toast while sitting on the floor with the day's papers spread around me. I read the papers from the front page onwards for the first time in a while. For the last few weeks, or maybe even longer, whenever I read the paper, I'd been flicking past the news just to get to the features and reviews. The news was full of things I didn't want to read about.

Graham rang me at ten o'clock. This was just after the morning editorial conference would have finished in the newsroom, so we always expected a call around this time. A phone call at ten meant a new brief. I held up my phone so Alex could see Graham's name flashing up in white. Alex rolled his eyes, slunk further down in the chair and used his own phone to switch the bluetooth speaker in the corner of the room to a jazz radio station and turned it up loud.

'Don't tell him I'm here,' Alex said before I answered.

I took the call in the kitchen, glancing at Judith's terrible, imposing vase as I answered.

'Morning Graham. Who's died?'

He laughed his throaty pub landlord chuckle down the line. 'Nobody yet. The day is young. How are you, Soph? Get a decent couple of days off? You've been filing some nice pieces. Is Alex with you?'

'He's here. How much of the drama has made it back to the office now?'

'You're clairvoyant. It's all a load of overblown nonsense really, but nonetheless – we all think he might need some space. I'm worried about him. How is he, do you think?'

'Right now he's being Serge Gainsbourg.'

'Mm. We're thinking of taking him off reviews.'

The jazz on the radio meant I had to raise my voice. I shut the kitchen door so Alex wouldn't hear. 'What? So he's really cancelled?'

Graham coughed. 'It's gardening leave, Sophie. That's what we're calling it. And did you know that Peter Ogilvie is ill? We wondered if Alex might like some time off on compassionate grounds.'

'How ill is he?'

'Malcolm's updating the obit today. I'm glad Alex has you there. I'd be nervous about him being alone at the moment. He needs someone with a level head around him.'

My phone was hot against my ear. My head did not feel level. I watched a pigeon land on the branch of the tree visible from the kitchen window. The branch it had chosen bent under its weight. There was already another, fatter pigeon sitting further along. There must be a nest nearby.

'There's something else. We don't want to take Alex off the brief and then have a hole in the paper. The editor's keen to get a replacement lined up. Listen, Sophie, the editor wants to have a woman do most of the theatre reviewing from now on, at least for while. A feminist, preferably. Someone who could show that the paper is taking this whole thing seriously. A great writer, obviously, with a decent critical style, but more nuance and sensitivity than Alex has sometimes. You know? And I agree with him. I suggested you, Sophie. You're already there. It would just be a matter of taking on a bit more work. As long as you could manage it. You could stop doing the little art reviews and just do the big theatre shows instead.'

The smaller pigeon flew off. As it pushed away from the branch, the leaves on the tree swung down and then up again, some of them fluttering to the ground like litter.

I thought about asking Graham if I had a choice. I wanted him to tell me that I didn't have a choice, I had to do it and that was that. But I knew Graham. If I'd told him I was reluctant, he would say I didn't have to do it if I didn't want to, and he'd send someone else up to come and stay in the flat and take on the remaining festival reviews, while I stayed on the exhibitions beat. There was plenty of space in the flat, after all.

There was a reason that Graham, and not Paul, had rung me. If it had been Paul, Paul would have told me I was doing it, and there was no other option. Graham had probably insisted on ringing. He had probably told everyone that he needed to make sure I was OK. He would want me to feel I could say no.

I didn't want that. In my mind, an image formed of my byline taking the place of Alex's in the paper. I imagined the pull-quotes being my own words, instead of better words chosen by the subs. I imagined the words *our new theatre critic* in the standfirst. I thought of having the page lead. I thought of being puffed on page one. In the end, I agreed almost too easily.

'It sounds like the plan that makes the most sense,' I said.

'Are you sure?'

'I'm sure.'

'You deserve an opportunity like this. I worry that some people at the paper have underestimated you.'

Was that true? Never mind Alex; I now wondered what they might all have been saying about *me* behind my back. 'But I think you'll do a great job,' Graham was saying.

I almost asked if they'd be paying me any more money for this, but I was pretty sure the answer would be no, and I didn't need the humiliation of having that confirmed. It wasn't as if I knew anywhere near as much about theatre as Alex did, anyway. I suspected they were only asking me because I was a woman and it was convenient. All I said was: 'Will you let me tell Alex? I think it might be better coming from me. And I can do it in person.'

'No. That's kind, but I've known Alex a long time. If he takes it badly on the phone, I'll take him out for a beer and talk it over. I'm his line manager, anyway. There's one more thing. Sophie?'

'Yes?'

'Look, this is a difficult situation. You'd tell me, wouldn't you, if Alex had ever done anything to make you uncomfortable? The people in HR aren't thrilled about all this. Alex has assured me personally that nothing has ever happened at work or with a colleague. I hope you feel you could tell me if anything *had* happened.'

I considered telling him. I really did.

'No,' I said. 'Nothing.'

I followed the sound of the jazz back to the living room.

Alex groaned. His own phone was ringing with Graham's name on the screen. 'So you didn't tell him I've died.'

Alex took the call in his room. I turned down the jazz and opened the window to let out some of the smoke from Alex's cigarettes. I couldn't see the tree with the pigeons in it from this window. Nests were for spring, so it couldn't be that, I thought. Maybe their baby had grown up and gone. Maybe there was nothing keeping those two pigeons together any more except for the fact they both liked the same tree. Maybe that was enough.

Alex threw open the living-room door sharply enough that it banged against the wall.

'Oliver Cromwell,' he said, lighting another cigarette. 'Usurper.'

'I could tell Graham I'm not going to do it.'

'I need a fucking drink.'

'It's not even ten thirty.'

But Alex was already going into the kitchen. I followed him. He was pulling bottles out of the cupboard. He picked out one with a picture of a missile on the label and cracked it open. I lingered in the doorway, biting a thumbnail.

'I knew they weren't happy, but I didn't think they'd pull the trigger, you know? I'm a good writer. I'm the best writer at the paper, and they know that. What happened to sticking by your journalists?'

'It's not over, though. It's just a break. They'll have you back soon.'

'Like fuck they will. Come on. This could really be the end. I'm really going to be that guy who used to be a theatre critic, and then after that he did nothing for the rest of his life. I'm not qualified for anything else. What am I going to do, write about houses in the Cotswolds for the property pages? Get a job in tech? Anytime anyone googles me, all this Hayley crap will come up. No other company is going to hire me once their HR sees my name. I never broke any laws. I didn't do anything wrong, but as far as anyone knows, I'm just an abuser who was a journalist once.'

He spat the words, pacing the room like a guard dog at a boundary. For the first time, I saw in Alex a vein of real violence. I shrank into the door frame. But he must have seen this coming, I thought. Surely, he must have considered the real possibility of it.

'Alex—'

'They said I had to get out of the flat today. I can't stay here if I'm not reviewing. They're not even paying for my train ticket back to London. What am I supposed to do, crawl back into some hole?'

'You can still stay here. I don't mind. I won't tell them.' Something occurred to me. 'Josh is coming up, but—'

'Oh, Josh, that makes me feel better.'

'If that's how you feel, maybe you *should* go,' I said, with a burst of momentum, because by insulting Josh he was insulting me.

'And let them get rid of me? Let them cancel me? All of it can get fucked,' and with that he picked up the monstrous vase on the table, heavy with water and flowers, holding it by its stupid little handles, and hurled it against the wall. It made an incredible noise as it smashed, the red clay smearing a streak of maroon across the magnolia paint and carving a deep notch into the plaster. We stared at each other in amazed horror. I didn't know what to do: try to clear up the shattered fragments, take him to task for the violence of it, or walk out and leave him there.

'That thing's worth tens of thousands,' I said, in the end.

'Bullshit,' said Alex, quietly. 'Just because someone would pay that much for it, doesn't mean it's worth anything at all.'

I started to pick up the flowers, their stems broken. A crack ran up to the ceiling from where the vase had hit the wall, and another small chunk of plaster fell from it onto the floor. Crooked laths were showing in the hole. Bits of ceramic lay in a pool of water that smelled of summer rot. Alex went out, and I didn't dare ask him where he was going, or when he'd be back.

As I was putting the shards of ceramic into a dish on the table, not knowing what else to do with them, one of them sliced open the edge of my palm in the shape of a check mark. I sucked the wound clean. I got an email on my phone from Graham with a list of twenty shows that I now needed to review. And then, at the end of the list, something else. *I forgot to say,* Graham wrote. *The editor's lost hope of Alex getting the Hayley interview. And in any case, he doesn't think it's a good idea for Alex to interview Hayley any more. But he still wants the piece. Can you pick that one up too? Thanks x*

WEEK TWO

Saturday, 12 August

14

The next morning, Alex wasn't there. I didn't know if he was asleep in his room, if he'd gone out early without me hearing, or if he hadn't come back the night before. His leather satchel was still on the living-room armchair, though.

The smear of the broken vase and the crack in the plaster looked worse at a day's remove, and my hand hurt. I didn't know if I should tell the paper about it and find out if they had some kind of insurance, or if I should try to fix it myself. The poor flowers were in the bin, and the ceramic fragments remained in the dish where I'd put them, looking oddly edible.

I emailed Lyla asking for an interview with Hayley. I couched my pitch in caveats. Reading it back, it was tremulous and scared. It was the kind of approach that PRs find easy to turn down.

> Hi Lyla, hope you're well! It's been crazy for us over here. I was wondering if Hayley Sinclair might be

available for any interview time over the next few days? I know she must be super busy just now!

I considered taking out the exclamation mark, but Lyla loves exclamation marks, so I left it in.

We were hoping to do a profile piece with her. We'd like to give her a chance to tell her side of the story and reclaim that space in the paper.

I'm not sure if you know, but Alex has been taken off reviews. I know that our paper may be the last place she wants to be right now, and her show is going from strength to strength! But it might be something that appeals to her? It would be me doing the interview, and you know me. We'd send a photographer too. We'd pitch it for the cover of the magazine supplement.

Let me know what you think? It'd be fab to meet up for another drink during the festival, either way x

I was never good at interview pitches. I have the same problem in the interviews themselves: I want people to like me too much. Maybe that's the kind of thing they teach you to get over at journalism school but, like most of my colleagues, I've never had any formal training. I remember once meeting a journalist from the US who told me all about her master's degree in journalism and her newspaper's rigorous dedicated fact-checking department, and she was very surprised at my lack of those things, and it gave me a fresh perspective on why people say the British press is trash.

In my experience, there are only two kinds of culture journalism: the first is where you spend a long time working on a topic you really care about, and try to do justice to the material, and then it gets widely ignored. The other kind is more common: you write whatever you've been told to write, as quickly as possible, and hope for the best.

And journalism is full of shame. Before AI transcription software was invented, transcribing my interviews used to take hours, because I spent most of the time having to pause the tape to claw at my face in embarrassment. Oh, my poorly phrased questions, my laughter in the wrong places, my miss of an obvious opportunity for a follow-up, my rudeness, my nerves, my clear lack of knowledge of the subject, my stupid voice!

But sometimes, when I was listening back, a moment would glimmer that I hadn't noticed when I was in the room. A moment when maybe I'd held back from a question, out of a desire to be nice, and the interviewee had responded by giving me more than I'd asked for. They would volunteer some story, some frustration or inspiration, that would expose slightly more of the person than they'd intended to reveal. Any interview is a transaction, but people can't help being people. Sometimes a connection happens without either of you realising it.

On my first day as Alex's replacement, there were two shows to see. One of them was a historical drama at the International Festival, called *The Uncivil Peace*, split across two six-hour performances, with a dinner break in between. Before that endurance test began, I'd been assigned to review what sounded like a fun performance art piece, not too far out of my critical comfort zone.

'The Chill Pope' was billed as a 'modern confession booth' on George Square. The idea, according to the Fringe programme, was that it was a supportive, inclusive, kind version of the traditional Roman Catholic confessional. *Come and confess anything you want in strictest confidence,* said the blurb. *The Chill Pope will absolve you of your sins, because there are no sins in Chillicism! Got something bothering you? Come and be embraced by a bestie who gets it, and be rewarded by a short performance on the theme of forgiveness.*

It was hot that day as I stood in the queue for the Chill Pope, with no shade and the smell of a hot dog van making the sweltering heat feel all the more oppressive. People were coming and going from show venues, getting drinks and setting down their plastic pint glasses on a carpet of plastic grass, next to a large plastic cow. Blackboards were set out and chalked with lists of the performers who would be on stage for the daily late-night comedy shows that night.

The Chill Pope's booth, which was constructed from two portaloos stuck together and painted all over with rainbows, was open for two hours in the morning. I had a printed press access pass in my crossbody bag.

'This is actually my second time coming,' said a woman in a sun dress in front of me in the queue. She was talking to a man who was wearing fishnet suspenders under denim shorts and had a spiked piercing in one ear. 'It was life-changing yesterday. I've never felt so accepted. It felt as though everything I'd ever felt shame about was just washed clean. I had to book another ticket straight away. Cheapest therapy ever.'

'Oh em gee,' said the guy. 'I need that for myself, for real.'

I took my notebook and pen out of my pocket and looked through my phone, absorbing nothing. I saw a post from someone I didn't follow, saying *When are Hayley Sinclair stans going to admit that* – but then the stream refreshed, the tweet disappeared and I couldn't find it again. When I looked up from the internet, a woman in her early twenties walked past carrying a tote bag that said:

THE ALEX LYONS EXPERIENCE

It was my turn next. The guy in the fishnets came out of his confessional in tears. He looked at me and tried to speak, but was too emotional. He held my forearm and said, 'You have no idea.'

I told him I was so happy for him. And I really was. He walked away, shaking his head and splaying his fingers in alternating tension and relief.

An usher wearing a lanyard opened the door for me when I showed my press pass and told me he'd knock after ten minutes so the next person could have a turn.

I sat down in the dark. It did have something of the portable toilet about it, something of that fake solitude. I sat down, the usher closed the door on me, and a grille rattled shut. It was dark in the booth. My knees almost touched the door. I could hear the muffled sounds of people outside.

A deep, meditative sigh came from a few inches to my right and made me shudder, and then a female voice began speaking in a deep, husky approximation of a fortune teller.

'Welcome, my child. Unburden your fabulous self in strictest confidence. There is nothing to fear. There is only love, forgiveness, and, perhaps, a song. What do you have to tell me, child?'

I wasn't sure what to say. At my first theatre review, I hadn't expected that I would be part of the performance. What would Alex make of this? I had imagined sitting in the safety of a dark theatre, writing notes and thoughts surrounded by the insulating cocoon of an audience.

'I-I don't really know what I'm doing,' I said.

'None of us does, child. Go on. In what ways have you wandered and been lost?'

'Well, I've been unfaithful to my partner,' I said. I don't know what possessed me to be so honest. Something about the seclusion of the booth, maybe.

'Monogamy is a construct,' said the voice of the Chill Pope, cheerfully. 'And we all have baggage and history, and reasons why we do things. Is there anything else?'

'Can I ask you something?'

'All questions are welcome here. I'm trauma-informed – I've done a day course.'

'Do you think that anyone involved in the arts is inherently monstrous?'

There was a silence from the Chill Pope. And then, 'I think we all of us have a monster within us somewhere.'

'I have this friend, and he did something terrible. Not just once, but lots of times. A lot of people got hurt, even if they didn't know they were being hurt at the time.'

'Speak freely, my child, so that you may be absolved.'

'Well, he's a reviewer, like me, and he wrote some bad reviews, and he got all that mixed up with his romantic life. Anyway, after all that, it somehow turned out that I was his only friend. I guess I liked that. And then, just lately, he's started to frighten me. Though I suppose, in a way, he's always frightened me. But even with everything he's done, with all the things I know about him that I wish I didn't know, I see him as something different from how I've seen other people talk about him. I see a person who maybe isn't sorry, but who is a person who could maybe *believe* he is sorry. But is that enough, after what he did to Hayley?'

The grill rattled open. It revealed a girl in a feathered rainbow-coloured wig, a sequined dress, and clown stage make-up in blue and orange. She was staring at me in horror.

'Are you talking about Alex Lyons? Are you friends with Alex Lyons? Here on a press ticket, are you? Going to give me one fucking star as well? Do you think what he did was right? Hayley is my friend, you piece of shit. Get out of my show. Go on, get out. Write about this if you want. I don't care. Anyone from your paper isn't welcome in here. Tom!' She rapped on the tinny wall of the booth. 'Open this door!'

The usher opened the door and I was spat out into George Square. Two or three people turned to look. I think they assumed it was part of the show.

I turned my phone off airplane mode. There was a text from Josh with the details of the train he'd booked that would bring him and Arlo up the following day. I stared at my phone for a few more seconds. There were no other messages.

I sent Graham an email. *Don't think the Chill Pope is worth covering after all*, I said. *Amateur student stuff. Can I just have an extra three hundred words for* The Uncivil Peace?

He emailed right back. *Whatever you think. You're the critic.*

The show I saw that afternoon at the EICC building was a long and involved historical drama and I spent most of it thinking longingly of the dinner break in the middle. During the interval, I went down to the bar to collect the free food and drink that had been laid on for critics – a cheese sandwich and a small plastic tumbler of warm white wine – and then just wandered around the corridors of this building that was like an endless computer simulation of an office corridor. Voices were coming through an open door. I stood a few paces down, cheese sandwich in one hand, wine in the other, listening.

They were rehearsing. I edged closer to the door while still trying not to be seen. I watched them for a while. There were four of them and they were doing some kind of warm-up game involving clapping and jumping and pointing at each other. It looked dorky, but also like fun. They looked like children playing.

Was this how Alex felt? The fourth wall blocking him out, all the time. A feeling that the real fun was happening somewhere else, somewhere he wasn't allowed to be.

I looked at Alex's Wikipedia page on my phone again, for the first time since that first week. A new section had been added: *Controversies*. There was a heavily cited paragraph outlining Hayley's show and linking to his original review. It felt like the kind of footnote that would be there for the rest of his life.

I went back into the show. I was sitting in a row behind a lot of other newspaper critics. I recognised one of them as a writer for a rival paper. Jan Haider was a distinguished woman in her sixties who had been doing this for a long time. She had a sharp blonde bob and leaned her chin on her hand with an eager, encouraging smile as she watched. I found myself emulating her posture. I hadn't ever been to the theatre with Alex. I wondered what he looked like when he was reviewing a play. I imagined him leaning back in his chair with his arms folded, not taking any notes, restlessly tapping one leg, annoying the other people in the aisle. Or maybe, if a show was good, he was intent, focused, moved. I didn't know.

The show was long and complicated. I felt too stupid to write about it, certain I was going to miss something essential. But I couldn't duck out of reviewing this one. There was a space in the paper tomorrow and it was my responsibility to fill it. My name would be there at the top. There were at least one or two people waiting to hear what I thought.

The main problem with the play was that there were lots of characters and I couldn't always work out how they related to one another. Alex's voice in my head: *just say that, then. Just say it made no fucking sense.*

I couldn't write that, though. Did I have a greater responsibility to the actors on stage, the company and crew who made this obviously high-budget and well-rehearsed show, or to the audience around me? Or to the people reading the paper, who would never see that particular production, but who kept up an interest in theatre and just wanted some opinions to chew over with their breakfast?

I came out of the show with a deadline of an hour to write what I thought and I'd written not a single thing in my notebook. My head was thick. I walked back to the flat and it was dark, lonely and empty there, still no evidence of Alex, his satchel still lying on the armchair. I stood by the door of his bedroom in my socks for a minute and heard nothing. I wasn't used to reviewing anything so late in the evening. I wasn't used to the night ending for everyone else, but continuing for me.

I ran a glass of tap water – Edinburgh water tasted of minerals – opened my laptop, and wrote. That was maybe the blessing of such a short deadline, compared to my normal, comparatively leisurely art deadlines: there wasn't a lot of time available to weigh up the nuances of the situation. In the end, I gave it five stars. I mean, probably if I'd understood it, I'd have given it five stars, right? And a lot of people had put a lot of effort into it. I thought I'd seen Jan Haider nodding in quiet awe during the curtain call. And the final monologue had been so impassioned I could see the spit arcing from the actor's mouth and catching the spotlight. I said it was a *blistering performance of an extraordinary new approach to historical drama* and I emailed it to the night editor before the last deadline for the paper going to press. I sat up a little longer, watching my inbox, until I received confirmation from the night editor. *Got it, thanks.* No notes. No questions. My piece would, that probably meant, run unchanged. I lay in bed in the dark until the adrenaline drained from my system.

My phone lit up again, with an email from Lyla Talbot. I had to read it three times before I could absorb what she was saying.

Hi Sophie! I've spoken to Hayley about it and she is interested in the idea of an interview with the paper. She remembers you being at the first revamped show. We could fix something up for Monday, if that would work with your deadline? xx

15

There was gloating online the next morning, when my review was posted online and printed in the paper, and it hardened the knot of guilt in me.

GUYS WE DID IT. Alex Lyons is over!

*

Can't believe we actually convinced that batshit newspaper to do something honourable for once, ig there's hope for us all

*

£100 to the first person who takes a pic of nepo baby sewer rat Alex Lyons crying in a gutter somewhere LOL

There was a post from a media blind gossip account, too:

Hearing from multiple sources that Alex Lyons has definitely been TAKEN OFF reviewing duties at least for the rest of the Edinburgh Festival due to recent events. I'm hearing it wasn't his decision. It's currently unclear if/when he'll return as the paper's theatre critic

And a post from Hayley:

What a day. I'm still waiting for an apology (watch this space. . .) but in the meantime, I'm feeling thankful for all the incredible women I've met and the stories they've shared *praying hands emoji* Tonight, we move again. Because misogynist male critics may always have a platform, but right now we have a stage. And this was never just about one person. It's a revolution! I just checked and there are a few tickets still available for the show tonight from the Fringe box office xx

So her show wasn't sold out that night. Another tweet appeared on my timeline, from Murray Maclean, only his fourth tweet ever.

The mob got their prize: the career of a young writer ended. Well, I think it's a damn shame.

It had been posted only a few hours before and had thousands of reposts. Was this a backlash? Was this why Hayley had agreed to the interview? I replied to Lyla and set up a time to meet Hayley. I suggested the National Museum of Scotland. Hayley wasn't yet famous or experienced enough to know that she could make me go wherever she felt most comfortable, on her territory and her terms. I chose the museum because it's always good to do a long-ish interview in an interesting place. It at least gives you something else to write about to fill space if the interview itself goes nowhere. And I had fond memories of the museum from when I'd lived in Edinburgh. I liked the models of prehistoric life in the basement, and the mysterious Bronze Age grave goods. The skulls hoarded in caves, and the tools made of bone.

I went out that morning, still without seeing Alex. This time his satchel was gone.

Josh and Arlo arrived at Waverley on the lunchtime train from Kings Cross. By that time, I had already seen one show, a two-man dramatisation of a Russian political scandal in the 1990s. I was one of eight people in the audience. The two actors were in their early twenties and one of them introduced the show by welcoming us to 'a period drama based on real historical events', which made me feel very old.

I waited on the station platform for Josh, my stomach heavy. There was a cool wind that blew down into the subterranean station from the streets above. I watched in the direction where I thought they might be coming from, trying to summon a sense of warm anticipation, and finding only fear. I wondered if I would cry when I saw Josh. In the end, I was facing the wrong direction, and I turned round only when I heard the sound of Arlo's voice.

I took Arlo from Josh's arms before I even acknowledged Josh, who was smiling and carrying an enormous bag on his back. I gathered my baby, now seeming so much bigger, into my arms, and covered his fuzzy head in kisses. He was holding his toy panda and he pulled away from me, scared, clutching the panda more tightly, and started to cry, but then he let his body relax into me, full of recognition and love and relief, and I felt like the worst dirt for leaving this little boy.

I pointed to a round white antique-looking lamp next to the station concourse.

'Look, Arlo bear,' I said. 'Moon.'

He looked puzzled and buried his shy face back into my shoulder.

'He doesn't really do that any more,' said Josh. 'He's into cars at the moment.'

'Oh.' A weight fell into my chest. 'Too much time without a strong female influence. Hello, by the way.'

'Hey. Missed you.' Josh pushed his glasses further back from where they'd slid down his nose and put his arms around me in a hug. I was holding Arlo so we had to hug sort of sideways, and I couldn't get my arm all the way around him because of his backpack, and then I wondered if I should kiss him, and it was a bit like meeting up with a cousin I hadn't seen for a while. I focused on Arlo to avoid looking in Josh's eyes.

Josh, too, looked different. His jaw was set wider than I remembered. Maybe I was just too used to seeing him only on video calls, and the reality of Josh in three dimensions upset the connections in my brain.

With Arlo in the pram, we walked the less hilly way back to the flat. The streets were so busy that manoeuvring the pram through the crowds felt like driving an HGV down a narrow cul-de-sac. There was a contortionist performing outside a pharmacy, his patter electronically amplified. We would go back to the flat and then go out for lunch, nowhere special, maybe the café on the upper floor of the Waterstones on Princes Street that had a view of the castle from its tall windows.

At the flat, Josh nodded towards the dent in the wall, and said, 'Nice place they've put you in', but he didn't ask anything more about it specifically, so I didn't tell him what had happened. It would take too much explaining. I changed Arlo into fresh clothes on the carpet. Alex still wasn't there.

Josh went to unpack. Alone with my baby, I kissed Arlo's two little feet, pudgy and clean. His skin smelled like mine. He giggled at me. *Silly mama,* I said. *She missed you so much.* It twisted my brain to think that these feet would one day be the feet of an adult man. Hairy on the top with rough skin and ugly toenails, probably, like Josh's. For now, Arlo was top to toe a *putto*. But for how long?

What sort of a man would he be? Would he be a man like Alex, tricking women into thinking he could give them what they wanted, only to maim them emotionally the moment they opened themselves up? Or would he be like Josh, who loved being the honourable moral centre of his own world, and whose infidelity was anyone's fault except his? Or would he be like me? That would be the worst.

For a while I just stared into Arlo's soft, dark eyes and he stared quietly into mine.

That night, after I'd filed all my reviews, I was exhausted. Josh had put Arlo down in the travel cot I'd found in one of the wardrobes. It was only at the point of going to bed that I realised Josh would want to share the bed with me. But the flat is so big, I almost said. There are so many other rooms. But how could I say that? All those nights of being alone in this bed made it feel unnatural to share it with him. It was so close it was invasive. I thought about how close I'd been with Alex. About how intimate it had felt to be alone in the flat with him. In bed with Josh, I wanted to curl my body up like a leaf in autumn. I wanted to hibernate from whatever this was.

Arlo woke early the next morning and I was the one who went to him. He stretched his little arms up towards me in his travel cot. I'd bought some Shredded Wheat and I took luxurious pleasure in feeding it to him as he sat on my lap at the table, looking out at the tree. I pointed to it and said, 'Tree!'

'Tree!' said Arlo.

Josh was making me a coffee.

'I've got this interview to do on Monday,' I said.

'So I'll take Arlo out at around noon?'

'You don't have to take him out at all. You could have him here. But I'll need to do some prep here, first. It's quite last minute and I haven't had time to do a lot of research and plan my questions. I'll need some time.'

'OK, I'll have Arlo. I thought we might go out to the National Museum. It's got a kids' area, hasn't it?'

'But that's where I'm interviewing Hayley.'

'What, in the kids' area at the museum?'

'No, but in the museum. You can't go there.'

'Why? You'll be in the café or something, won't you? And then if Arlo needs you, we know where you are.'

'But you can't just come and see me, Josh. I'm working.'

Arlo dropped his spoon on the floor, leaving a smear of milk and a lump of wet mashed wheat. I cleaned it up with some kitchen roll.

'You won't know we're there,' said Josh. He was looking through his phone. 'Did you know about this?'

He held it out for me to see. It was a post from the BBC's *Newsnight* account, trailing an exclusive interview to be aired that night, featuring Alex Lyons.

That evening, after we'd got Arlo into bed, we watched Alex on *Newsnight*. Josh had gone out to get beers and crisps in, as if it was some kind of sporting event. It was so strange seeing Alex on TV. Possibly it was genetic, but, like his mother, he was one of those people who looked better on TV than he did in real life. When he appeared on screen, he seemed put-together and energised, very different from how he'd been the last time I'd seen him, when he'd smashed the vase, when he'd been powered by chaos.

He was being interviewed in an Edinburgh studio by a presenter I hadn't seen before, who was presumably covering for the usual hosts over their summer holiday. Pamela Tang was about the same age as us, and Alex, sitting in his chair as the camera panned across the studio, seemed relaxed in her company, glad that she wasn't one of the normal presenters, and he was already falling back on his flirty smiles, his proven charm. Pamela, though, was impervious. She gave a potted introduction to what Alex had done, how Hayley had responded, the backlash, the cultural conversation.

'Alex Lyons, thank you for joining us. Why have you decided to speak now?'

'Thank you for having me, Pamela. Er, well,' said Alex. 'I feel there's a need to set the record straight. This whole thing has got out of hand. I've been getting abuse. And, so far, I've been very restrained in not responding to it.'

'Let's focus on the facts. We've had Hayley Sinclair in this studio. Ms Sinclair told us that after you'd written a one-star review of her show, and before it appeared in the newspaper, you drank with her in a bar, took her back to your flat, and had sex with her, all without revealing your identity or that you'd seen her show. Is that correct?'

'That's – that's not quite how I'd put it, and—'

'But it's accurate?'

'Essentially, yes, that is accurate, but the reviews I write are completely separate from my personal life.'

'Do you have any regrets about how you handled things?'

'Pamela, I think what people don't understand is that showbusiness is tough, and you have to be thick-skinned. Criticism is part of the business. Everyone wants a five-star review, but five-star raves would be meaningless without one-star reviews to give them balance. What can a critic do if a performer puts on a bad show?'

'Mr Lyons—'

'It's not my fault when someone apparently can't separate their art from the critical response to it. Our responsibility as critics is to our readers, not to the performer. We're not writing school reports here. We're elevating the culture. And can I just say, I stand by my original review. I'm sorry that Hayley was upset, but the truth is that her original show was really bad. No, it's true. The fact that she's made it so much better now, or so everyone tells me, means that my review had a positive effect. I can take some of the credit. If I hadn't pointed out the flaws in her original work, she never would have improved. So, Hayley, if you're watching, you're very welcome.'

'He sounds like a politician,' said Josh, opening the crisps.

'This isn't just about the one-star review, though,' said Pamela Tang. 'Do you regret having a sexual—'

'It's entirely about the one-star review, because if I'd given her five stars she wouldn't have made a show about me.'

'I'll ask again. Do you regret having a sexual relationship with the person whose show you were reviewing, under those circumstances?'

'Well,' said Alex. 'It wasn't ideal.'

'Not ideal?'

'Obviously not, but if I'd slept with her and then given her five stars, *that* would have been a conflict of interest, but nobody would ever know about it, and we wouldn't even be here having this conversation. But that's not what happened. My review was written before I'd even met this person socially. So it was completely objective. I just think this is a non-story that's blown up out of all proportion during silly season.'

'You're known for writing quite personal, negative reviews. Is that fair?'

'What do you mean by fair? What does any of this mean, really? This is all just a show, too, isn't it, for the people watching at home? They want to make me the villain. But I'm a victim in all this, too. I'm the one who's been hounded for weeks. How is that fair? Have I really done anything wrong?'

I scrolled through social media on my phone.

my jaw is ON THE FLOOR with the gall of this mf on newsnight rn

*

Men in media really do think they can just treat people like shit and get away with it. Props to the interviewer for nailing Alex Lyons to the wall on this

*

High time these media cockroaches get what they deserve. Well done Hayley.

*

ok but i have something to say about alex lyons [a screengrab image of Alex in profile, looking like a model]

*

think what you like about alex lyons but that hayley girl has really milked this whole situation imo

'Don't you think,' said Pamela, 'that women have a right to speak up when damaging things like this happen to them?'

'But she's dragged my name through the mud, and potentially ended my career, when I haven't even done anything illegal. I haven't abused anyone. I haven't done anything without consent. Is it fair to pull up every instance from my private life for public consumption and appraisal just because I've hurt a girl's feelings? And put me in the stocks for it?'

He was jumpy now, leaning forwards with a barely restrained, panicky anger. The sheen of self-confidence had already cracked.

'At least he's not swearing as much as he usually does,'

said Josh. 'I don't know how you've managed to stand being stuck up here with him for so long. Another beer?'

I stood behind where Josh was sitting on the sofa, in a reversal of how Alex and I had watched the first livestream of Hayley's show on my laptop. Josh cracked the cap off another bottle of IPA for me. Somehow it made my mouth feel more dry.

'Don't you understand why you've been criticised?' said Pamela Tang. 'People are saying you've been treating women poorly for what sounds like your whole adult life.'

'But that should be private. Not to presume anything, Pamela, and I'm sure you're a saint, but imagine if everyone you've ever dated decided to tell the world all your worst moments? It's not as if I'm proud of it.'

Pamela rested the tip of her pen on her notes, selecting her next question. 'Let me ask you this. What do you think a relationship between a professional critic and a performer should look like?'

'But it's not professional. This is a classic mistake people make, Pamela, but I'm sure you know as well as I do, that journalism isn't a *profession*, but a trade. There's no such thing as a professional critic. Our trade is in stories, and, for a critic, opinions. That's what we make and sell. Nobody ever said it was honourable.'

'That sounds as though you think there shouldn't be any standards or ethics involved in journalism at all?'

'What does a "free press" mean, Pamela?'

I imagined him having the same kind of conversation around the dinner table with the Harwoods. I saw the fifteen-year-old Alex in his eyes. He couldn't hear how he really sounded.

'What about Hayley Sinclair's right to free expression?'

'Well, no. That's . . . that's different.'

'And isn't there a duty of care, here,' Pamela continued, 'when you are in a position of power, with a platform in a national newspaper? A lot of people would say that your review was unreasonable in the first place, and then the way you treated Ms Sinclair was downright cruel.'

'Everyone's acting as if nothing like this has ever happened before. Since when did journalists have to be perfect human beings to be allowed to write what they think? Some of the best journalists who ever wrote had messy personal lives. I know at least three journalists who are cheating on their spouses with people they met at work right now.'

I bit my finger instead of a crisp by accident. It hurt.

'Is that better than what I did?' Alex went on. 'What's really happened here? Two people had sex and one of them decided they don't like the other one. Tale as old as time.'

'So you think everyone should just leave you alone?'

'Yes. Basically.' He glanced at the camera.

'It's been reported that you've been suspended by your newspaper – is that correct?'

'Well, it's quite a complicated situation, involving being on leave for personal reasons.'

'We're almost out of time. Hayley Sinclair may well be watching this interview, along with the other women who've taken part in her show and made their own accusations against you. Is there anything you'd like to say to them?' said Pamela. 'Do you think you owe anyone an apology?'

Sweat was visible on Alex's linen shirt. One of his curls had come loose and was over his forehead. 'No,' he said.

His face was unsure, his eyes red, his expression wildly adrift.

'Alex Lyons,' said Pamela, turning away from him, her notebook and pen in her hand as the camera followed her to the next story, leaving Alex behind. 'Thank you very much.'

WEEK THREE

Saturday, 19 August

16

Some people online thought that Alex had made some good points. Mostly, though, anyone talking about it said that the interview had confirmed their worst opinions of him. And it did have the unfortunate effect, for Alex, of re-igniting some of the debate about him that might otherwise have been starting to fizzle out.

Alex came back to the flat late after the broadcast and prowled into the kitchen. He assumed I'd watched it, but said he didn't want to know my opinion, and he didn't acknowledge Josh at all. Then he went to bed. The next day he slept late, and when he woke, he avoided speaking to anyone. We were now in a position where there were three people staying in the flat who, technically, were not supposed to be there, none of whom wanted to leave. I couldn't tell the paper about the wall damage from the smashed vase in case they sent someone from the letting agency to assess it for repair, and discovered not just one female critic staying there, but three undocumented male companions, one of whom was under two years old.

There was a distance between me and Josh. I cringed when he touched me and I could see that it hurt him as he withdrew his hand, confused, not knowing how to ask what was wrong. He said he thought he might stay in Edinburgh for a little longer, because he didn't have anything urgent that he had to be back at home for, and no teaching commitments over the summer. OK, I said. Privately, I just wanted him to leave Arlo with me and go. But I had to work, and I couldn't take Arlo to the shows with me. If I could just get through to the end of the festival, I kept telling myself, things would be clearer then. Decisions could be made.

As Alex spiralled, I too felt increasingly detached from reality. On my phone, as I stood in queues waiting for theatre shows to open their doors, I watched a lot of videos online of extreme natural events. Storms at sea where ships were sucked down into deep yawning canyons of water. Crocodiles lurking unseen in muddy rivers, twisting their lithe spines to slam their jaws towards a kayak.

The next night was Critics' Drinks. Josh stayed at the flat with Arlo, so I had to go on my own, even though I had an invitation with a plus one. Alex had vanished again. I suspected he was out drinking somewhere. I'd never been important enough to be invited to Critics' Drinks before, but this year Alex was out, and I was in. I received the digital watermarked invitation on the morning of the party. This wasn't a snub, because everyone received it on the morning of the party. It was that kind of studiedly casual affair only for people who were in town, to squeeze in an appearance between shows. It was at the Playfair Library, a grand old room with white marble busts of famous men marking the ends of rows of book stacks so important they had to be kept behind wires.

The feel was very different from the Summerhall party. This event was organised by someone at the Book Festival and the guest list was elite. Not just critics from the UK, but people who wrote for the *New Yorker*, the *Economist* and *Der Spiegel*. There would be Pulitzer winners there. There were people who considered themselves people of letters. Within minutes of my arrival, dressed in a black maxi dress, the most formal item of clothing I had with me, I saw an actor who was known to be pursuing a second career as an auteur-director, speaking with conviction to an editor at *Vogue Italia*. I stood near a waiter with a tray of canapés, in a state of paralysis, hoping my terror would be mistaken for aloofness.

Stuart MacAskill rescued me. 'It's Alex Lyons's stunt double,' he said, swooping in with an air kiss. 'What about that car-crash on *Newsnight*! I was gnawing off my own hands.'

We went out to the balcony together and looked at the castle. It was lit up in weird colours, green and orange with a flash of purple. The Royal Edinburgh Military Tattoo was, like every night during the festival, getting started in the specially installed stands above the city, heralding its beginning with booms and flashes.

All we seemed to be able to talk about was Alex. It had become a habit, like discussing the weather. It was more comfortable than talking about anything else.

'I'm surprised you've stuck with him and haven't gone on Hayley's show to denounce him yourself,' said Stuart.

'Are you spending the whole festival with him? I never see you out with anyone else. You're never free for a drink with me. Is Alex your full-time job now?'

I said it wasn't like that, and that I'd been busy reviewing shows, but I felt the heat of guilt.

'I dunno babe, that's what it *looks* like,' he said. 'Is it one of those things where you're the only person who *understands* him? It reminds me of those women who write to serial killers in prison. If it were me, I'd have told him to fuck off out of the flat the second I found out what he'd done to that poor girl. Alex isn't some tortured genius – he's not Beethoven. He's just another sexist, straight white guy hack. He's fucked over a load of intelligent, creative women who deserved better. There are thousands of Alexes.' I didn't know what to say. It was like being told off by a teacher. Stuart sipped his drink, a knowing look in his eyes. 'I've been wondering if you're spending all this time in Alex's head because there's something in *your* head that you're avoiding.'

'It doesn't feel like that,' I said. 'There's really nothing going on in my head.'

'And what about Hayley? I saw her coming out of her show the other day. She doesn't look well. She's had this big cultural moment explode in, what, two weeks? A bomb has gone off in her life. But once the gunpowder's all spent, what's left? There's a story there, too.'

This troubled me. Whenever I'd seen Hayley, I'd thought she looked glossy and radiant, effortlessly winning her own war. Now I wondered if my camera had been trained on the wrong subject entirely.

'I don't think she's as willing as Alex is to let me into her head.'

'Worth a try, maybe, for the newbie theatre critic. How are you finding it all?'

'I don't know. Nobody ever built a statue of a critic, did they?'

'I hate it when people say that. It's not true! There's a statue of Roger Ebert in Illinois. There's a statue of Northrop Frye in Toronto. They're making a new one of Ruskin right now, for God's sake. You'll be next.'

'Only after they've erected one of you in the West End of Glasgow.'

'Jesus, I can't think of anything worse.'

'No sculptor could do justice to your physique,' I said, with affection.

'Or my mystique! And what if they only do it after I'm dead? I wouldn't even be able to review it. What's the point?'

We were both laughing now. It was a nice feeling. I was remembering what it felt like to have real friends.

'Well, nobody's in it for the statues,' said Stuart. 'You know, Alex isn't a critic any more, but I've been thinking he hasn't been a critic for a while. It's as if he doesn't even like theatre these days. That's when it's time to stop. A critic should go to every show hoping it's going to be five stars and believing it could be. Because how lucky are we to have theatre? Thousands of years of it, and it's not getting old yet! People putting on a show to entertain us, to make us think and cry and laugh, to devastate us. I know I sound daft. But theatre is joy, Sophie. Pure fucking joy.'

It was very far from how I felt about theatre. 'I'm not sure if being a critic is for me,' I said.

'Well,' said Stuart, 'if you ever get sick of the paper, I was talking to someone yesterday who's starting a new visual arts festival in London and they're looking for a programmer. He asked me if I knew anyone with great taste who hadn't ever pissed off any major artists. I told him about you.'

'For the job?' It seemed so unlikely.

'He actually already knew you. Said he'd read some feature you did about the Venice Biennale. He's gone back to London today, but he said he'd get in touch with you. Hang on, I'll send you his details.'

He got out his phone and forwarded me the contact. It felt like a crack of light.

That's when Judith entered the room, like a soundwave. Her fame rippled through everyone, changing the dimensions of the space. And I was the first person she saw.

'Darling,' she said as she kissed me on both cheeks. 'It's so good to see you.'

Her attention glowed onto me like a beam of August sun. Stuart politely melted into another conversation and Judith and I talked a little about the festival, the shows we'd seen, until she changed the subject abruptly, clutching me by the shoulder and addressing me with an alarming directness, as if, in the whole room, it was only the two of us.

'Darling, did you know you're looking so careworn and serious? I miss that playful scepticism I so loved in your face from our first meeting. It's quite gone.' She briefly placed a cool finger under my chin and lifted it, inspecting me. 'Are you ill?'

'I don't think so?' I put my own hand to my throat, as if to check. I didn't feel ill, but if Judith thought I was, maybe she was right.

'I must come and pick up that vase. Or perhaps you

can keep it. I've been thinking of you. You and Alex aren't – No?' She didn't give me time to answer. It was as if she already knew, better than I did. 'I hope you don't think poorly of me, darling. The blame for a man's mistakes always falls on the mother – for not equipping him with the proper emotional faculties, or whatever it is. But good wombs have borne bad sons. Not that Alex is bad, no – he's just a player in search of a play. I always thought he could have been a marvellous actor. But instead he's a spectator, adrift in mediocrity. It pulls at one, this sense that one should have done better. It's all right for the men, that's what I wish Alex understood. They simply go on and on, from leading man to wise old sage, and the roles never dry up, the acclaim only gets more reverential. For us women, it's impossible. If you're bewitching as the maiden, nobody wants you when you're the mother or the crone. Unless you're willing for them to laugh at you. Unless you're happy to hear them say, did you see how old she's looking now? Did you know she was once a great beauty? Of course, they say it anyway.' She paused. She clutched my arm, her eyes piercing. 'Think nobly of me. Won't you?'

I nodded. Her monologue held me rapt. I would have agreed to anything, forgiven her anything. This conversation wasn't about Alex at all; it was more like a series of reflective surfaces in which she might better admire her own image. She constantly flitted into and out of performance, and it was unnerving not to be able to tell which mode she was in at any moment. And I felt her judgement of Alex's life of mediocrity fall on me, too. Any life that wasn't in pursuit of mass adoration was unthinkable to her.

As I was thinking this, the focus of her eyes moved slightly to the left, over my shoulder. Barely perceptibly, her attention had shifted. The warm light of her presence was cooling on me and brightening on someone else.

'David, darling! Have you written something divine for me to read on my flight? I haven't forgotten!'

Some variant of playwright or screenwriter with a scruff of grey stubble was looming with the intent of speaking to her. My moment had gone. I felt the chill of her lost gaze. Was this how Alex had felt, as a child, when his mother's friends had come to their house with all their glamour and their stage presence, and taken his mother away from him, into their world, where he couldn't follow?

My mother, too, spent too much time inside other people's heads. When I was in my teens, I used to read the newspapers that the paperboy brought round while I ate my Coco Pops before school, while my mother was seeing her first therapy client of the day. I always had to keep out of the way when she was with a client. It was important that they didn't see too much of her home life, to comprehend her as a rounded human. She took their sessions in a purpose-built wood and glass shed at the end of the garden. She had planted a sensory garden in front of it full of tactile, fragrant plants.

I loved walking up and down the path, rubbing lavender buds and thyme leaves between my fingers, feeling the pointed tips of the tall, swishing grasses. I wasn't allowed to do that on the bright summer mornings when my mother was speaking to people for their 8 a.m. appointments. But it was OK. I had the papers.

Stuart came back over, wanting to know gossip from Judith, hoping for dropped names. He was disappointed to hear we'd only really talked about Alex. I wanted to change the subject, so I said I couldn't believe it was almost the end of the festival already.

'Ah, the festival ends, but theatre never stops,' said Stuart. 'There's always more. The show doesn't just go on, it goes on and on *and on*. Next month there'll be new shows opening, and then it's the Christmas season. There's always another press night. Another theatremaker who's made something and wants you to see it. Everyone desperate for people to like what they've made. We're all still children, wanting our parents to look at the picture we've drawn. We never grow out of that feeling.'

There was one other person at the party I recognised: Mehdi, the paper's comedy reviewer. I'd only met him at the Christmas party, when he'd intimidated me with the seniority of the elder critic. He recognised me now, though, and sauntered over to greet us with an embrace of familiarity that acknowledged the fact that, by being invited here, I'd ascended to a higher media plane, and he now saw me as an equal. Mehdi knew Stuart as well, and we spent some pleasant time accepting more wine and talking about the craziest and most fantastic and most appalling shows we'd seen. Mehdi was a judge for the comedy awards that year, so he'd been seeing six shows a day or more.

'How's Alex doing, Soph?' Mehdi spoke through a mouthful of canapé. 'Coping with the fame? I haven't seen him since week zero.'

'He's not doing great.'

'Shit, really?'

Mehdi never came into the office. He was technically freelance. He'd started out reviewing poetry but had somehow ended up making a sideways move into comedy. He said they weren't so dissimilar. Both depended on rhythm and timing. He was a generation older than Alex and me and going through a divorce, and that night he had the bloodshot eyes and slight snuffle that characterise the underslept days of the late festival. Probably he was on something as well.

'Has he got somewhere to stay? Is he going back to London?'

'He's refusing to leave the flat at the moment.'

'In a sulk? Classic Alex. Drama queen.'

I thought about the smashed vase. It felt like more than a sulk.

'Where are you staying, Mehdi?' said Stuart. 'Not in the paper's haunted suite of rooms with the kids this year?'

'Nah, I've done my time in that dump. Got a mate in the New Town who lets me stay in a fancy four-poster bed now. I'm living the life. He's got a spare room there, actually, since an actor who was staying's gone home. If Alex isn't going back to London yet, he could move out of the flat and bunk up with me?'

Mehdi and I ended up leaving the party and walking across town to the flat together, so he could put it to Alex in person. I did warn him that I didn't even know if Alex would be there, and there was no point texting him, because he wouldn't answer. Alex's movements had become unknowable to me. He was now almost nocturnal, for one thing. I knew that Josh would be there, though, with a sleeping Arlo, and was apprehensive about intruding on their peace.

In fact, Alex was there. Josh was in the bedroom and Alex was smoking in the living room, reading Kafka's *The*

Trial and listening to obnoxiously loud free jazz, which sounded like a musical panic attack and which Arlo was somehow sleeping through.

Alex seemed pleased to see Mehdi at first, but held me back when we were going to the kitchen for drinks and whispered, 'What did you bring that nutter back here for? I'm surprised he's not totally spangled out of his mind already tonight. Comedy critics are mental.'

The free jazz clattered on through the speakers. Josh had emerged and looked on edge. He'd be worried about whether the music was going to wake Arlo.

'He wants to offer you a place to stay,' I said to Alex, as Mehdi was talking to Josh about poetry. With the jazz, the drinks, the smoke, the sleeping child in a nearby room, it felt like a domestic surrealist version of a 60s New York art club. I'd drunk too much already. I sat heavily in a chair.

'Sophie said you might want a place to crash, mate?' Mehdi said, raising his voice over the sound of a squealing saxophone and frantically fingered double bass.

'Nah mate, you're all right.'

'What happened to the wall?' Mehdi pushed his index finger into the dented plaster and more of it crumbled away under his touch.

'I was wondering that,' said Josh.

'I threw a vase at Sophie's head,' said Alex.

I glanced towards Josh, who blanched, but said nothing, terminally non-confrontational. I folded my arms. 'That isn't true.'

'Only because I missed.'

'Fucking hell, Alex,' said Mehdi. 'Everyone knows you're a bellend, but wind it in a bit, yeah? We're meant to be on your side.'

'On my side?' Alex shouted so loudly that Arlo did wake up then. I wasn't about to move, so Josh went into the bedroom to comfort him. Alex went on, all but screaming now over the insane jazz: 'I didn't see you coming over when all this kicked off. Sophie was the only one here. Every night, just me and her. She's the only one who cared at all.'

He was so loud, Josh must have been able to hear him from the bedroom. I felt icy and weightless, as if my internal organs had all vanished.

'I'm offering you somewhere to stay, you arsehole,' said Mehdi. 'Wish I hadn't bothered now. Stay here, for all I care. You'll be in the shit when they find out about that wall. No wonder you've got nowhere else to go. Prick.'

The free jazz kept sounding as though it might be on the verge of screeching towards a coherent melody and then swerving sway from it. Mehdi let himself out into the night.

'Alex, he was being nice,' I said. 'He was trying to help.'

Alex was pulling on his jacket. 'I'm going out to get more cigs. See you in the morning.'

17

In the morning, unusually, Alex was awake before me. Leaving Josh in bed, I went into the kitchen carrying Arlo, and Alex was in there. In fact, it looked as though he hadn't slept because he was still wearing his clothes from the night before.

I made Arlo some porridge at the stove. Arlo surveyed Alex with curiosity from the safety of my shoulder.

'I've been invited to appear on a US talk show,' Alex said.

'Oh yeah?' It was difficult for me to pour from the packet of oats and the large plastic bottle of milk with one hand. Arlo gurgled in my ear as I ignited the gas stove to set the porridge simmering. It had been a while since Alex had given me any kind of news. We were still acting as if nothing had happened, but it was getting harder with Josh in the house. To me, it felt as if the truth was constantly present in the flat, like background white noise, gradually getting louder.

'They want to do an interview with me. Probably somewhere in between segments on abortion law and gun rights. Listen to this pitch: *We're all huge fans and we'd love to hear more about your beliefs and your side of the story. We love that you're honest and that you don't care about offending people, and we'd love to hear more from you about how women like Hayley so often owe their careers to men like you! Would you like to speak about all of this to our very sympathetic audience?*'

'Jesus.' I stirred Arlo's porridge and poured it into a bowl. I swirled some honey into it. 'And would you?'

'I'm not talking to anybody who unironically uses the word "vaccinista". I don't want to deliver a manifesto. I just want people to stop acting like my life is over.'

'It doesn't sound like they think it's over, if they're asking you to go on TV.'

'It's all just eulogies for a career I can't have any more. That's not the only invitation I got this morning, and it isn't even 9 a.m. There's all these emails from radio PRs, too.'

He rubbed his eyes. They were red. I sat at the other end of the kitchen table with Arlo on my lap, spooning warm porridge into his mouth. He'd stopped being interested in Alex and was now only interested in his breakfast.

Alex looked at me as if he was about to say something, but I spoke first.

'You could tell them you don't want any of that, though. You could tell them you don't share their beliefs, whatever they are.'

'What if I do, though, and I just didn't realise?'

I shrugged. People who claimed to be on his side had started picketing Hayley's show. Josh had said he'd seen them waiting outside her venue the day before, a handful of people with professional-looking placards printed with slogans saying things like FREE PRESS and MEN ARE NOT

A CRIME. Some of the protesters were men with barbed wire tattoos and bald, meaty heads, but there were women among them too.

At the same time, Hayley's show was also inspiring a wave of articles written in newspapers by women who felt, for the first time, that they could speak out about terrible things their own exes had done to them. Things that would never see a police prosecution, but that nonetheless had changed their lives for the worse. There were think pieces and long reads by eminent female writers and critics in online publications I admired. It started to feel as though these women didn't want judgement, or a reckoning. They wanted something more meaningful and more personal than that, something that couldn't be measured, and maybe couldn't ever happen.

'Soph,' said Alex. He was looking at me strangely. 'Can I ask you—'

Josh came into the room, causing Arlo to smile a big, porridgey smile at him.

'Coffee?' he said in a pleasant voice, though looking watchfully at Alex. Alex got up and left without saying anything more.

I was due to meet Hayley in the atrium of the National Museum at noon. The museum would have light and space, two things I needed. At the museum, I sat on a small bench looking up at the white ironwork that arched overhead. It was like being in the bleached insides of a giant whale. The floor was busy with people.

Reading my phone on the way there, I'd seen a picture online of a pop star who was touring in London and had gone on stage the night before wearing a t-shirt printed with the picture of Hayley's face from her poster. I was curious about what version of Hayley would be there to meet me. Was Stuart right about her? We'd only have an hour together, Lyla had told me over email, and then Hayley would have to go and do a radio interview for a network in the US.

When Hayley appeared, she looked serene, holding a steel water bottle.

'Sophie!' she hugged me. I stared at her for a moment too long before I responded, taking her in, feeling the invisible weight of Alex between us in a way that she couldn't possibly know. She was as warm as Judith, but more raw and fragile. She said it was crazy to see me again. I agreed.

'You were part of that first show,' she said. 'What a night. Feels like it was months ago, right? I didn't know if you'd maybe be on his side, or whatever. But then I saw you'd taken his job, so obviously not. The paper seems to have made a decision, at least.'

'Yeah. Exactly,' I said. 'Well, would you like to have a walk around?' I put my phone on airplane mode and set the voice recorder app going, holding it in my hand so it could pick up our conversation.

We went down into the basement to the prehistoric gallery, because Hayley asked me to lead the way and I told her it was my favourite part of the museum. It was also the quietest part, and it was, as I'd hoped, empty of people down there. There were carved Pictish stones and tiny fragments of a lost society: bone needles, decorative beads, the remains of a brooch. Some carved balls that, the plaque next to them said, were for unknown purposes, perhaps ritual use. There was something of the crypt about this gallery. We stood in front of a glass case full of grave goods.

'Should these really be in a museum?' said Hayley. 'There are human skulls and bones here. Feels like they should've stayed in the ground.'

The thought hadn't occurred to me before. She stood and tilted her head to one side as she contemplated the exhibit. She reminded me in that moment of the way my mother used to stand in front of paintings at galleries. Absorbing them.

I asked Hayley a standard set of soft, easy opening questions. You have to do this when you interview anyone: ask them the things they're expecting you to ask. It helps the subject to relax, and then they say more interesting stuff later. So I asked her the questions I knew she had already answered lots of times before: about the show and her hopes for it. She repeated all the same things she'd said during the other media interviews she'd given, as I'd expected, though as she was saying them, I got the feeling she was staying guarded, not really listening to her own answers. As she was talking, I was searching her face for glimpses of what Stuart said he'd seen. Hayley was energised and bright, that was true. There was also, though, a greyness to her skin and her eyes.

'Can you tell me a bit about where you grew up?' I asked, trying to make this sound like an offhand question. There actually wasn't much information about this available online, so I was interested to know.

'Sure. I grew up in Connecticut until I was fifteen, when my parents, who were evangelicals, moved to the UK to plant a new church in North London. I was into it. I sang in the worship band. But I *loved* being in the drama club at my school, so I applied to drama school instead of college. That was where I got more involved in experimental theatre. When my mom passed while I was at college, the church kind of just fell away.'

'I'm really sorry. My mother died, too.'

'Well, then you know. I'm sorry for your loss.'

'Thanks.'

We sat in a silent, heavy moment, hearing only the distant echoing of other museum-goers' footsteps, and I felt the responsibility of needing to dig us out of this conversational ditch. 'How did your family feel about your studies?'

'Oh, they were supportive, even if they didn't always understand what I was doing or why. They pray for me, you know.'

That hadn't worked. We were still mired in gloom. It was time for a really nice question, to get the interview on a more positive footing again, so I scanned my notebook for my list of prepared questions, and chose this one: 'What does it feel like to be the sudden star of the festival this year?'

This was a peach of a question. An invitation for her to say something non-committal, self-flattering and humble. Usually, this is the sort of question journalists avoid asking, because the answer would reveal nothing new or tactile, and it's the sort of question that interviewees love most to be asked, because it's safe, impersonal, and focused on the work. It's the same as questions like 'Was it fun working on the movie?' and 'Were you excited when you were cast?' These questions yield a few anecdotes that have already been rehearsed with a PR, and little else. All Hayley had to say, here, was that it was amazing, and she never expected it, and we'd be back on track to get some nice quotes to fill out the piece.

Instead, she turned to me and fixed me with her intense, pale, conviction-filled face. 'You want to know what it's like?'

And that's when it all spilled out of her, as if she'd been wanting to tell someone how it really was, for a long time.

'Well, I'm staying in this shithole flat in the Old Town,' she said. 'I mean, it's OK, but it's like this tiny box room at the top of a tenement above a kebab shop and it stinks. I'm subletting from this guy called Sammy who plays in a jazz manouche band. Every night, pretty much, they have friends over to smoke and drink and fuck each other.'

'Ah. Well, have they seen the show?'

'Yeah, Sammy didn't get why I switched my show to be all about, quote, "some douchebag". But after a few days, they all got it. I mean, right away, it was unstoppable. Everyone was talking about it. We had this party with all Sammy's musician friends. People on the streets could hear the music through the open window of the flat and they buzzed the doorbell and came up to join the party. It got pretty crazy. Someone brought a bottle of absinthe they'd swiped from their job at a bar. Someone else brought tequila and a saxophone. One girl came in this feathered headdress and, like, Pope costume, and after an hour we were best friends. It was that kind of night.'

I thought about the dark, smoky flat I'd shared with Alex for the last few weeks. Hayley's sounded a lot more fun.

'Sounds like it was kind of a release,' I said.

'Well, I definitely drank way too much.' Hayley was still staring right at me as she spoke. Her intensity really was compelling once she got going on a topic. 'I ended up standing on a table, singing "Stand by Your Man" in my underwear. And then everyone was writing stuff on my body with someone's black eyeliner. Someone else wrote a list of the names of warrior women – Boudicca, Medea, Joan of Arc – down my back. Sammy drew a heart around my belly button. His girlfriend kissed me. I just felt wanted, you know? Valued. The next night, when I went on stage, I felt as though I'd been lifted there by the will of everyone I knew, reclaiming some ancient feminine power.'

'Wow,' I said.

'Yeah. It didn't last, though, that feeling. I've been having these dreams. There was this one dream where I was having sex with Alex live on stage in front of a full house of people yelling. That one freaked me out so much.'

'Was there ever a point,' I said, 'where you considered stopping the show?'

'Oh my God, every night. But I'd sunk so much into it already. The show was booked for a whole run, and the tickets were sold. The people running the venue said that promoters and PRs were asking to come. I signed with a new agent. There were new reasons to keep going every night, more people invested all the time. I've never been this flattered. I didn't know where the brakes were.'

'And what's it like?' I said, leaning towards her. 'I mean, it's fascinating, for people like me, who've never been through what you have. What's it like to get, suddenly, all this . . .' I searched for the right word '. . . vindication, from so many people?'

'Is it vindication? I don't know any more. It's all happened so fast. The shows are sold out, but it's not like

I'm seeing any money from that. All the ticket sales go to the venue. I'm still in a ton of debt. Nobody brings a show to Edinburgh to get rich, and everyone loses money, even people with beyond successful shows.'

'I hadn't thought of that,' I said, which now seemed stupid. 'But if it's not about the money, what do you hope people will get from the show?'

She thought for a moment. 'At first it was more about me than it was about them. But oh my God, Sophie, you have no idea. After every show, these amazing people from the audience come up to me to take me by the hand, look into my eyes, and tell me how much what I'm doing means to them. They thank me for being brave when they couldn't be. They tell me their own stories. It's nothing to do with Alex. I've listened to people tell me about being assaulted, raped, their birth traumas, their childhood abuse. Someone made a painting of me and gave it to me. And the things they send me to burn on stage. I mean, holy shit. It started out small, just newspaper reviews and like, a leather bracelet belonging to someone's ex, but then it got to be photographs and clothes and pieces of entire lives – I feel responsible for all of it. People come to me to fix what happened to them. And I don't know how.'

There was a long silence. I glanced down at the voice-recording app on my phone. We'd been speaking for almost an hour already. Hayley wasn't finished.

'Some of it feels worse than anything in my show. It blurs everything so I can't see, any more, a clear scale from wrong to more wrong. It all blends together into this huge mass of human hurt. I don't even know what to make of my own trauma any more.'

'Is it trauma?' I said.

'Well, if it is, it's a trauma that's given me a new life. I sometimes feel like a comic book superheroine whose origin story involved sexual assault. As if female power could only ever be conferred through male harm, you know. I always hated those movies.

'I can't reconcile these two ways of thinking about all this. It's like two flints that spark when I rub them together. On the one hand, there's the memory of how I felt with Alex, before any of this happened. I felt like he got me, you know? I felt held.

'But then there's the humiliation of that morning, and the feeling that any worth or talent I had ever had was snatched away from me, and that what I'd believed, just a few hours before, had been a trick.' She put her hand on my arm, bringing her face close to mine in the cold, empty museum of ancient human life. 'Why do I even keep doing this show when it still hurts? Will it ever feel better?'

I laid my pen down on my open notebook, on which I had written not a single word. For a moment, I couldn't breathe. I was somewhere else, an intrusive thought of my mother, in her bed in those last few days when she had forgotten why she was ill, and where she was, and that she could no longer stand. I remembered her trying to get out of bed, and saying those exact same words – *will it ever feel better?* – with the fear of a small child in her colourless face.

I shut my notebook.

Hayley looked down at her water bottle. She seemed desperately alone. I felt as though this was a moment when I should hug her. I didn't.

'But I think you've done something incredible,' I said.

'For what it's worth. Art should make you feel as if the person who made it is speaking directly to you. And for that to happen, there needs to be, underneath everything, some real, true, deep hurt, something which rubbed away all your protective surfaces.'

'This is what people like Alex don't get,' said Hayley. 'Making art is terrible, a lot of the time. So much rejection, so much disappointment. Someone like Alex, who's never been rejected in his fucking life, whose name has opened every door for him, he can't understand that. He says whatever he wants and he has no idea of the messy reality of life for the people with big plans, and weird brains, and good intentions, who spend their days making beautiful new things. I knew my climate show wasn't, like, the greatest show ever. But it was important to me and to my friend who wrote it with me. Even if it wasn't a five-star show, shouldn't I have been allowed to make it anyway? To try something new? Can I even still be an actress after this? Or do I just have to tell this story forever?'

I turned off the voice recorder. I definitely had enough material, though how the hell I was going to turn it into a newspaper feature, I had no idea. 'Hayley, I have to ask. Not for the paper. For me. What actually happened that night with Alex?'

We were side by side on the white stone bench. I could smell the strawberry in her hair. She unscrewed the top of her water bottle, and drank.

'It's in the show,' she said.

'We're not at the show now.'

She screwed the top back onto the bottle and placed it slowly, carefully, into her threadbare satchel. She crossed her arms and leaned forwards again, as if she had a stomach ache.

'People always think I never want to see him again. But it's not like that. If anything, I can't believe he never even came to see the new show. Every night, I wonder if he'll be there. You know what really fucking sucks? That night we were together, I cried on his shoulder in bed. I'd been so worried about my show. And he held me. He said it would be OK. He said the show would be a hit. It helped. And all that time, he knew it wouldn't be OK. He knew that his review was already on the way to the printer. What kind of a person does that?'

This was new. This was worse. I thought I'd known who Alex was and the kind of hurts he caused. I hadn't known anything, not really.

'Why *didn't* that end up in the show?' I asked.

'What,' said Hayley. 'Like I wanted people to *pity* me?'

A member of the museum staff walked past with a pointedness that caused me to realise there was a school group arriving, standing hopefully near a case of Bronze Age arrowheads, looking for spare seats. Our time was up.

18

When Hayley had gone, I went to find Josh and Arlo, who were in the museum's children's section. It was designed to be a sensory area, and so it had no natural light. It was definitely a sensory experience for me. There was a buggy park in one corner and an echo of children's screams ricocheting around the walls. A five-year-old girl was tearing up and down a pattern of round pads in the floor that made a pentatonic scale when she stamped on them. Josh was sitting with Arlo on his lap as Arlo ran a tentative, fascinated hand over the lumpy texture of a large piece of tree bark. 'Tree,' he was saying.

I went over with my arms outstretched and scooped him up. He protested at being separated from the tree bark.

Josh tried to hold my hand on the way back to the flat. He offered to put Arlo in the buggy but I said I wanted to carry him, and Arlo wanted that too. I breathed in the little bronze wisps of his hair and loved the way he leaned into me, turning his shy little face towards all the people on the streets, smiling to old ladies, who smiled back and waved joyously as if they were toddlers, too.

I had the afternoon off from reviewing shows so I could write up the interview. Hayley's photoshoot would be the next day, somewhere powerful and edgy and atmospheric. Paul Ellis didn't know exactly where, that was just the brief he'd given the picture desk.

Josh went out to get some supermarket supplies and I was alone with Arlo for an hour. We sat at the window watching the people and buses go by. He'd taken to gripping me so tightly, his fingers left little red marks on my arms and my neck.

That evening, I went to see another play. This one was an original piece of site-specific theatre about migrants, put on in a shipping container. The cast were students in a university drama society, mostly white, with no evidence provided in the programme that they had links to any migrant communities at all. It was written by someone called Giles Lambotham. The script was a chain of clichés: 'I'm just trying to seek a better life for us, Miguel!'; 'Death will mean nothing once we reach our promised land'; 'Britain will be an oasis compared to the hell we are leaving!' It went on.

They meant well. I knotted my fingers into my hair and slowly tugged it against my scalp, more and more insistently, until it really hurt quite a lot, just to help me dissociate from the experience.

When it was finally over, I headed back to the flat and opened my laptop. I had never hated anything more, felt more embarrassed for the existence of something. I was beginning to understand how Alex felt when he got back to another blank page after yet another show and needed to find something to say. And yet, what Hayley had said about the messy hope of the people she knew who made theatre chewed at me.

I could never have given the show five stars. I knew that. But I *could* have given it three: it was an ambitious idea. It was an important topic. Their hearts were in the right place. It was an issue we should be talking about, and they had something to say, even if that something was not complex or nuanced or new.

But the acting was melodramatic and, actually, racist. This was a bunch of privileged white university kids. The script had no progression. They'd found a shipping container to be the set, but the design had stopped there. It was hard to escape the fact that this was a bunch of students shouting platitudes in a Scottish car park.

And maybe, despite everything Hayley had said about how hard it was to try making something new, just for the love of it, something had hardened in me over the last few weeks.

I eased my denim jacket off and hung it on the kitchen chair in the empty flat. There was a rectangular weight in one of the pockets that I hadn't noticed when I'd been wearing it. I pulled out one of Josh's lighters, the gold one with the letter S entwined with filigree.

My deadline was close. What would be the point in trying to be kind to these people? In trying to indulge their project, which was doomed from the moment they stepped on stage? They were students, and being a student is for learning. They had a lot to learn. But was this the time for it? And what did audiences have to learn from them?

I thought about their parents, and how proud they

would be of their children, performing a show at the world's biggest arts festival. Getting their names in a national newspaper. How much they wanted them to succeed. The power I had to crush that. The power I had to ruin their morning. Their whole day. To make them think again about a career in performance before they'd even started. If this writer and director, and these actors, were cursed never to find success in their careers, would it be kinder to steer them towards a different course now, before they'd invested too much?

But maybe I didn't have that power. Maybe their mothers wouldn't even read this paper. Maybe the students wouldn't, either.

I was thinking too much about the performers. I needed to think more about the audience, or rather the readers who might become an audience. People doing a show at the festival had invested a lot of money, and time, creative energy and good faith to bring their work here. But people in the audience, who had come up for a holiday, had invested their time, money, and good faith, too.

I would be complicit in a deception if I told them something was good when it so obviously wasn't. And then, even worse perhaps, the value of my own opinion would be corroded. People would, gradually, trust me a little less. I owed it to readers to be honest. I owed people the truth.

As I started to type, the directness came more easily. A sharpness, newly formed, sparkled inside me. If it was cruelty, it wasn't something that had grown overnight. It was something that had always been there, something about me I'd always feared and tried to suppress, and which had at last been revealed.

I thought of the fury in Hayley's eyes and wondered if

she'd felt it too: that same ancient, buried instinct for cruelty. I remembered hearing something on the radio once about the surest precursor to revenge being humiliation. An embarrassed child lashes out at their parents. A disgraced army regroups and is more vicious in the counterattack. Its soldiers commit more war crimes.

I decided to be honest. I wrote a list of all the problems with the show. At the end of the list, I realised I'd almost got to the word count of the slot already. I wrote a short paragraph for the beginning about the context of the show, what the information in the Fringe programme led audiences to expect, and how the show itself had let down those expectations. Then I really had made it to the word count. I re-read the piece. It wasn't as mean-spirited as the kind of reviews that Alex used to write. At least, I didn't think it was. It was clear and straight. Like a disappointed teacher writing a school report for a promising child who just needed to try a little harder to fulfil their potential, I was more in sorrow than in anger.

I emailed it to the duty editor and copied in Graham. I wrote the rating at the top of the email: ONE STAR.

It was very late, and Graham would have gone home from the newsroom by now. But he replied directly to my email, less than three minutes after I'd filed. The email consisted of one word: *Wow!*

19

The next morning, Josh took Arlo to an indoor play centre and I walked around Edinburgh for a while to find a café where I could keep working on my interview with Hayley. It was raining a warm summer drizzle and the daylight had a seeping dinginess to it. The city felt worn out. A family of tourists unloaded outside a hotel. They had enough luggage with them for a few days. For them, the festival was beginning today. For all the reviewers and performers, it was already dying.

   I wanted to see some places I hadn't been to for years, to inhabit them again as the person I was now. A shop selling art prints that I'd liked had moved across town. A place where I used to see indie folk bands was still putting on gigs. On the Royal Mile, a topless guy was riding a unicycle along a clothesline in front of a semicircle of people applauding politely. I stopped in an independent bookshop and enjoyed the indulgence of reading the first page of several different contemporary novels that I had no intention of buying. As I walked along the Grassmarket, sunshine cut through the drizzle and hit Edinburgh Castle on its great rock above me with such sharpness that I stopped and stared at it, amazed at how it warmed the city into colour. Suddenly I wished I had a sketchbook and some watercolours to capture it exactly as I was seeing it. It's what my mother would have done. But I didn't, so I took out my phone, took a photo, and posted it on Instagram.

I walked past what had once been a standard comics store and was now a shop selling Wizarding World merchandise. Everything seemed tidier than it had been when I'd lived here ten years ago. It was me that was messier.

I passed a chain coffee shop and saw Hayley in the window. She was sitting on a stool, looking through her phone, not seeing me. A fine layer of sweat sheened her hair and skin. Her face was dragged down by whatever she was thinking about. I could just make out the edge of her phone screen. It looked as though she was reading a Twitter thread. She seemed older even than when I'd seen her at the museum. Her hand worried at one of her earrings. Stuart was right about the toll the month had taken on her. I didn't see her any more as a kind of incandescently beautiful avenging angel. I saw bruising.

There was a run of tatty posters for shows along the wall next to the bus stop, some of them stickered over with narrow white rectangles of paper printed with black stars, only ever in constellations of four or five, peeling at the corners. I saw a poster for *The Uncivil Peace* and jolted to notice a sticker placed on it that said: '★★★★★ – SOPHIE RIGDEN', and the name of my paper. I bent my head and picked up speed, as if people might recognise me from it.

As I walked down Princes Street with my headphones in, I scrolled through my phone. I'd already got some likes for the picture I posted. Otherwise, my various social media feeds showed a series of posts that assumed complete knowledge of a developing situation without naming any names.

Too many people on this app need to go and touch grass. Part of the problem of this entire mess is that what should always have stayed online has spilled out into real life. Yeah what he did was bad but it wasn't ILLEGAL and she's just milking this too much now.

*

Hey girls, it's all good if you have sex with someone who secretly hates you, because you can be famous! Thinking of all the comedians, writers and performers today who have been working towards something for years and never got a shot. Turns out talent wasn't as important as sleeping with the right person, after all

*

Am I the only one who's deeply uncomfortable with this whole thing? Feels like the sort of drama that should have been a private falling out between two people. If she was really upset she could have complained directly to the paper. And she's got famous because of it which is probably what she wanted all along

*

I actually feel sorry for Hayley still. Nobody knows what's going on in her life rn

*

Smh white feminist tears will get you anywhere

As I sat in a café with my laptop, editing what I'd written the day before, cutting and pasting quotes from the interview and knitting together all the thoughts I'd had about the show, about Hayley as a person, about the strangeness of this entire moment, I found it was coming together more smoothly than any piece I'd written previously. Maybe the one-star review had opened up a new vein in me. I'd broken through something. Fuck it, I thought, if I'm a critic I might as well be honest. I wasn't both-sidesing – I was trying to find a clear-eyed, close-up truth, without puff or flattery. I knew this whole situation better than anyone else did by now. It was my story, my beat. And I liked the words that were coming out. I just wasn't sure if I liked the person writing them.

I would proofread the interview and send it to Graham later. After I saved the draft, Josh messaged me a picture of Arlo smiling as he tottered through an art gallery. I sent him a heart emoji in response, then looked through my phone for the contact at the new arts festival that Stuart had given me. I sent him an email and ordered another coffee, which I drank looking out at the rain. He replied within minutes, suggesting we meet when I was back in London.

I was stunned. But before I could respond, I had a message from Graham. He asked if I'd heard from Alex. I realised then that I hadn't seen Alex all day. Or the day before, come to think of it, since before I'd left the flat to interview Hayley. Graham said that he'd just picked up a message from Alex, sent earlier that day. In his message, Alex had said that he was sorry, but he just couldn't do this any more.

Is he with you, Sophie? Graham wrote. *Can you check if he's OK?*

20

Alex wasn't at the flat. Josh was still out with Arlo and Alex's laptop was on the kitchen table. I opened it. It woke from standby to his emails, open on the last message that Alex had received.

Hi Alex,
    Thanks for your message. Yeah, I've seen what's been going on with this show in Edinburgh. I hope you're OK. It seems like a lot. I did get a message from Hayley asking if I had anything I wanted to share with her for her project because someone had told her that we were together for a few years. I don't know who told her that, and I haven't replied to her. I don't think that's something that I'd want to do – get up on stage, or have my words read out by hundreds of people. That's never been my thing. But then I saw you on *Newsnight*, and I wondered if you could really believe all the things you were saying.
    I did watch one of Hayley's shows online and I was

upset by it, to be honest. It brought back a lot of things from when we were together and when we split up that I found hard to process at the time, and I think I'm only now realising the effect they all had on me.

I've been seeing a new therapist who said that all addiction stems from an inability to face your own emotions. It's helped me understand my relationship with drinking after what happened, but it also made me think about you, and wonder what you might not be facing?

I don't want to presume. The time for us to have these conversations is actually over now, and I don't want to open up that whole thing again. But I wanted to reply to you because all this has made me feel as though there was maybe a door that was still open somewhere, and for the record, I'd like it to be shut.

It's hard to put it into words, the thing that happened and how it felt. I still don't know, really, why you didn't come with me that day. I think it was already over between you and me when I made the appointment anyway.

But why didn't you come, really? Why did you leave me to go through it on my own? Why did you gaslight me afterwards and make out that I hadn't told you where it was, or what time? We both know that wasn't true.

What some of these other women in your life have been saying about you scares me, Alex. It makes me worry that you might not be capable of caring about anyone. That's terrifying, and it's not the Alex that I thought I knew for three years. There was a time when we were happy, and I imagined the whole future with you. I never thought there would be a time when it would be hard to talk to you at all.

I have a lot of regrets about that time. The thing that really hurts about it even now, though, is that I am actually grateful it happened. I'm relieved that it showed me I didn't have to be tied to you by something neither of us wanted. I'm glad, even if I had to pay for that release mechanism with pain, and loss, and guilt.

I'm doing really well now. I didn't feel as though I needed to be part of some show. But, at the same time, I couldn't stand the thought that you might have gone on through your life thinking that, maybe, at least, you never really hurt me. Because you did.

Don't feel you need to reply to this. I don't need to hear any more of your opinions on what happened or what could have been different. If you do reply, I won't read it.

I hope you're doing better now too.

Soraya

I opened the Find My Phone app on the laptop. It showed that Alex's phone, presumably with Alex attached to it, was on top of Calton Hill, on the other side of the city centre.

I half-walked and half-ran through the drizzle, and walked up to the top of the hill under the low, grim clouds bringing the afternoon an unnatural early darkness, past people talking and laughing and drinking. You could often see the whole city from up there, but today it was mostly obscured by grey mist. The castle was already lit up for the evening in its weird colours. There was the expanse of sea to the north. The city lights speckled through the gloomy daytime rain like yellow stars.

I found Alex sitting on the ground, hugging his knees in a grassy hollow at the very top of the hill, in the shadow of the Greek temple monument. At first, I'd thought he was a junkie, or a pile of coats, until I recognised the curls of his hair. He was tilted awkwardly to one side and his hands were fumbling at a cigarette.

I sat down next to him, the rainy ground soaking through the seat of my jeans. He smelled of smoke, wet clothes from yesterday, alcohol, and faintly of vomit.

'Graham sent me to find you,' I said.

He mumbled something at me.

'What?'

'I said, so you're an investigative reporter now.'

'I'll find a cab. We'll go back to the flat.'

'No, I'm all right. Leave me alone, please.' He was less drunk than I'd initially thought. He was capable of speech, for one thing.

'Where have you been?'

'The Royal Infirmary.'

'What? Are you OK?'

'Not for me. For my dad. He was supposed to be in a play but he's too sick for that now. There was stuff I thought I should ask him. Not sure I even know what. It sounds weird, but I wanted to tell him that I tried on his shoes once, when I was sixteen. He'd left them at my mum's house, I don't know when, must have been when I was little. I didn't think they'd fit, but they were the exact right size. These really nice oxblood-coloured brogues. I thought I might keep them. Then I looked in the mirror, and they were ridiculous on me, in my ripped jeans and Ramones t-shirt or whatever the hell I was wearing then. They fit me but they didn't fit me, you know?

'I didn't say any of that to him, anyway. I just sat there for a long time while he was asleep, then he woke up, and he saw me there, and he didn't say hello or anything. It was so weird. He just said: "Our revels now are ended."'

'From *The Tempest*,' I said.

Alex rolled his eyes, like, *duh*. 'Yeah. And so I was like, "The actors were all spirits after all." It was so pretentious. But then he was crying and stuff.

'"My boy," he was saying to me, "You are my boy. I did something right." And he tried to hold my hand, but I had to move the cannula thing out of the way first. And you know what I wanted to say? I wanted to say no. I wanted to say, you have it all wrong, and, actually, how dare you? Any love I have for anything comes from my mother, not from you. *You* weren't there. *She* took me to the theatre and filled our house with books. All your absence gave me was absence. That's what I wanted to say.'

'But you didn't?'

Alex shook his head. 'I held his hand. I thought he was going to say something else about my childhood or some shit. And then he said, "What do you think they'll write about me, Alex? Do you think they'll put me in the obituaries pages? Perhaps they'll write that I was a good actor. Do you think they'd put that in the papers?" I said I was sure they would. I was sure they'd say he brought the house down. Then he went back to sleep, and I just leaned back in my chair, looking at the yellow ceiling tiles. Who in the NHS chose that fucking colour? Who thought dying people would want to look at that?

'The nurses came and checked him over, and I went for a walk, and I ended up back at the flat. I checked my emails and then – it doesn't matter, but I had to get a drink. I started to get convinced that my dad had died. I sat in Princes Street Gardens wondering if *I* wanted to die, but then I had this awful thought that if I did die, someone might write an obit for me that was actually all about Hayley and my mother. I don't remember much after that. Fuck, it's cold.'

He leaned his elbows into his knees.

'Well, if you do die,' I said. 'I'll probably write the obit.'

He laughed. 'Thanks. Good of you. Right now I feel like Aubrey and Maturin, chasing the *Acheron* through the sea fog and getting blown up again and again.'

'Christ, what is it with men and *Master and Commander*?'

'Sophie,' he said. 'The other day—'

'Oh, you don't have to – we're OK.' My voice sounded unnaturally bright to me. I wanted him to stop talking about this as quickly as possible.

'We're OK?'

'Yeah. Of course. I mean, it's nothing.' Whatever it was, I couldn't stand the idea of him trying to make it better.

'Sure. Cool. I mean, that's what I thought, so.'

He smiled weakly. He looked very tired. He stood up then, a little unsteady, and spat on the ground. I walked with him slowly down the hill. He leaned on my shoulder, stumbling now and then. I convinced a cab driver to take us home but, in the cab, the stink of Alex meant I had to open two windows. I gave the driver a generous tip. When we got back into the empty flat, he headed into his bedroom, and I followed. I took off his shoes and socks and his sodden coat and pulled the duvet over him. He turned away from me. The flat was so quiet without Arlo or Josh. The rain threw itself madly at the windows. The lines of Alex's body under the sheets were sharp and angular. It felt like a long time since my hands had felt his body. It felt as if it had happened to two different people.

'Saw you gave that show one star,' Alex mumbled as I left the room. 'Nice piece. Funny.'

'Thanks.' My pleasure at this surprised me. I realised I hated that review. Five stars, one stars, it didn't matter. I didn't like reviewing at all.

Why are you like this? I didn't say it to Alex. It was a question I still couldn't answer. And it wasn't just Alex. When I asked myself why Alex was the way he was, I also wanted to know why other men were like this – why *Josh* was like this. Why had Josh slept with someone else?

As I stood in the kitchen, my breathing was rapid and ragged, and it wouldn't slow down. The strangeness of the last few hours, the last few weeks, was creeping into the air and taking me over like a change in the weather.

A tide was dragging me out. The wound that had been within me since my mother died was growing still, with every day that I woke up and washed dishes and fed the baby and answered emails and tried to move forwards through my life. An emotional ulcer that I was now, increasingly, convinced would never heal.

The pain of it hit me first somewhere in the mouth. The sting and burn of grief, like citrus and saltiness and sunburn on raw skin. Everyone was wrong, including me. I'd become obsessed with Alex's life not because I wanted to control him, and not because I was in love with him. I'd held him, been almost as close to him as physically possible, and it hadn't answered anything at all. I didn't hate him. I didn't begrudge him anything. Why was that, when everyone else felt the opposite? Was it just because he was, despite all his sins, still alive? He had kept on living, when other people who were so much more deserving of life, good and kind people, people who made beautiful things, people I wrote obituaries for every week, were dead. Who made that decision? Who could I complain to about that?

Alex had all this life in him. So much of it. He was full of blood and salt and water and semen and bile. For me, everything was an effort. And there he was, careening through the world so carelessly, wrecking everything as he went.

The more I'd watched him that month, the more I'd thought, well, why not? Why not leave a trail of wild destruction through your only life?

I'd worked so hard at not missing my mother. I thought if I started to miss her too deliberately, too freely, it would open up a whirlpool in my life that would pull everything into it. Now, that was happening.

Arlo still had his other grandmother, Josh's mother, a woman that I, really, in comparison, barely knew. I had a sudden, desperate need to hold Arlo, to gather him into me, to hook my hands onto him as if he were a tree root on the edge of the swirling water.

I hated that Arlo wouldn't ever know my mother. He wouldn't ever be a little boy perched in the kitchen of her house, his grandma's house, baking shortbread rounds. He wouldn't ever splash through her rainy garden in his wellies, picking a fistful of indigo sweet peas for the table with her, while she showed him the holly tree where there was a blackbird. He wouldn't ever know how much he missed, in missing her. His time on Earth missed hers by inches.

If I'd had children earlier. The thought prickled evilly at the edges of my mind. It was a thought I'd swallowed down and been refusing to think for those three brief, endless years since her death. If I'd had children earlier, there would have been some time for everyone to be together. If I'd known, then, the date that my mother's life would be over, what different decisions would I have made?

I sat on the kitchen floor with the lights off and the sky darkening at the window, holding Arlo's toy panda in my hand, then bringing it up to my face, pressing it against my forehead, and I cried. I cried so rarely that it terrified me, and I was ugly about it, too, snotty and gulping. My body shook.

I cried until Josh let himself in through the door. He dropped his borrowed key on the hallway table. He came into the kitchen and knelt beside me. Arlo tottered towards me, babbling a confused greeting in toddler language.

'Hey,' said Josh. 'What's happened?'

'How can she be dead when I still need her?'

Josh put his arms around me. As he held me, in my ear he murmured, 'I know, I know, I know.' I leaned into him. He was warm and real.

Arlo leaned in to hug me too. He looked so scared and serious. I cuddled him. 'Mama's all right,' I said, swallowing. 'She's just being silly.'

Arlo wriggled away. 'Look!' He pointed out of the window to a round and glowing street lamp below that had just switched itself on in the early, cloud-brought dusk. 'Moon!'

21

Josh put Arlo to bed. The flat was quiet. I boiled the kettle and the roar of it filled the kitchen before clicking off into bubbling diminuendo, fading into the jangling sound of heavy rain against the windows. I made us each a mug of peppermint tea. Through the raw jungle terror of my own grief, there was a thinning of the trees. Could I leave the paper? Was it possible to build a more stitched-together life, improvising each step towards the next? Was it possible to have Arlo as part of my life, instead of all of it? Was that an obscene thing for a mother to want? Perhaps it was something I wanted and couldn't ever have. To consume the generation above and be consumed by what follows.

'When the festival's over,' Josh said, coming back into the room, 'I was thinking, let's go to your mum's grave together. You haven't been since they installed the headstone, have you? We can take sweet peas. We can take Arlo for the first time.'

'It wouldn't mean anything to him yet,' I said. I sat at

the table, holding my mug of tea in both hands, inhaling the mint-scented steam through my nose like an ancient medicine.

Josh picked up his mug of tea from beside the kettle. 'It would mean something to us.'

He stayed standing by the sink. He paused, as if considering whether or not to say something.

'Sophie.' His gaze was steady on me. He put the mug of tea back down on the counter and spoke very softly. So softly that it was hard even to hear him against the sound of the rain. I recognised this as a moment of unusual weight, one of those moments where I became sharply aware of the colour of the light, the sounds of the room, the feeling of my skin. A moment that, even before it happened, I already sensed I would remember for a long time. 'Has something happened between you and Alex?'

Fear thrilled through me like caffeine, and I knew then it was a fear of myself, of my own terrible impulses. All the many weaknesses that for years I'd lacquered over with self-deprecation, and held down under thick anxiety, fizzed to the surface. They arranged themselves plainly before me. My selfishness, my snobbery. My need to be liked. My need to be wanted.

I thought about not telling him. I thought about lying. But I hadn't, up to this point, ever lied to him, and starting now would feel like another step away from the person I wanted to be.

'I'm so sorry,' I said.

There was a fleck of mint leaf in my tea. It twirled a little dance under the murky water. I wondered if this was it, if this was finally the re-opening of the path, and Josh would really, truly leave. I thought of Arlo, of things being just him and me forever. Or would Josh win some kind of custody battle, I thought, frantically, and I would be alone?

'Oh God,' Josh was saying. He ran both his hands through his hair. 'Where is he now? Is he here?'

'Does it matter?'

'I kind of want to punch him in the fucking face.'

'Josh, he's passed out. He's drunk. He's pathetic. Just, please don't.' The thought of them in a fight was so terrifyingly crazy it was almost funny. What was he going to do, beat Alex senseless while Arlo slept in the next room? It was impossible.

'Did it happen in the flat?'

'No, it wasn't here.'

'Is it over? You and me?'

'I don't know. I don't know what to say.'

'You could say you still love me? God knows I still love you. It wouldn't hurt to hear it.'

In that sudden, bitter crack of sincerity I glimpsed the fullness of his hurt and humiliation. His bruised and patient life. It took the breath from me.

'But, before,' I said. 'You did this. You did this to me first. I don't want to drag it all up again now, I don't want that, but you—'

'No, OK, let's talk about it.' Something about his presence was exactly like how Hayley had been, in this same room, when she'd discovered Alex's review in the paper. He had that same spark in him. 'I've let you paint me as the bad guy for all this time, as the guy who should just be grateful that you took me back. You never wanted to talk about anything else that was going on at the time, the circumstances, or even since. With your mum, and with work, and having the baby, and with everything.'

'Josh, I can't—'

'Don't we at least owe it to Arlo to talk about this? I can forgive you – I am willing to forgive this – if you're actually willing to forgive me. I'm not just going to leave. I'm not going to leave you here.'

The mention of Arlo ruptured something in me and I couldn't move from the table.

'You left before,' I said. 'You left me alone when he was just a baby. I was so hurt, and so sad and desperate, and you didn't even see it. You just went back to work and left me there to deal with everything. Life went on for you, the same as it always had. And for me, everything was different.'

'But how do you think it felt for me to leave you like that?'

Josh was wounded, primal, exhilarated. He started talking about things I'd never let myself listen to before. He talked about what had happened with Coralie. He talked about how scared he'd been when Arlo was born. He spoke with a great physical effort, and in the pauses between his phrases there were wide expanses of painful hope. I felt in them the extent of his loneliness, his mortification, how he tempered it now with a furious, injured dignity, how he had suspected something of me ever since he'd arrived in Edinburgh and seen the way Alex and I were, how he hadn't wanted to accept the possibility of it being true. And how all of it, he saw now, went back much further in our lives than just this August.

'Two weeks after Arlo was born,' he was saying, 'when I had to leave the two of you alone, and spend all day with academics and students wrapped up in their own lives – it was the lowest I'd ever been. I'd left you at home, bleeding and sad and betrayed. I got to the office on that first day, shut the door and cried.

'I was terrified that something would happen to Arlo or to you. I was doing that research project reading all the old death records. Halfway through a lecture, I started getting insane intrusive thoughts, hallucinations even. I could see you with your skin blotchy with some terminal disease. I could see Arlo's body, cold and still. I even started thinking about the marble monument that, if I'd been an eighteenth-century merchant, I'd have made in your memory. I was really crazy. I felt violently protective, to a scary extent. I couldn't stop thinking about the ways I'd tear apart anyone who hurt you.

'But I was also amazed by how strong you were. I wanted to do everything for you, but you were on top of all of it. Whenever I did the laundry or the washing up, you did it again after me, because I'd messed it up somehow, and you were obviously upset that I'd done it wrong. And when I asked you how I should do it, you snapped at me that I should stop asking you how to do every little thing.

'I didn't want to make life worse for you, so I just stopped asking, because that seemed like what you wanted. And you loved Arlo so much. You were everything he needed. Sometimes it was as if I wasn't even necessary. I was this incidental figure in his life. But it was OK. I made myself OK with that, because I told myself it was temporary.

'But these last few weeks, while you've been away, and it's just been me and Arlo, I've had some pretty dark thoughts. Sometimes he cries just because all he wants is you, and I can't even comfort him, not really, because I feel exactly the same. I've been taking him to the corner shop to buy the paper as soon as we get up at 6 a.m. so I can point out your name, and show him the tiny photo of your face in your byline picture, and I say to Arlo, 'Who's that?' so that Arlo can say 'Mama!' and blow kisses to you. It's for him, but it's also for me. I want to see your face too. I've been missing you for so much longer than just the last three weeks. Where have you been all this time? Where have I been?'

There was a glow to his honesty in the dim kitchen. He wasn't pleading a case. He was setting out a record. If he'd come towards me at that moment, I would have held his face in my hands. I wanted to feel the heat of his skin under mine. But he stayed on the other side of the kitchen table, standing with one hand on the counter, gripping it as if it might fall away from him, and I shrank into my chair, kept there by the force of my own shame.

I remembered when my mother was in the hospice, a modern building that she hated, and Josh had brought round old books from university libraries across London for her. He'd left tiny, soft leatherbound editions of sonnet collections and essays beside her bed, carefully arranged next to the bud vase I'd put there, so she had flowers and poetry beside her. And when she was too weak to read them herself, he read the poems to her, while I lay on the bed beside her and closed my eyes, holding her hand. After she died, he filled the Daunt Books tote bag he'd bought on one of our first dates with the books she'd loved, and he brought them to the funeral. He'd said it was so that they would be near her as we said goodbye.

I'd forgotten that. I'd forgotten so much. All of it lost in a fog of grief, this whole time.

His tea was cold. He hadn't drunk any of it. Mine, too,

was untouched. You can drink hot tea and you can drink iced tea but you can't drink it at room temperature. It just doesn't work.

'I've never loved anyone else,' he said. 'I don't think I ever could. Tell me, how come you could spend so much time with Alex, who's done these terrible things, and listen to his side of the story, and you couldn't ever bring yourself to listen to mine? You excuse his behaviour – and you couldn't forgive me?'

I didn't know what to say. There seemed to be so much to say, and so little. I felt millions of years old. Josh was staring at me with a marbled mixture of pain and relief. He didn't have to be the bad guy now. There was no good or bad, not any more. He was so alive, so full of fight. How could I have thought he didn't care? How could I have mistaken his love for something weak, something already lost? It had never dimmed. His face was a mirror of my own betrayal. I saw things I'd long since buried in myself rising to the surface, finding a way out.

It was as if I'd been looking through a cathedral window from the outside at my life for all this time, seeing only a muddy set of dark, dull, obscure panes. And now I was on the inside, with sunlight flowing towards me, making a bright, clear image of the multicoloured glass.

22

The next day was my last day in Edinburgh and the last night of Hayley's show. When I got up, the door to Alex's room was open but he wasn't there. That morning, the final Saturday of the Fringe, our paper's front page splashed with an exclusive about a TV presenter who'd been discovered sexting a teenager. For the first time in weeks, there wasn't a single piece in any of the papers about Alex. The glare was starting to dim on his life, and the stage lights were coming up somewhere else.

I texted Graham to say that I'd seen Alex the night before and he was OK. He replied: *Phew. I thought I might see if he fancies writing obits for a while.*

Good idea, I replied, *as long as he doesn't start giving star ratings to the dead.*

Josh said he'd take Arlo out to the park for the morning so I could work in peace and file my final copy before the train home the next day. Josh paused at the door before he left and looked me in the eyes for long enough to make me look back at him, really look. I saw, there, something

I hadn't realised I'd been looking for. In his face, I didn't see a reflection of my obsessiveness, my self-hatred, my desperation to look at anything except my own hurt. Instead, I saw him. I kissed him, and he kissed me back, his hand in my hair.

About twenty minutes after they'd left, Alex came back into the kitchen, smoking a cigarette. He opened the window and stood beside it, blowing the smoke vaguely towards the open air. I kept looking at my laptop. It felt disloyal to acknowledge him at all, but I couldn't tell him to get out.

'I was thinking,' Alex said. 'I should go and see Hayley's last show tonight.'

I looked up from my laptop then. 'Why?' But really, by now, I already knew why. I had, I think, been expecting this.

Alex took his creased old wallet out of his pocket and was fiddling with something in it, opening and closing it. 'The only show I've ever seen her in was that disaster three weeks ago. Now, apparently, she's Nelson Mandela. What kind of critic would I be if I *didn't* go and see it? It's a show about *my life*.'

'What if someone recognises you?'

'It's dying down now, all this, isn't it? There isn't anything in the papers about it at all today. Maybe it'll just be a really good show. Maybe I'll come out of it thinking she made some good points, and that this Alex Lyons prick deserves everything he gets. Anyway, I went to the box office in person. Told them my name and showed them my media pass and wouldn't you know it, they had two returns left.'

*

Alex left me a ticket and said he'd meet me there, but when I got to the theatre I didn't see him. I suppose I was a bit early. The anti-Hayley picketers were there outside, but they were mooching around looking at their phones with their placards leaning against the railings, and they didn't look up as I walked past. I went down into the basement. The stage was much more elaborate than it had been when I'd attended that first show. There was a pyrotechnic rig, and jagged scenery flats in jewel colours, and sweeping curtains of thick fabric at the back. There was the silver metal bin on the stage, now blackened inside and at the rim from where she'd been burning newspapers and clothes and possessions every night. It was full of stuff. Some newspapers and something that could have been a lacy bra strap poked out of the top.

To the right was the door that Hayley came through to enter the stage. The venue had an end-of-term feel. Everything was shabby and greying and overheated. It was as if the building had a hangover.

Alex still wasn't there. Maybe he just hadn't shown up. There were so many people. Without enough chairs for everyone, some people were standing at the back, three or four rows deep, pushed up against the black walls. I didn't know anyone in the audience, but I felt part of something, even if it was the end. The music on the speakers was like the hype music played when wrestlers enter the ring.

The lights dimmed, and still no Alex. Hayley stepped through the dark red curtains at the back of the stage to immediate applause and whooping from the crowd. Instead of dying down so the show could start, the applause got louder. She had two handheld microphones, presumably one for her and another for whichever guest would be joining her tonight. There were two chairs on stage. I wondered if there would be a return of one of the previous contributors, India Morris maybe, or maybe even Lavinia, in person. The temperature in the room seemed to rise with the sound of applause. I was aware of the narrowness of my seat, and how hemmed in I was on both sides by people. The woman on my left had brought a little foil packet of butter popcorn, and she offered me some. I took a handful.

'Ladies and gentlemen,' said Hayley, and the cheering faded. 'This is our final show!' The cheering started up again. This time there was stamping of feet, too, like gathering thunder. The vibration went right through me.

Instead of performing the first part of her show, the part that was the same every night, where she would recite Alex's review, Hayley stood still. She seemed to look right at me, and smiled.

'I can see some familiar faces in the audience. Thank you so much, old friends and new, for sticking with me on this crazy ride all this month. I never, ever thought, when I first brought my little show up to Edinburgh, that it would end up like this. It's like a dream.'

There was more applause.

'So,' she continued. 'This is the Alex Lyons Experience. It's always been about what happened to me, and the guy that did it, and all the other horrible things he's done and got away with, until now. And then, somewhere along the way, that changed. The show became bigger than both of us. It became about all of you, as much as it was ever about me. But, ever since the first time I performed this show, one very important character has been missing.

Well, not any more. I've got a surprise for you tonight. Our last show will feature a new headline act. The man himself. Alex Lyons.'

There was no cheering. The auditorium was instead filled with confused, silent dismay. Not least mine. Was this a joke? How had she contacted him? Why had he agreed?

'Before Alex comes on stage, you're probably wondering why he's here. Why, after spending three weeks telling you this guy was to be avoided at all costs, would I invite him onto this stage and give him a platform?' She was nervous, I realised. There was a tremor in her voice. She seemed smaller than the last time I saw her. She swallowed, gathered herself.

'Well, I did an interview the other day for a newspaper where I was talking about the show and what an incredible ride it's been, and how honoured I am to have so many women tell me they feel empowered by it, and it made me think: what do I want to happen to this guy?

'At first, I just wanted as many people as possible to know what he'd done to me, and for him not to do the same thing to anyone else. But now, what do I want? Do I want him to crawl into a hole and never come back out? Do I want him never to work as a critic again? Well, yeah, sort of. But that's happened before. We call out men who do awful things, they appear in the news for a few weeks and then disappear. Sometimes their careers are over, sometimes they stay quiet for a while and then flare up again, like a bad rash. But does anything really change? The same thing keeps happening. Over and over again. And the lives of the women who call these men out get eaten up.

'This show has been mind-blowing, and validating, and so powerful for me personally, but it's also been exhausting. I can't keep doing this. So I thought maybe what I actually want is to hear him say that what he did was wrong. And not just say it, but mean it. And maybe if this one guy, who has hurt so many people, can do that, then my show will have achieved something more than just reminding everyone of the things men are capable of, until the next time a man makes the news.

'So, I got Alex Lyons's number from my agent and, late last night, I called him. I had the feeling that this would never really be over unless I found out if he understood how much he'd hurt me and the amazing women who have shared this stage.

'Ladies and gentlemen,' she said. 'Alex Lyons.'

Nobody applauded. The door to the left side of the stage opened. And through it, wearing his black leather jacket, looking pale, running his hands through his hair, into the silent spotlight stepped Alex.

He folded his arms, shifting from foot to foot, an uncertain half-smile on his face. His eyes searched the room, the stage lights shortening his visual range. For a moment, they faced each other, a little closer than strangers would stand. Hayley looked right into Alex's eyes. There was a second where the quietness thickened.

She handed him a microphone and they sat opposite one another in two black chairs. My mind ran through questions she could ask Alex, questions that I hadn't thought to ask him. Or questions that I had asked, but that might get different answers when Hayley asked them.

'Last week,' said Hayley, 'you were on TV defending yourself. Now you're here. What's changed?'

I knew, now, what Hayley wanted. It wasn't, as I'd assumed right at the start of the month, that she never wanted to see Alex again. She had wanted to see him, but differently. What would it mean for her if the festival ended and Alex had still only ever seen that one bad show, that one side of her, that one performance in which he had found no value?

He'd lied to me about why he was coming to the show, I realised, because he'd wanted me to be there, too. And probably also because he didn't want me to tell him not to do it.

Alex held the microphone to his mouth and spoke initially as if unsure whether his voice would really be amplified. 'Well,' he said. His voice boomed too loud, and he winced at the feedback. He cleared his throat and moved the mic further from his lips. 'Honestly, when you called me last night, I'd already had a really shit day.' He looked as though he was choosing his words carefully, an unfamiliar and uncanny sight. He looked like a three-day-old helium balloon, beginning to wrinkle and dip. His skin was grey. He seemed so tired. 'This whole month I've been attacked, in ways that haven't always been fair. But then I heard from someone else. I won't say her name. She hasn't been on your show, but she wrote to me. And it made me see things differently. It made me think – wow, I guess her life really would have been better if she'd never met me. A lot better.'

Whatever Hayley had been expecting him to say, it wasn't this. 'And to this brave woman,' said Hayley, looking out into the audience, as if she might find her there, 'and to all the extraordinary women I've had with me on this show, can you summon up an apology?'

Bring The House Down

'Yes. Absolutely.' He didn't hesitate. There was a brief, astonished beat of silence through the theatre.

'You haven't actually said the word sorry, though,' said Hayley. That thought had been occurring to me too. I wondered if she was regretting inviting him here. She looked uncertain. There was an uncertainness in the audience, too, an anxiety, as if, together, all two hundred of us had become one great nervous beast that might turn, or lash out, or bolt. Hayley must have sensed it, too.

'OK, I'm sorry to all those women,' said Alex. He blinked in the stage lights.

'Well,' said Hayley. 'It only took us a couple dozen shows to get here. But what are you actually sorry for? What you did to them? What you did to me?'

'I think what happened between you and me was a different thing.' Alex shifted in his chair. I winced. In the auditorium there was some disbelieving tutting. Someone booed.

'No, wait,' said Hayley, holding out a hand to shush the audience. 'What do you mean, different?'

'I mean, we weren't in a relationship. It was just one night. And now look at all this.' He gestured to the audience. 'This is going OK. You've turned it to your advantage. And as a critic, I applaud that. You can go and do whatever you like now, because of what happened between us. Whereas before, you had a show that . . .' he paused. I could see him choosing the most polite words; another uncanny sight. I could see him almost saying *a show that fucking sucked*. Instead, he said, 'A show that not many people would have come to see.'

'So, you think that what you did was OK because it all turned out fine for me?'

'I didn't say that. But you had one morning of feeling bad and then you turned it into a successful show. Great job. I've had a whole month of the entire country thinking I'm the actual devil. I don't think you know how that feels.'

'You think that's all it was? One morning of feeling bad?' Hayley was furious all over again. 'Have you learned anything? Why did you even come here tonight? Just to have one last chance to get back at me?'

No, I thought, it wasn't that. It was one last chance for self-respect. But Alex had a slightly different answer.

'No,' he said. 'I mean, I could have done what other men do in this situation. I could have checked into some luxe rehab for my mental health for a few months and got some doctors to say that none of this is my fault. That it's all just because I'm so properly, medically unwell, a truly sick man, and poor me, I need to be left alone to recover. I could have given everyone a sob story. My dad's in a hospital in Edinburgh dying at the moment and I haven't even fucking mentioned that. Or I could have moved to another country and changed my name. Or I could just have said, OK, Hayley, you win, you shamed me into realising how bad I really am, and now I'm going to banish myself for years and think about what I've done, whipping myself and repenting in the wilderness. I've thought about doing all that. I have. But I decided to come here tonight.

'And I could have come here and said that there are loads of guys who've done far worse than me, guys who really do belong in jail, who get off on their plans to do terrible things that I wouldn't even want to say out loud. And I could have said that you should all really be taking *them* to task, not me.

'But look, Hayley. It was wrong not to tell you about the review right at the start. I should have told you. And I wanted to come here and say that, in public. The stuff about my relationships is a different thing. And for that, I know a lot of people want me to say, OK, you got me, I'm a massive sexist, misogynist, terrible person.' He took a deep breath. 'And, honestly, I wouldn't have come onto this stage tonight if your show hadn't brought up some very uncomfortable truths for me. And I have learned things about myself. But that doesn't mean I have to accept that everything you've said about me is right and you're an angel. Haven't you ever done something you regret? Why am I the only one who has to learn something here?'

Hayley looked as though she'd found an answer she'd been searching for, but not one she'd hoped for. Mostly, she looked done with all of it. 'I'll tell you what I've learned. After that first night of the show, I could have just given up. Left Edinburgh and gone crying back home. And for a moment there, I really fucking wanted to. But on this stage right now, I'm so glad I didn't. And from speaking to everybody I've had up here over the last month, I guess I've learned that women are the strongest creatures on the planet. And I've learned that whatever happens, however terrible you feel, whatever people are saying about you – you've got to finish your damn show.'

Hayley stood up and walked towards the metal can full of stuff to burn. On that cue, music started thumping through the speakers and the bright white stage lighting changed to a red gel. She lit a match from a box she pulled out of her pocket, and held it high above her head, then brought it down to touch the edge of the newspaper at the top of the pile and let it ignite.

Hayley didn't see it right away, but I did. A long yellow flame licked up one of the red curtains of the backdrop behind her. I don't know what the curtain was made of, but the narrow flame scrambled right up it in a second, like a cat climbing a wall. I became more acutely aware of how crowded the room felt, how old the building was.

Nobody in the audience moved. They thought it was part of the show, I realised. This was typical Fringe to them: a small room, an element of danger and unpredictability and improvisation. Everyone knew the show had a fire in it. Hayley had burned something every night, so this must just be the grand finale. This would all be smoothed out in the West End transfer, they'd be thinking.

Hayley turned and saw the flames. 'Oh, shit,' she said. She looked around her for a fire extinguisher, a blanket, anything, but there was nothing. She looked to Alex, but he only reflected her bewildered gaze.

All the curtain was blazing now and still nobody in the audience moved. The woman with the popcorn next to me was frozen, her hand halfway to her mouth. Thick grey smoke billowed horizontally along the ceiling. Alex and Hayley both looked around for some member of staff who knew what to do. A smoke alarm began to blare.

Then everyone seemed to move at once. I stood up. The stage manager ran out with a fire extinguisher and shouted at everyone to get to the fire exit. Someone screamed, and everyone was pushing towards the back of the room where the stairs were. But there were so many people, and only one way out of the basement, back up the dark staircase. Everyone was standing now, pushing their way into each other. There was more smoke and a lot of people between me and the exit. The stage manager abandoned the fire extinguisher, dropping it on the ground with a clang, and I couldn't believe how quickly this was happening. It felt like only a few seconds since Hayley had struck the match.

Glass shattered in the lighting rig and huge flames rippled across the ceiling. Every breath was becoming an effort. All my muscles felt slow, heavy, as if I were in a film on half speed, or a sleep paralysis dream. I tried to move towards the door, but it was the strangest thing, my whole body was exhausted, and every chair I tried to move was too heavy, and the people who couldn't yet reach the exit were turning in different directions, looking for another way out, but there wasn't one. The heat was so intense that my eyes hurt. I couldn't see Hayley or Alex. I crouched low to the ground. The lighting rig crashed to the floor. The lights cut out.

My head seared with pain, and I had no idea which direction the door was in any more. People were shouting, and I thought I heard Alex behind me, but I could see so little that it felt as though the space was empty of everyone except me. I tried to get to the door, but my hands found only walls and chairs and pillars.

I could die here, I thought. I could die here, today, in this absurd place, and my picture would be printed alongside Alex's and Hayley's in all the papers.

And then in my mind was Arlo, and the terrible thought of leaving him behind, leaving him the way my mother had left me, without him ever having the chance to know me. With another crash behind me and a roar of gathering heat, I pushed towards my last approximation of where I thought the door must be. And then my hands and knees hit the stairs, and, on all fours, I climbed them.

Coughing, stumbling, I was outside. Gasping at the air brought cold fresh pain into my lungs. The first person I saw in my swimming vision was Hayley, standing ahead of me, backlit in the blue flashing lights of a wall of ambulances. She saw me, caught my eye in a wild glance, held it for a moment.

Someone else grabbed my arm, a firefighter that for one mad second I thought was a spaceman in his beige suit and yellow helmet, and he shouted in my face: 'Is there anyone else in there?'

I tried to speak but could only produce a hacking, painful cough.

He said again, 'How many are still in there?'

'Alex,' I managed to say, though my mouth didn't seem to be making any of the right sounds. 'Alex is in there.'

As if he'd know who Alex was. He called to the other firefighters and two of them went into the building behind me. I knelt on the edge of the kerb. A police officer helped me up and took me behind a cordon and people were all around, watching the venue as smoke clouded through the windows. The street was full of every kind of emergency vehicle, and fire alarms and sirens sang in my ears. My lungs ached and dragged, and my eyes stung so much I could only keep them open for a second at a time.

'Far too many people,' someone was saying. It was the woman who'd had the popcorn. 'The capacity is only eighty and it must have been double that.'

'Accident waiting to happen,' said a man.

My whole body violently shook. I was very cold.

More firefighters were unspooling hoses but they weren't dousing anything yet. There were a lot of people standing around. Smoke was coming out of the windows now. Police were evacuating people from the buildings on either side. They were asking people to leave.

I stayed. I sat on the low wall opposite the theatre, shivering, more numb than cold now. I imagined still being stuck in that basement as the smoke swirled into my lungs and the heat peeled my skin.

I took out my phone and messaged Josh. *There's just been a fire at the theatre. I got out OK but I think the whole building might go up. I just wanted to say . . .*

I paused. I didn't know what I wanted to say. It was more what I wanted to hear. I abandoned the message. I selected Josh's name from my contacts list and called him.

When he answered and said my name as if it were a question, I started to cry.

He offered to bring Arlo and come and meet me, but I said no. I needed to stay. If Alex didn't come out, I wanted to be the one to tell his mother. Maybe I should try to contact her now. A TV news crew arrived in its own white van, and now the whole road was blocked. I wanted to tell them to go away, but I knew they had to be there, too. Someone had to see the story so they could tell it.

In that time, to me, Alex was both alive and dead. What would have happened if his life and Hayley's hadn't led them both here? Where else might the world have taken them? Hayley had made herself the protagonist of this show that was her life, but for the protagonist, things always get worse.

There's nothing like writing obituaries to teach you that death is everywhere. Whether or not you're famous enough to have a newspaper obit written about you, somewhere, after your death, there will be a summary written of your life, and it will not be written by you. Someone else, whether someone you love or just the person who types up the council death notices, will weigh up the most important things you left behind, the people you knew, the prints you left in the mud. And that summary will exist alongside the summaries of all the other people who died the same day. And it will be read, for a while. And then it will be forgotten.

Does it matter what they say? Or does it only matter that you made the choices you were always going to make, and you were never, ever, going to have enough time?

At last, Alex emerged from the building, held up by two firefighters. I got to my feet. I wanted him to see me, to have someone to aim for. I called out his name. And he saw me then and smiled. A little what-now smile. A little fucking-hell smile.

One of the ambulance staff tried to put a silver foil blanket around his shoulders and asked if they could check him over. He said he was OK. He said his lungs had seen worse. There were dozens of people walking around aimlessly or standing and staring at the fire. I waited where Alex could see me through the crowds. He came and sat next to me on the edge of the wall and doubled over, wheezing, coughing, and I watched the building as fire started to eat away the roof.

He said he'd waited to leave because he suddenly imagined what it would be like to get out and then discover someone else had been left behind while he survived. And he couldn't bear the idea of forever hating himself even more than he already did.

He wasn't a hero, not even an anti-hero: he didn't save

anyone's life, you understand. That's very important. But it's true that he was the last one out of the building.

The paramedics offered again to take Alex to hospital, but he insisted he was fine. I said I'd take him home.

As we walked up the street, I shoved his shoulder with my hand.

'At least we've saved Graham some paperwork for next year,' I said. 'HR's never going to let anyone come to the festival again.'

'Are you joking? They'll fucking *love* it. They've had to extract people from war zones before. This is nothing. Maybe I'll be a case study on the next Extreme Reporting Environments training day. Now everyone might finally believe me that theatre is dangerous.'

Both of our voices were deepened, hoarse and cracked with smoke. My arms and legs were still heavy. As we walked back towards the flat, I refreshed the BBC News app on my phone, my thumb pulling it down and down. There was patchy phone service. It was probably because it was the last night of the festival, and thousands of people were gathering on Princes Street.

The app refreshed.

Firefighters in Edinburgh are working to put out a fire in a historic pub, theatre space and festival venue, it said. There was a photograph of smoke blending with the night clouds, the luminous livery of emergency vehicles on the street, the tiger-flick orange of flames coming through the roof of the building, the pub sign hanging off the wall. I clicked through to a video from the scene. In the corner of the video, I saw the shadow of Alex, limping towards me.

'Oh God,' I said. 'We should tell the news desk we're here. We should file a story.'

'Oh yeah! We are the news! Again!' The grubbiness of Alex's cheeks, and his mad, matted hair, made his eyes look unnaturally bright. They'd lost their laziness now. They were wild.

'Shouldn't we be writing about this?' I said.

'Fuck that.' Alex switched off his phone. 'I need a drink. And I'm going to buy some more cigarettes. You coming?'

'Your lungs haven't suffered enough?'

I got a message from Josh.

Just seen the news. Looks worse than you made it sound on the phone!

Then, a second later, another message.

I'm glad you're OK.

Another pause. And then:

I love you.

I hesitated. I stopped walking. 'I think I'm going to go straight back to the flat.'

Alex stopped too, and looked at me as if he'd misheard, or hadn't quite understood the words I was using.

'Oh,' he said. And I thought I saw, somewhere behind his eyes, the smallest movement of a shadow, like the falling of a curtain. But it was dark, and I wasn't sure. He blinked and it was gone. 'OK. Yeah. I'll be in that bar down the road, if you change your mind. If I don't see you before your train, I'll see you back at the newsroom. We can pretend we were never here.'

I hugged him. He smelled of burning buildings. He held on half a second longer than I did. I started walking in the other direction. I felt bruised, burned, awake.

'Hey,' Alex called after me. 'What would you say if you had to write a review of everything that's happened this month?'

I stopped. I thought about it. 'I feel so much older,' I said. It was starting to rain. 'Where would you even start? It would have to be hundreds of pages.'

'Never mind that,' said Alex. 'How many stars?'

23

Nobody died in the fire, which people said was a miracle. The building was lost entirely. In the weeks afterwards, I was obsessed with reading about other fires in entertainment venues. I read that on average you only have about three minutes to get out of a space that's gone up like that before the smoke overwhelms you. That sent a deep shudder through me.

In London, Alex went back to work at the paper, putting in newsroom shifts every day, writing obits and advertising copy and some of the endless trivial cultural news stories we put out in the lead-up to Christmas. I sent him an email a few weeks later, after I'd left the paper and was getting ready to start my new job at the festival. I just asked how things were going. He replied after twenty minutes:

Hey Soph,
   Being on obits is like being Charon, ferrying the souls of the dead across the Styx, except now I have

to sit at the desk next to the commercial team. And everyone is called Karen. It's agony.

I miss the flat. Sometimes I think it's the most intimate thing I've ever done and I wish it could have gone on forever.

But I'm sorry, for what it's worth. Sorry for bringing you down.

Alex

I didn't reply.

It's an image from the end of the festival that returns to me now, from when I took the train south at the end of August with Josh and Arlo, my throat still sore from the smoke, my limbs still heavy. My interview with Hayley was in the Sunday magazine supplement tucked inside the paper that day. I bought a copy in the big newsagent and stationery shop at Waverley station, along with, on impulse, a mini sketchbook and a set of drawing pencils. Once we were on the train, I laid it all out on the table among Arlo's baby snacks and toys as we rattled along the coast towards London. Hayley's picture was on the cover of the magazine, on a pink backdrop, glossy and delectable, served up again for readers to admire or judge. The supplement had gone to print the previous Wednesday so there was no mention of the fire in the interview. It was already out of date.

Arlo stood his chunky legs up on my lap and reached his little hands towards the sea beyond the train windows, and Josh stroked my arm across the table.

As I read my own words, they were already unfamiliar to me. I wouldn't ever write another newspaper feature. My eyes hurt too much now from looking at other people in all that detail, like how lacemakers' eyes a century ago were ruined from too much close-up work with not enough light.

But I didn't read that piece with any sense of embarrassment or defeat, as I would once have done. I knew the piece was good, clear and direct. It wasn't fawning. It showed Hayley's work, this moment in her life, as if through a jeweller's loupe, paying attention to the structure behind the sparkle. It was sharp where it needed to be. It was funny and creative and strong. It recorded Hayley's accomplishments and my own as an interviewer. And it was fair.

I'm not so vain that I'll tell you exactly which sentences, as I read them back, made me feel this way. But it read, to me, like the completion of an apprenticeship to a trade. One I never wanted to work at again.

After she read it, Hayley sent me an email inviting me to have dinner with her in London. She was writing an original drama for TV and set to appear on a late-night show in the US in the next few weeks.

She had been absolved of responsibility for the fire because it turned out that, although it had looked as if her lighting of the match onstage had started it, the official investigation discovered it was in fact caused by longstanding faulty electrics at the back of the stage. That didn't stop people saying it was Hayley's fault though. It had looked as if Hayley caused it all.

So many of the feelings I had during that August in Edinburgh – the vivid desires, the psychological contortions, the shuddering retches – had felt deep-set and terminal. But afterwards, in the few weeks before starting my new job at the art festival, as summer became autumn, they faded away entirely, and the world seemed coloured differently.

I took long walks through London, looking for wide open skies. The air was cool in a way that made me want to press my palms against it. I made several trips to stand in front of the Rothkos at the Tate, absorbing their energy like a low musical vibration.

I can't be a fair critic of anything, not least my own life. It was only after I'd left the paper, and found space from the daily churn of opinions, that I could see it: I'd spent so much time in a state of perpetual response, existing as one long reaction to what other people had already done. I'd thought that was how we all were. The inevitable way of being in the world.

But response can either look backwards or try to go forwards. I'd always been looking back. Now the light was changing, I wanted to take what had come before and use its momentum to go on.

On a Monday morning in October I sat by the Thames in the sun. I had my sketchbook and I was drawing the buildings on the other side. I pencilled their phantoms on the paper and washed them bold with paint. They were their own, and they were mine.

Now I hold my life in my hands and feel its warmth. I breathe gently on the embers. I make them glow.

Acknowledgements

To everyone whose work I've ever reviewed: thank you for making something worth talking about. I'm sorry if I got it wrong at the time.

Thank you to:

My wonderful agent Rachel Yeoh, who has flawless taste and tireless enthusiasm, and who read the manuscript on the train, took it into her heart and made everything happen.

The four brilliant, witty and imaginative women who became this book's muses as well as its editors: Cara Reilly, Amy Perkins, Meredith Pal and Jo Thompson.

Bill Thomas, Lee Boudreaux, Lily Dondoshansky, Elena Hershey, Vimi Santokhi, Felecia O'Connell, Rita Madrigal, Jess Deitcher, Gianna Antolos, Casey Hampton and everyone at Doubleday.

Oliver Munday for the beautiful US cover design.

Beth Coates, Francine Brody, Anne O'Brien, Susanna

Peden, Tanuja Shelar, Jabin Ali, Lipfon Tang, Harriet Williams, Sabina Lewis, Holly Martin, Eleanor Slater and everyone at The Borough Press, Ellie Game for the gorgeous UK cover design, and Isabelle Farah for bringing the audiobook to life.

Nicole Winstanley, Kristin Cochrane, Brittany Larkin, Beth Cockeram, Jasmin Shin and everyone at Penguin Canada.

Olivia Maidment, Valentina Paulmichl, Hannah Kettles, Hannah Ladds, Casey Dexter, Madeleine Milburn, and everyone at the Madeleine Milburn Agency.

I am grateful to The Society of Authors and the Authors' Foundation for the Taner Baybars Award, which did not directly enable me to write this book, but did enable me to write a different, much worse book first, so it kind of helped me to write this book too.

Stu Hanger for the fire expertise.

For feedback and discussion at every stage: Rowan Hisayo Buchanan, Suzannah Dunn, Jennie Godfrey, all the CBC writers, the City Lit Advanced Fiction Workshop, Georgina Leadbetter, Robert Leadbetter, Isobel Norris and Jennifer Kaytin Robinson.

All the great, anonymous journalists I've worked with who are definitely not the inspiration for this book. And Martin Chilton, the most human editor on Fleet Street.

Alice Vincent for the voice notes, emotional support, infinite wisdom and well-timed cherry brownies.

A million and nine thanks, always, to Rosie Kellagher and James Runcie.

And, of course, Marilyn Imrie. I'm sorry this book was written a little late for you to read it – but then, I only wrote it because of you. You're on every page.

My amazing children, without whom maybe a little more of this book could have been written in daylight, but without anywhere near as much love.

And to Sean, who was willing to talk this book through endlessly, and made it so much better, and who is nothing like any of the men in it, and who is in fact the best, funniest person in the world, and who makes everything feel possible and good.